THE FIELD AGENT

THE AGENT BENNET SAGA
BOOK 1

FriesenPress

Suite 300 - 990 Fort St
Victoria, BC, V8V 3K2
Canada

www.friesenpress.com

ISBN
978-1-5255-9347-5 (Hardcover)
978-1-5255-9346-8 (Paperback)
978-1-5255-9348-2 (eBook)

1. YOUNG ADULT FICTION, ACTION & ADVENTURE

Distributed to the trade by The Ingram Book Company

THE FIELD AGENT

BOOK 1 OF THE
AGENT BENNET SAGA

R. S. TWELLS

Dedicated to me,
for proving to myself that
I can finish something.

TABLE OF CONTENTS

CHAPTER 1

"Let's go through it again," I said, spinning around in my chair in the back of the van to face my brother, Collin.

"Alright, boss," Collin said with a grin. "Three times ain't enough?"

"Not when it comes to explosives." I crossed my arms over my chest and stared him down, waiting for him to go on.

Collin put on his backpack, adjusting the straps to fit him perfectly. Unlike the paper, pens, notebooks, and textbooks the other teenagers in the school would have in their backpacks, Collin's held a gun, knives, and a specialized tool kit.

"Go in, defuse the bomb, go home, eat pudding," Collin said, counting each item on his fingers. "I believe that is everything. Right, Bennet?"

Before the sun had even risen, one of our teachers, Agent Asher, had come into our room and given us our assignment. They had intercepted information that a bomb had been placed in a private school in DC—one of those swanky schools where politicians always sent their kids. We were taken to a plane and flown to the location. All this happened in such a rush that Agent Asher wouldn't even let me pee until we had reached cruising altitude. Our home, *cleverly* named the Orphanage, for that's what we were, was far behind us, and I was

1

dreading what I would miss in our university-level biology class.

I rolled my eyes at Collin. "There are a couple of details in between those steps. Besides, you can't eat pudding before noon. Have a little class."

The driver of the van, Baker, looked back at us in disgust. "Why the heck did they send you two to deal with this?" he asked. "They should have sent someone who had actually graduated instead of 'the opposite twins.'"

"The opposite twins" was what everyone at the Orphanage called us once they realized Collin would always win in a physical fight, and I would be better off fighting behind the controls of a robot. We were quickly sorted into our prospective career paths. Collin would grow up to work out in the field, and I would be his trusted earpiece, working from the Orphanage and dealing with the technical side of things.

"Well," Collin said with a smirk, "the best of the best weren't available, so they got the best of the mediocre instead."

"That's us!" I agreed, and we each gave a little wave toward Baker.

Baker, though a rather grumpy guy, was a pretty good driver, so unfortunately, the Orphanage kept him around. He could drive anything with wheels and almost anything without. Back when he was still in training, the Orphanage had tested him as a getaway driver in a heist in New York City. By the time he got out of city limits with no cops in sight, there was no damage to the car, and his heart rate had never elevated. Since he was clearly overqualified for this particular job, I figured he'd been sent to babysit us.

"It's a simple 'in-and-out' job," Baker said. "Get it over with so we can go home. I've got better places to be." He turned back to the newspaper he was reading.

Baker usually got along with Collin; me, not so much. There was probably some important sports game on TV he was missing. Don't ask me which one, because I'm more of a comic-book guy.

I picked up a tiny box and tossed it to Collin. "Put these on," I ordered.

Opening the box, he carefully took out a microchip no bigger than a grain of rice and stuck it in his ear. It was so small that even if anyone looked closely, they'd only see earwax. He took out the second chip the box contained, opened his mouth, and stuck it on his bottom left molar. Once our adult teeth came in, we'd had dental surgery to be able to house the chip perfectly.

The two chips ensured that he could hear me, and I could hear him. He was ready to go defuse a bomb.

Unfortunately, whoever had equipped this van must have been in a hurry: There were no body cameras. It wasn't the end of the world. I would just have to hack into the security cameras to keep an eye on him.

Turning back to my computer to read our notes, I said to Collin, "According to the information the Orphanage got, the bomb is set to go off in thirty minutes. They want this job done without alerting anyone, so some politician doesn't decide to start a war or something silly. Walk into that school as if you belong."

Collin and I had gone on many assignments together, but we had never been on one that risked so many lives. Still, there was no need to panic.

Straightening up from double-knotting his shoes, Collin said, "Bennet, it's going to be okay. You're in my ear the whole time. Anything I don't know, you can talk me through." He gave me a reassuring smile before adding, "Besides, Baker is here to keep you company. What could go wrong?"

Turning around, he opened the back door of the van and hopped out into the street to officially begin our first assignment that could possibly end with a bang.

Now it was my turn to work. Typing madly away, I wormed my way into the school's security system. It was a five-minute walk from the van to the school, giving Collin twenty-five minutes to locate and defuse the bomb. Collin had a knack for goofing off during assignments. This time I prayed he would use his time wisely.

Finding the bomb shouldn't be a problem. The Orphanage had developed a simple device—disguised as a watch—to track down such items by detecting the materials used to make them. The watch also had a tiny camera in it, so I wouldn't be completely blind if Collin went somewhere with no security cameras. It just sucked when the wearer of the watch would flail their arms around, making it impossible to see anything. Collin was in good hands *finding* the bomb, but it was up to him to get rid of it.

I was trying not to grumble over the fact that the Orphanage could have sent Charlotte, a girl in our year who specialized in bombs. At a young age, she'd done quite well in chemistry. The Orphanage thought she would excel in the labs. It turned out she just really liked to blow things up. Who better to send on a bomb assignment than someone who lived to tinker with them?

The Orphanage had collected me and my twin brother from the childcare system after our parents died in a car accident shortly after we were born. They were hoping for the first set of twin field agents and were excited to see what that would look like. Once they realized that I had no coordination when it came to practically anything, their dreams shattered. They decided to take advantage of my love of hacking instead.

One great thing about the Orphanage is that they play to people's strengths. They aren't going to force you to do something you are terrible at; like Charlotte with explosives or Baker with driving, they want everyone to excel.

"Come in, Bennet." Collin came through loud and clear in my headset. "I have an entrance in sight, and I am taking it. Find me in the southeast corridor."

"Copy that," I replied, switching my computer screen and finding the correct camera. I got to work programming a looped feed to ensure that no one would ever know Collin had been there. "I see you coming in through the door. Switch your watch on in three, two, one."

I saw Collin tap his watch, making a screen pop up on my

computer that would allow me to help him find the bomb. Collin took the nearest staircase up, two steps at a time. The school was already getting crowded. The school day would be starting at the exact moment the bomb was scheduled to go off. How perfect.

"Imagine this," Collin whispered for only me to hear.

"Imagine what?" I asked, only half paying attention because Collin's watch was streaming a lot of information my way that was a lot more interesting than my brother.

"This." He moved his hands slightly to show he meant his surroundings. "Going to school every day. Having homework and normal friends."

"Why aren't our friends normal?" I asked, already knowing the answer. No sixteen-year-old should be able to perform open-heart surgery.

"You know what I mean."

I sighed. He was playing this game for my benefit. The Orphanage usually didn't let me go on location for assignments. I typically worked in the office back home since, apparently, I daydreamed too much. On my first Orphanage assignments, I was like a dog chasing a squirrel. I got distracted by the mundane. It's why my favorite characters in my comic books were always the superhero's best friend. They were the ones without any powers who got to live a mostly normal life. In all honesty, I made a terrible agent even when I was only in training.

I used to joke that I would quit and go join Google. I would say that Google treated their employees better, giving them on-site massage rooms, allowing them to bring in their pets, and even encouraging naps. Collin would laugh, but I could see that the thought of me leaving hurt him. Of course, in reality, I could never leave him. Maybe when we retired I could, but right now I had to make sure Collin and I graduated training.

I played along with him even though it kind of hurt, knowing I could never have a normal life. "We live at our school, we have insane amounts of homework, and our friends are our roommates. It's basically the exact same things except we have assault rifles."

"Sure, we get homework," Collin responded, and I could see him smiling in the security footage, "but it's university-level math, not tenth-grade math. Imagine going to football practice and going to school dances—"

I cut him off. "Imagine having all of that and being completely bored. Face it, Collin, you can't sit still for more than five minutes, and you love feeling like James Bond or Jason Bourne. Besides, if we did have parents and went to a normal school every day with jobs at McDonald's on the weekend, you might be a football star, but I would be the dork who got shoved in a locker."

I heard him laugh as I watched him pass between rows of lockers on either side, his watch not showing any signs of the bomb. I barely paid attention to him as he went on. "People don't get shoved into lockers anymore. That was more of an '80s thing, or something that happened in movies—I think. You would have sat on the floor with Chuck, eating lunch while trying to figure out the school's secure Wi-Fi password."

Now it was my turn to laugh, because that sounded exactly like what would have happened.

Back home at the Orphanage, Chuck was my best friend. We got along well, because when we first started doing physical training at age five, we realized that we were the two slowest runners of our year. We would run together and talk about who we would rather be, Spider-Man or the Hulk. Usually, we both picked Spider-Man, but on days that we got beaten in every round of hand-to-hand combat training, we would joke about becoming the Hulk.

"You make school sound so glamorous," I said sarcastically. "Focus on the assignment. I don't have to remind you that our conversation is being recorded." Last time we were on an assignment together, we got in trouble for telling too many jokes during a stakeout.

The little clock in the corner of my screen was ticking down, getting a little too close to zero for comfort. Collin needed to move faster. I just wanted this to be over with.

Collin disappeared from the security camera. I switched to another one and he reappeared, heading downstairs, done with the top floor. The school was getting even busier as the start of the day edged closer. It was fifteen minutes away, to be exact.

Baker got up out of the driver's seat and came back to look at the computer. "Tell your brother to hurry up."

"Shouldn't you stay in the front seat, ready to go?" I countered. He was making me nervous, hovering over my shoulder.

Baker let out a low whistle and leaned closer to the screen. "You two are so similar, yet completely different."

"Tell me something I don't know, Baker."

Collin and I had the same brown eyes, the same height of six-foot-one, and the same dark-brown hair. If someone were to look quickly at us, they would easily get us mixed up. But we were called "the opposite twins" for more reasons than just his love of being a field agent and my skills with a keyboard. He walked a little faster than me, and with purpose. His hair was shorter; I liked to sport a scruffy look. But probably the most obvious difference was that he had more muscle mass than me. I only did the weight training that was mandatory while Collin went above and beyond. He could probably lift a car off of a kid if it came down to it.

"Collin, you have ten minutes remaining." I waited a second for a reply, but nothing came through. "Collin, do you copy? You only have ten minutes." I felt myself itching to run out of the van and toward Collin. I needed to get him out of there before it was too late.

"Got it," he replied. "I've got the bomb's location."

CHAPTER 2

Collin slowly turned the knob of the door to the janitor's closet, then carefully eased the door open. I felt myself release a breath I hadn't known I was holding.

"I'm turning the camera on the watch on in three, two, one," Collin told me.

A little screen popped up, showcasing his chin. It wasn't a flattering angle.

He walked through the door and disappeared from the security cameras. Now I would only be able to see through the tiny camera. I cursed it and vowed to try and come up with a better design. For someone working as an earpiece, this was terrible. Leave it to engineering to come up with something like this, only keeping the field agents in mind and not the ones who are trying to talk them through everything.

Mops and brooms, along with cans of paint and cleaning supplies, cluttered the small room. Collin reached into his backpack and pulled out a flashlight. Clicking it on, he looked around.

"I don't see it, but it's supposed to be in here." Collin turned frantically around in the small space. He started knocking over cleaning supplies, pulling mops off hooks, and flipping buckets over.

Baker moved behind me and headed back to his seat. Apparently, trying to locate a bomb was boring to him. Before sitting down, he grumbled, "Tell him to hurry up."

"Not helping!" I yelled at him, but also unfortunately into my headset. "Sorry, Collin."

"It's fine, just help me," he complained.

"Just relax and keep looking. It has to be there. Check under the sink."

The light hit the space under the sink. Nothing was there. As he quickly flashed the light around the room, I noticed the door. A couple of large jackets hung there.

"Check the jackets!" I shouted.

Collin grabbed the jackets off the door and placed them on the floor. He shook them out, and I noticed his hands were shaking as he reached into the pockets.

He never got nervous on an assignment. My heartbeat quickened, and my palms began to sweat.

In the last jacket he searched, he finally found what we were looking for. He placed it carefully on the floor and knelt beside it.

"Remember, Collin," I chimed in, "stop the timer, then defuse it. We spent a whole month learning about bombs, so just relax and remember what they taught us."

He got to work figuring out how to stop the clock. The bomb itself looked really complex. There was an old-fashioned alarm clock connected by dozens of wires to a tiny metal box and a tablet computer. The clock read 8:25, and the alarm hand pointed to 8:30. We had five minutes to stop the bomb.

Collin must have noticed the time as well, because he was already on his feet and heading out of the closet.

"What are you doing?" I asked, confused.

He dashed down the hall and pulled the fire alarm. Immediately there was a loud ringing in my ear. In response to my brother's actions, I proceeded to make sure the fire department was on its way, as well as alerting the Orphanage. Confused students and teachers made their way to the nearest exits.

I was no longer sitting in my chair but standing in front of my workstation. A piece of me wanted Collin to exit the building with the rest of the students, but I knew he would never do that. Whoever said working with family was easy clearly didn't work in a job where death was around every corner.

I tried to control my panic as Collin hurried back to the janitor's closet. "You're cutting it kind of close," I told him.

"You think?"

"You've saved the students. You can save yourself now." I tapped my foot nervously on the floor of the van, the sound echoing.

"Our assignment is to make sure this doesn't go off, and that is what we are going to do." From his backpack, he pulled out a tiny cord. Connecting it to his watch, he flipped the bomb carefully around in his hands, examining the tablet. Once he found the correct slot, he slid the other end of the cord into the tablet. He watched—and I waited—to see if the screen would come to life.

Seconds ticked by, and nothing happened. I let out a sigh of relief. At least his actions hadn't set off the bomb. On the downside, if it had worked, the watch would have started transmitting information from the device to my computer. I could have possibly been more help then.

Collin continued to stare at his watch, hoping something would happen. I was just about to tell him to unplug it when something appeared on one of my screens.

"Hold on a second," I told Collin.

"What have you got?"

I got to work to see what I could access from the device, but I was locked out. The watch was definitely going nuts, uploading file after file to me, but no matter how hard I tried to work my magic on the keyboard, I couldn't get in.

And then, suddenly, I could. Line after line of red coding appeared on my screen.

Ha! I thought. *Give me a computer, and I can do anything.*

At least, I thought I could, but even working as fast as I could to catch up with the virus-like code that was multiplying and keeping me locked out of the tablet, I was always a step behind. On my screen, my green code slowly started to mix in with the red. I felt confident that I could turn the tables eventually, given the time—but did I have that time?

"Bennet," Collin interrupted, "you can't shut me out just because a fancy thing is happening on your computer that I can't see or understand. Talk to me. What's happening?"

I continued to ignore him. Sweat formed on my brow. I had to work faster!

But then the screen displaying Collin's footage started to cut in and out, and I stopped typing. It would take me hours to work through all the layers between me and whatever was making the bomb tick. We didn't have hours; we had minutes. I wasn't going to be able to get any information off of it from here. If—when—Collin succeeded in preventing the bomb's detonation, I would make sure he brought me back everything. I could have my fun with it then, finding out everything about its previous owner.

I quickly ordered Collin, "Unplug the tablet from your watch. It's a dead end."

"Got it."

All of the red coding on my screen disappeared, leaving me feeling useless. "We're out of time. Get back to the van," I ordered.

"Give me a minute." And with that, Collin ever-so-elegantly ripped the clock off of the rest of the device. Apparently, we were not going to be delicate with the object that could blow up the entire school.

The tablet screen came to life, counting backward from three minutes.

"Well, that didn't work," Collin said.

"This isn't a guessing game," I groaned, putting my head in my hands. "Try cutting a wire to the tablet."

"Which one?"

"Red. Always red."

He hesitated. "Are *you* guessing?"

"Maybe," I replied without lifting my head. Agent Asher had taught us that, when in doubt, "red is rad," which rhymed with "bad." A terrible saying, but he said it worked for him because most people associated red with bad.

Collin put down the bomb and pulled a pair of wire cutters from his backpack. He gently tugged at the red wire, then carefully put the cutters into position.

Snip.

I turned my attention back to the tablet, only to be disappointed that the time was at two minutes and counting.

"Get out, please," I begged.

"We've still got time." Collin now had a screwdriver in his hand and was working at the back of the tablet. "I can do this. I can save the school."

Sweat rolled down my face. "You've saved the students, now save yourself!" I cried.

Ignoring me, he sat down and peeled the back off of the tablet. "Bennet, relax. We can do this."

The fire alarm was still ringing in the background, and I could hear an approaching fire-engine siren.

"There are two chips that don't match the rest of the design. What's your call?" he said.

I gave in. "Take them both out, but make sure you keep them. This is the last thing you try, and then you leave. Run as fast as you can."

One minute and counting.

Collin gently removed the chips, one at a time. When he took the second one out, the timer stopped counting down at forty-five seconds.

"The school is secured," Collin stated.

I reached for my chair and sat down, relief flooding through me. I smiled, realizing that these kids could still go to school tomorrow and live their normal lives.

"How's it going back there?" Baker asked, not looking up from his newspaper.

I let out a laugh in response.

"Alright, Bennet, the bomb is defused, and I am on my way to the van with the leftovers." Collin put the pieces of the bomb carefully into a container and put it in his backpack. A bombproof box awaited the device once he got back to the van.

He stood up and walked to the closet door.

As he reached the threshold, my world exploded.

CHAPTER 3

The ground shook. The computer screens went blank. Static roared in my headset, making me rip it off.

Baker was on the radio, calling the Orphanage for more backup. I heard shouts from outside the van but couldn't make out any of the words. As chaos erupted around me, my body wouldn't move. I was frozen, unsure of what had just happened, or how to react.

"Agent Collin is down. I repeat, Agent Collin is down," Baker shouted into the radio.

What did he mean by down? The screens went blank. We couldn't know anything for sure.

"The device has detonated. Send immediate aid, as well as agents to retrieve Agent Collin's body before it is discovered."

Baker might as well have been speaking a foreign language. What he was saying was impossible. Collin was great at his job. We had less than two years before we graduated. He'd gotten out of the school. He must have.

I felt myself moving, but not by my own will.

"Bennet!" Baker was shaking me, trying to get my attention. I could see the panic in his eyes, but I couldn't reciprocate it. "Bennet, we need to go *now*."

We couldn't leave yet. Collin wasn't back. None of this made sense. Baker was back on the radio. "Agent Bennet is conscious but unresponsive. Probably gone into shock."

This time I was able to overhear the response. "Get yourself and Agent Bennet out of there. The assignment is over. Agents are minutes away. They'll deal with the mess," the voice on the radio said. "Bring Agent Bennet safely back to the Orphanage."

Whoever was on the other end of the radio sounded sad. I couldn't make out who it was, and I wasn't going to wait around to find out.

I got out of my chair and headed for the back of the van. As I opened the door and hopped out into the street, I heard Baker scream my name. Then I was sprinting toward where I prayed to find my brother.

I wasn't the only person on the street running. Others were heading in the same direction, toward the smoke and cries that filled the air. I rounded the corner and discovered crowds of people had formed around the crumbled school.

Students were holding up other students, helping them get as far away from the rubble as possible before any more crashed down. The students who had been closest to the destroyed school were covered in dust. Some had their hands over their ears, probably hoping for the ringing to stop. Others were trying to dig a hole at the front door, presumably to rescue someone. Backpacks lay on the ground, abandoned. Broken glass and what might have been textbooks were scattered off to the side.

My head ached, and I gasped for breath. This couldn't be real. How could something so small have such horrific effects?

The fire department was putting out fires and starting to work toward uncovering those trapped. Pulling the fire alarm had gotten most people out, but not all. Teachers were trying to do roll calls, but their attempts were swept away in the chaos. Students looked around, trying to find their friends, and I noticed teachers were doing the same. No matter how prepared the school might have been for the fire alarm going off, it could never have been prepared for this.

I stumbled through the crowd, making my way around the school to the side where I knew Collin would be. Collin would be working hard to help those around him, as my training was demanding me to do. I promised myself I would help as soon as I knew my brother was safe.

The dust was still settling. Some of the people around me were coughing as I made my way along, constantly on the lookout for a boy my height and with the same brown hair.

"Hey, have you seen Claire?" a girl who could have been my age asked. Her face had tiny pieces of glass in it. I wanted to reach up and help her get them out. She didn't seem to notice the pain she should have been in. Perhaps the same shock that Baker said I was in was coursing through this girl, too.

"Who?" I asked, dazed. My mind was focused on one thing, making it hard to pay attention to anything else.

"Claire? Have you seen her?" she begged.

The poor girl must have thought I went to her school. Tripping over rubble and stumbling forward, I shook my head. I prayed that her friend was all right, but I had to keep moving. I left her there, turning in circles, looking for help.

I made my way to where Collin would have been when my computers went blank. There was so much debris in my way. The school was nothing but pieces of a broken puzzle.

My hands shook and my eyes watered at the thought of finding my brother's body. What would I do without him at the Orphanage? Sure, there was Chuck and others from my year, but Collin and I were special. At the American Orphanage, there were no other agents who were related. Collin and I were a research project to see how well twins could work together. Half of me would be gone without him there.

I needed to control myself and focus on finding my brother. *Alive.*

Without a second thought, I started to climb the rubble to where I thought he could be. I wouldn't stop looking for him even if I had to turn over every last piece of this place. I climbed over broken pieces of wood that could have belonged to a teacher's desk, shards of glass, and what looked like a fridge. I balanced carefully as I jumped from one spot to another. I was getting closer—or so I hoped.

Tripping over a piece of the roof, I fell to my knees. Catching myself with my hands, I scraped them along some broken wood, cutting open my right palm.

I screamed out in pain.

Slightly defeated, I sat there for a second to catch my breath. I couldn't wait too long. Collin would never give up on me, and I wouldn't give up on him.

I started digging my way down. I lifted whatever was in my way and tossed it to the side. He was down there somewhere, and I was going to find him. The farther I dug, the more my hand bled. Everything I touched turned red.

With every part of the school I moved, my hope waned. After ten minutes of digging, it dawned on me what had truly happened. I sat there motionlessly, and again the tears rolled slowly down my cheeks.

Baker knew it. He'd told the Orphanage, so they knew. I should have known right away. I should have accepted the truth.

Collin was carrying the bomb in his backpack.

With one final effort, I lifted whatever I could and moved it out of my way, searching through two stories of shattered high school to find anything of my brother. I could maybe be at peace if I could find a shoe or his backpack or even him. I refused to believe that he could be here one second and then the next, completely gone. There had to be some trace of him.

I tried telling myself that I would give him a lung if he needed it. I'm sure the Orphanage doctors could find some way to make that work. I would even give him one of my legs if both of his got blasted off. He just needed to be alive.

I was so deep into the mess that no one was going to be able to spot me. The back-and-forth in my mind about whether or not Collin was alive was exhausting. I lay down and wondered how long it would take for help to come.

"Bennet," a voice called.

I perked up. "Collin?" I shouted. It had to be Collin.

I sat up and dug harder, pushing aside everything in my way. I knew the strength kicking in was adrenaline, and I would be in a lot of pain later, but it would be worth it.

My right hand felt like it was on fire. I knew my hand would heal eventually, but who knew how much air Collin had down there?

"Bennet." I heard the same voice, but louder.

I must be getting closer.

I put my back against a piece of broken wall and used my legs to kick away what looked like a column. It took a couple of tries, but it started to slowly give. I jumped down to where the column had stood, in the hope that I could spot him.

There was nothing there.

"Agent Bennet." Now the voice was right behind me, and it wasn't my brother's voice.

Baker's hands reached out for me, and I pushed away. There was no way Baker was going to get in my way. I kicked out at his legs to knock him off-balance. Surprised at my attack, he stumbled backward but managed to regain his footing on the uneven rubble. Then he grabbed my hands and turned me to face him.

I stopped trying to pull free and scramble away when I noticed the look on his face. Always-grumpy Baker looked sad.

I shook my head and whispered, "No." The truth was finally sinking in. "No, no, no," was all I could say.

"You saw the screen, Bennet. He was at the center of the blow. He's gone."

The only thing I could move was my head. I continued to shake it. "No, no, no."

"Bennet, we need to go. The Orphanage is sending agents to sort through this mess, but right now, our job is to get back. Can you do that?" Baker asked.

I didn't remember him ever treating me this nicely before. He wasn't one for soft, soothing, comforting tones.

I plucked up the courage to say, "But we could look. There might be something. He could still be down there."

I saw Baker's expression fall further. "I'm sorry, Bennet. Collin's dead."

I froze. Neither of us had said the word "dead" yet. We had said "gone" or "down," but not "dead."

The weight of that word hit me like a ton of bricks. I shifted on my feet and Baker let go of my hands, thinking I was agreeing to head back to the van. Focusing on taking a step, I wavered. Looking down, I noticed the ground was getting closer.

Then the uneven surface smacked against my face as my legs gave out.

"Whoa, buddy," Baker muttered, grabbing my right arm and placing it around his shoulder. Blood from my hand smeared on his shirt. "I've got Agent Bennet, and we are heading back to the Orphanage as we speak," he spoke out loud, clearly wearing a communication unit. He slowly led us through the rubble.

Things were not any better on the outskirts of the mess. Ambulances had shown up and were busy helping students deal with injuries that would heal up in a matter of weeks, maybe days. My injury would never heal. Thirty minutes had passed since the bomb went off, and the chaos it had left behind would last a lot longer for me.

Students, teachers, and bystanders had their phones out, taking pictures or videos to post on Instagram—pictures and videos that would ensure this horrid moment would last forever.

We finally reached the van. Baker opened the back door and lifted me in. Seating me in my chair, he buckled me in and gave my arm a pat.

My body was motionless. Nothing around me seemed important anymore.

Baker headed to the driver's seat. He started the engine, then slightly turned his head to look at me. "Everything will be okay," he said softly. "Not today, but one day it will be."

CHAPTER 4

My chair was cold underneath me. I was sitting in the auditorium, which was large enough to hold all of the American agents of the Orphanage, whether they had already graduated or were still in training. Chuck was sitting next to me, not saying anything. We were waiting for the final statement to be read so that we could get on with the rest of our evening as normal.

Well, everyone else would get on with the rest of their evening. I didn't know if I could ever feel normal again. A big part of my life had been torn away, and yet, I was expected to sit in this auditorium and act professional.

People started to file in and take their assigned seats. We sat in groups according to age. I was one of the agents born in 2001, meaning I sat in the '01 section. We were near the back since we had not graduated yet. Once we graduated, and as we got older, we would slowly move closer to the front. It was a way to show respect to the agents who had given many years of service. Sitting near the back was better for today, though, because it would hopefully mean fewer eyes burning into the back of my head, watching how I would react.

I wasn't looking forward to hearing Collin's final statement. Around September of every year, all the agents, no matter how old, had to rewrite theirs from the previous year. It was basically the Orphanage's version of a will, but since we didn't actually own anything to give away, we left everyone with one last word. In the past, agents had professed their love or written how they desired for us to discover the mystery of who we were, since the core of our identity was never truly having an identity. Others had been less poetic and had just shared a joke.

Collin's, I worried, would simply be a joke.

Staring toward the front of the auditorium, I heard someone sit down next to me. I didn't want to take my eyes off the stage, where the Chief, the head of the American Orphanage, would read Collin's last words.

The chair beside me squeaked as whoever was sitting beside me started to make themselves more comfortable. I finally turned that way.

"Hey man," said Austen, a guy from my year. "How you holding up?"

How am I holding up? How was I supposed to answer that? If anyone from my year had died, I would be doing bad, but this was my brother! Of course, my heart was shattered. How did he think I was going to answer his question? With a simple "fine"?

"Fine," I replied. My voice sounded like it belonged to someone else, someone broken, someone who had nothing to live for.

Austen took my answer as an end to our conversation and turned his attention to Chuck. "How is the hospital going, Chuck?"

Chuck was studying to be a doctor. The Orphanage had put him on that path when we were ten years old, running through an obstacle course, where I, being me, had managed to dislocate my shoulder. We had been reading countless medical books in class, but my confidence in Chuck's ability to pop my arm back into its socket was nonexistent. Still, I had sat still as he grabbed my arm and managed to successfully put it back in place. The Orphanage noticed his quick reaction to the situation—and his efficiency—and started grooming him to work in the hospital.

Out of the corner of my eye, I saw him look toward me with a sympathetic smile. He always knew when I needed some peace and quiet, and right now was one of those moments. On the other hand, he also knew that, out of respect, he should answer Austen. After all, he would be the future Chief once the current one retired.

"Things have been alright. Agent Copper is still in rough shape after the incident in Belgium. Doctor Caleb is letting me treat all of Agent Copper's burns, and I think he will be back out in the field within a month, as good as new," Chuck told Austen.

Austen nodded and turned his gaze toward Charlotte and Jane, who had just walked in and taken their seats in our section. The three started a conversation about Charlotte's recent assignment to France, which gave me the perfect excuse to zone out.

Seats were filling up faster, and the start of today's events was closing in. I didn't know if I was ready to hear what Collin had wanted us to hear. I thought about all the people he had affected. He'd made the '01 boys' dorm room better by moving the beds to the wall and out of the way to start games like soccer or handball. Austen and Collin would get up early every Monday and practice their knife-throwing skills. Collin watched Sunday football with Baker and a few other guys from older years in their dorms, and now that was over. Collin and I had talked of the things we would do once we retired, and now that would never come to pass. It was all over. All the good memories were just that: memories.

My heart felt heavy in my chest. Tears formed in my eyes as a horrible image came to mind. Though I would never have another conversation with Collin, another pudding cup, I would always see him. He would be staring back at me from every mirror I looked in. Even worse, the reminder of him would be sitting in the same class as me every single day.

And speak of the devil, she walked down our row at that moment and sat right next to Chuck without saying one word to me or turning to look in my direction.

Darcy.

Darcy hadn't spoken to me since the incident. In the hallways, I wasn't sure if I was avoiding her, or if she was avoiding me. It was probably me avoiding her. The guilt of losing her boyfriend was more than I could bear.

Collin and Darcy had been dating for almost a year. They were an interesting couple, to say the least. Both worked incredibly hard as field agents, both trained nonstop, and both had decided to risk their professional relationship and start dating each other. Dating was, of course, permitted by the Orphanage—I mean, who could stop such a thing?—but it wasn't exactly encouraged.

Technically, they were both field agents, but Darcy specialized in something not many dared: She was an assassin.

Why on Earth someone would want to kill people for a living was beyond me. I much preferred saving innocent lives or helping to advance society through knowledge.

I had nothing against agents being assassins, but it was mind-boggling to me. I couldn't imagine how hard it would be to basically be a "trigger."

Here at the Orphanage, we only had a handful of assassins. Their job was to point and shoot. There was certainly a personality that went along with being an assassin, and Darcy had it. She was quiet but aggressive, certain of her every move but seemed to always be waiting for orders. Needless to say, she scared me.

Collin had been able to look past all of the scariness the title of assassin carried when he became interested in Darcy. It was funny: One day, Darcy was just another girl that we trained with, and overnight, she became something more.

The two were rather rational when it came to their relationship. They sat with each other at most meals and trained with each other, but they never questioned each other when they needed to do things separately. I guess that goes with the territory of a secret organization.

When Collin and Darcy started dating, I found it uncomfortable to hang out with them. Maybe it was because they were both confident in who they were and what they wanted. It could have been because Darcy was the terror born of every horror film shoved into a sixteen-year-old girl's body. But I think the most likely reason was that, in truth, I was terrified of the opposite gender.

It wasn't like I would always tag along with Collin and Darcy. I would try and eat lunch with them, and we would usually watch a movie together on a Sunday night when we were all home. I just figured that, with time, I would relax around the two of them. I guess I would never find out.

Shifting my weight in order to cross my legs, I tried to come up with something to say to her. I racked my brain, but it was like I could no longer form complete sentences.

Everyone from our year was finally sitting in our section, and around us, the seats were mostly filled. Some agents were on assignments, and so their seats remained empty. Everyone tried their best to pay their respects to a fallen agent, but orders didn't always allow for that. The final statement was a tradition as old as the Orphanage itself, dating back to 1826.

Lucas, a rather active boy from our year who seemed to move faster than his brain could keep up, was tapping his foot aggressively, making a noise every time his toe hit the ground. Every single tap made me jump in my skin. Every time he hit the floor, I flinched. Every noise was too loud, and I couldn't find the words or the strength to ask him to stop. Every tap seemed to send me right back to that horrible day.

Chuck sat still beside me, not talking. My palms were sweating, and I felt claustrophobic. The air was getting thick. I grabbed onto Chuck's arm. Chuck didn't flinch at all. Even if he didn't say much, he was a great support.

The murmuring in the hall stopped as Benjamin, the Chief of the American Orphanage, walked onto the stage.

CHAPTER 5

THE ORPHANAGE
DECEMBER 13
7:30 P.M.

"Thank you for coming today for the final statement of Training Agent Collin from the year '01," the Chief said, putting two file folders on the podium. One was black, one red. The black one held Collin's final statement. In the red one was the report of our last assignment.

The Chief wore his usual outfit: a suit and tie. Chief Benjamin thought of it as a uniform. He said you need to dress to impress. I preferred to stay comfortable in jeans and a sweatshirt. Thankfully, we got to choose our daily wear. For assignments, we had to go with what the task called for.

My tight heart tightened even more as I looked at how thin the folder holding Collin's statement was. I prayed that whatever was in there was single-spaced and in a four-point font. I held on to the hope that there was a letter specifically for me. I would cherish that letter and read it every morning when I got up and every night before bed. I would memorize it and recite it in the shower and speak the words when I couldn't bring myself to do anything else. That letter would give me hope to go on.

All of us in the auditorium were silent, just as we were trained to be; we were not a group to fill in the silence with murmurs and unnecessary side comments. We sat still and waited. Things tended to go faster when everyone was quiet, and when someone's life depended on swiftness, it helped to have a quiet group to brief. I never understood scenes in movies where teachers had a hard time silencing their classes in order to be heard. If the students stayed quiet, they'd be done their classes that much faster.

The Chief took a pair of reading glasses from his left jacket pocket. Holding them in his hand, he said to us, "Training Agent Collin '01 was on his way to becoming a strong agent. He tested well in his physical training and responded quickly in tight situations. He was someone I was looking forward to seeing graduate. He will be missed by many and not forgotten."

My cheeks became wet. I counted the passing seconds to give myself something to focus on other than people's eyes darting in my direction. From a room full of agents, I expected a more subtle approach.

"Now," the Chief continued, "I will recount Training Agent Collin's last minutes during his assignment." He opened the red folder, just as slim as the black one holding Collin's final statement. Given my attachment to the issue, Agent Baker had written the report, although I was later briefed on it. I was grateful to him since, for the past week, I had mostly resembled a zombie.

Both of the folders would go into Collin's records, containing all the information gathered on Collin since our arrival. Those records would then be placed in a special vault housing the records from all deceased agents. It was our version of a burial ground, since most of the bodies—like Collin's—never made it home.

The Chief cleared his throat, put on his glasses, and began to read. "At 0600, we intercepted information pointing to a bomb in a Washington high school. The decision was made to send Training Agent Collin to retrieve the bomb, with Training Agent Bennet accompanying to act as his on-site earpiece. Agent Baker went along as their overseer. At 0800, Training Agent Collin made his way to the high school..."

No one in the audience seemed to flinch as the horrible events unfolded. I didn't dare close my eyes for fear that the images from that day would play out in my mind, just as they did every night as I slept. I released Chuck's arm, put my hands on my legs, and focused on not fidgeting, all while not losing count of the passing seconds. Two minutes and seven seconds. Not long at all, yet it felt like an eternity.

"At 0805, Training Agent Collin entered the school and searched for the bomb. At 0825, Training Agent Collin found the bomb hidden in a janitor's closet and proceeded to attempt to defuse it. After pulling the fire alarm to ensure the safety of the civilians, Training Agent Collin was able to stop the timer with forty-five seconds remaining. However, the stopped timer proved to be a decoy. The bomb detonated at exactly 0830, killing Training Agent Collin instantly." There was no change in the Chief's tone as he spoke. He sounded as if he were giving a briefing for an assignment. He had done this too many times, so it was probably best for him that he didn't get emotional during these readings.

The Chief put the report back inside the red folder and set it to the side of the podium.

I wasn't sure if I was ready for what was to come next. I braced myself for the worst. As long as Collin's statement wasn't read, I could imagine it said almost anything. It could talk about beloved memories between the two of us. He could have written about how he wanted me to eat the pudding he'd stashed under his bed, which was long gone—the cleaning crew had come the day he died and cleared out his belongings. Maybe he'd written some final farewell to Darcy.

Selfishly, I prayed that he would have more to say to me than to Darcy. With my luck, more than half of what he had written would be about his undying love for Darcy, and there'd just be a line or two for me. But it was hard for me to *not* be selfish. He was my other half, my twin.

The part of me that wanted this to be over was now silenced completely by the part of me that was too scared to hear what he had written. In this blissful ignorance, his statement could say whatever I wanted it to say.

I had lost count. I thought around three minutes and fifteen seconds had passed since I had begun counting. My fingers began to look for something to do. It was hard to keep them still when they were so used to moving swiftly over a keyboard.

Out of the corner of my eye, I saw Austen take his phone out of his pocket—something you never did in any sort of meeting, especially a final-statement reading. He held it low to his leg and tilted it in my direction. I glanced at it.

"It will be okay," the screen read.

Taking a deep breath, I looked at Austen. He gave me a half-smile before turning his attention back to the stage.

Nothing would ever be okay again, but how could he understand that?

"Now," the Chief's voice boomed across the auditorium, "on to the final statement of Training Agent Collin '01." He opened the black folder. Picking up the single sheet of paper it held, the last paper to ever go into Collin's records, he read Collin's words. "'This is a weird thing to be writing while I am still alive. I guess most people feel that way when writing these things. Every year we write these, and every year I'm not too sure what to say. I am grateful for my time at the Orphanage and hope my death was honorable. I am assuming Bennet is still alive, so please take good care of him. Get him away from a computer every now and then and make sure he drinks water, because the amount of Coke he drinks is going to kill him.'"

I wanted to laugh, I truly did, but nothing would come. It sounded like something Collin would write. His statement was longer than a sentence, and he had kept it on the light side. I knew I had also tried to keep my final statement light-hearted to avoid too much potential heartache for Collin. I'd even added a medical joke for Chuck and something about Darcy having to take care of Collin for me.

I was practically on the edge of my seat as the Chief continued to read. "'I would say I miss everyone, but I'm dead.'" A chuckle ran through the room, forcing the Chief to pause briefly. He gave us a disapproving look over the top of his reading glasses, then resumed. "'Enjoy the little things and keep saving the world. We work hard to leave the world better than we found it, and I feel like, in my own way, I have done that. Goodbye and farewell, fellow agents.'"

The Chief put the paper down and looked out across the auditorium. "Will Training Agent Bennet please come to the stage to receive a letter from the deceased?"

My breath caught. All eyes were now definitely turned in my direction. Chuck stood, took my arm, and helped me to my feet. I made my way out of my row, bumping into people's knees, then shuffled slowly up the long aisle, glancing from side to side at everyone I passed. My feet weighed me down like a ton of bricks, making it difficult to move. Seconds felt like an eternity, but I eventually found my way to the stage. Quickly wiping away tears, I climbed the stairs to the right of the stage and walked toward the Chief.

The room was silent. I reached the Chief and stopped, waiting for him to make the next move.

Picking up a sealed white envelope, he held it out to me. "Your brother has one last letter for you. You may read it on your own time."

I nodded, unable to say anything, and took the letter from him. It was hard to believe something so small could carry so much weight. This letter was a special gift from Collin. This would be what would remind me of him daily when I missed him more than I could handle.

Tearing my gaze away from the letter, I thanked the Chief with a slight nod and made my way offstage and back to my seat. I didn't know where to put the letter, so I just held it with both hands.

"You are all dismissed," the Chief said. He picked up the file folders and walked offstage.

Around me, people began to stand up and make their way down the aisles. I looked up at Chuck for some reassurance after this emotional rollercoaster and noticed the seat next to him was already empty. Darcy was long gone.

Chuck looked at me with a soft smile. "How about you read your letter, and I set up a movie in our dorm? I have some candy from a recent assignment we can eat."

"Thanks," I said.

I sat back, waiting for the room to clear; it would be needed for nothing else today, so I was guaranteed privacy. I stuck my finger into one of the corners of the sealed envelope flap and quickly pulled across to open it. Pulling out the piece of paper inside, I opened it and held it up.

The tears began again as I read:

Hello brother,

I am so sorry. It is unfair that you live with part of you missing. I know if the tables were turned that I would be a blubbering mess without you. You were the best brother I could ever ask for. Though we were opposite in almost everything, we were a perfect match.

I must confess something, brother. I have known your secret for far too long, and it is time we got it out in the open. I know you don't like it here. I see your eyes light up every time we leave the Orphanage. You talk about our parents as if you knew them when, in fact, we do not have a single memory of them. I know it is too late for a chance at a normal family, but there is still a chance for you to have a future where you could have a piece of happiness. We aren't prisoners here, as you sometimes dramatically say. Once you graduate, you can leave and still make the world a better place, just not as an agent. Go work at Google and use their nap pods. Make friends who don't solve the world's problems before breakfast. Leave now if you think it would help you heal. If I could have one wish, it would be to see you find the normal that you were always searching for.

I love you, brother,

Collin

Dropping the letter on the floor, I put my face in my hands. My breath came in gasps, and I had to fight to keep a cry from escaping. I silently wished that I had died instead of Collin. It was unfair to him to wish such a thing, but this pain was more than I could bear.

Picking up his letter and folding it back up, I stuck it in my pants pocket.

I couldn't leave, no matter how true Collin's words were. The Orphanage was my home. Everywhere I looked, I could bring up a memory of Collin. If I left this place behind, it would be like leaving Collin behind.

Trying to be rational, I weighed the pros and cons of living a normal life.

Pro: I get to work at Google.

Con: I leave Collin behind.

Pro: I get to eat whatever I want, when I want.

Con: I leave Collin behind.

Pro: I don't have to maintain my fitness level.

Con: I leave Collin behind.

How could I leave my twin brother behind? He wanted me to leave, but now more than ever, I needed to stay.

Getting up from my seat, I headed toward my dorm room. I walked swiftly, avoiding people and any sympathetic word they might have had for me. There was too much going on in my head to deal with another reassuring smile from someone who would never understand what I was going through. None of these people could know what losing a sibling was like, and I never wished for them to. I wouldn't have wished it on my worst enemy.

Finally, I turned the corner into the hallway where my dorm room was located. The door was open. I walked into the room and looked around at the five beds lining the walls. Two were taken up by Chuck and me, and another two by Austen and Lucas, who was training to become an engineer. The last bed had belonged to Collin. It was beside mine and now served as a reminder of his absence—at least, it would until the Orphanage managed to snag a new training agent from another Orphanage.

Chuck said nothing when I plopped down beside him on his bed. All he did was offer me a gummy bear. I was ready to lose track of time and thought while watching movies for the rest of the evening.

Before Chuck clicked play, I glanced back at Collin's bed.

The cons outweighed the pros. I couldn't leave home. I couldn't leave Collin.

JANUARY

FEBRUARY

CHAPTER 6

"Good job, Baker. Start your walk to the backup car and make your way to the safe house. Agent Hannah has the plane prepped and ready." I sat back in my chair and watched Baker walking away from a burning car.

On one computer, I had begun some paperwork, and on another, I continued to track Baker. There was no way I was going to let him out of my sight until he was home safe. Most earpieces didn't worry much about making sure their agent got home after the assignment was finished. Not many had lost their agent on the return trip. Baker was used to having me as his earpiece and knew I wouldn't stop communicating with him until he was home.

Since returning to classes, I had buried myself in my studies, staying as busy as I could. I tried my best to hide my tears when they rose to the surface. Sometimes I would pass it off as stress over an assignment. Most of the time, the tears came when I was looking at my reflection in my computer screen, a reflection I had once shared with my brother.

I was determined to prove my worth as an earpiece and show that I was a capable agent. The only problem was that half the agents thought I had gone mad, and the other half thought I was still grieving.

They all tried to avoid having me as their earpiece. It was hard to get my training hours in when no one wanted me.

Luckily, Baker had taken me under his wing. He had agreed to let me train as his earpiece as long as I got him home safely, which was really nice of him, because before the incident, we didn't do much of anything together.

Baker hopped into the backup car that had been hidden under a tarp in the forest and started it up. "I know my way to the safe house, and I would rather listen to music than you and your commentary, so I'm signing off for now. Gold stars for this assignment, kid."

"Thanks, Baker," I replied. "Your route is clear, and I'll cut your music if anything comes up. Have a good drive."

His country music blasted, and I quickly moved to lower the volume on my end.

The Spanish countryside was still as Baker ripped down the road. The special chemical some chemist here had come up with was making fast work of burning the car Baker had left behind. Baker had to drench the car in the chemical and set it on fire. In a matter of minutes, it would be nothing but dust on the ground. Any sign of that drug dealer was quickly disappearing. Tomorrow, evidence would pop up and point to a rival drug dealer who was conveniently unconscious in his home at the moment. Baker had taken care of that one earlier today, mixing some pretty powerful sleeping drugs into his afternoon coffee. The local cops would have no problems finding him. Two birds with one stone. These two drug dealers were making life terrible for countless local teenagers. Hopefully, with them out of the way, those teenagers would be able to put their lives back on track.

Switching my attention to homework from the other day, I scratched my head in frustration. Last Friday, in world-economics class, we'd had to look through different companies' statements to see whether or not anyone was illegally shifting funds. It wasn't exactly rocket science, but it was time-consuming. There were mountains of paperwork to sort through.

Austen and Jane were probably already done. Austen was a wizard with paperwork, because the Chief had him going through endless amounts of it, studying every piece to familiarize himself with the ins and outs of the Orphanage. Jane, on the other hand, was training to work somewhere like Wall Street as a financial analyst, though why on Earth someone would want to have anything to do with finances was beyond me. Jane had always been gifted with the ability to look at any math problem and solve it in seconds, with or without a calculator. She was also one of those lucky people gifted with incredibly good looks and intelligence. It was unfair.

Every class at the Orphanage always had five boys and five girls. Our year was the exception since, at the moment, the Chief still hadn't replaced Collin. The American Orphanage loved having five and five while agents were in training. After we graduated, agents would slowly start to die off or retire, making things uneven.

Recruiting was an interesting task. A few agents' jobs were to travel the world in search of recently orphaned babies and take them, leaving no trace of their having ever existed.

The other Orphanages around the world did things a bit differently. The one in England liked positions to pass from father to son. In the past fifty years, they had also started to pass it along to their daughters, but that was a stretch for them. They were the only one that wasn't called the Orphanage, for none of the agents there were actually orphans. They were called the Agency, and thought they had the superior title. England wasn't much fun. The China Orphanage was all girls and was where the American Orphanage had gotten Mary, a girl from my year who was a very handy mechanic. The Orphanage in India was very interesting, in that they waited until homeless kids were five. They watched to see who the best pickpockets were, offered them a better life, and started their training. It was strange, because they either had tons of kids in a single year or as few as one, depending on who they found in the streets. Last but not least, the Russian Orphanage seemed to have a lot of recruits, but we never talked about how they operated. All I knew was that they were always there when we needed them, and they were usually some of the best.

There were five Orphanages in total, each with its own traditions and each tradition stupider than the last. For instance, the American and British organizations took the naming of new recruits very seriously. When the organizations began in 1826, recruits were named after characters from the Bible. In 1902, with those names starting to get overused, the two groups decided to name the recruits after characters in either Shakespeare's plays or the Bible. Then, in 1981, the Chiefs (although they denied it) had a few too many drinks and decided to create a new tradition, with recruits each year being named after characters from a different book. They tried to keep it strictly to classical books, but they had a hard time keeping to that after they decided to let the graduating class pick the book for the new batch of recruits.

Unfortunately, by the time it came around to name my year, the ever-creative graduation class had picked a classic, by Jane Austen. We got named after people from *Pride and Prejudice*.

I was looking forward to when my graduating year would get to pick the book for the new recruits. Collin wanted to go with *The Gunpowder Plot*, but no one was on board with that one. The rest of the '01s thought that book was boring, even though Collin would forever claim it was his favorite. The only thing I could say was that it was better than *Twilight*. What could have possibly possessed the '98s to pick that book, no one would ever know.

"You ready for lunch?"

Startled, I jumped in my chair and twisted around. Chuck was standing right behind me, a smile on his face. Glancing at my watch, I noted the time and started to pack up my tablet in order to keep tabs on Baker while I was at lunch with Chuck.

"Yeah, I'm ready," I responded, getting up and following Chuck. I had been working away in what we called the office: a place where earpieces could help their agents safely through their assignments.

Earpieces rarely had to be on location. In my case, I had a feeling I would be stuck at home until I graduated, and then probably for a while after that. Apparently, having a mental breakdown in the field doesn't look good on your resume.

We kept pace with each other as we walked in silence, heading toward the elevator to go to the cafeteria, which was our usual routine when we were working a week of specialized fieldwork. As long as Chuck wasn't helping in some sort of surgery, and I wasn't needed at my keyboard, he came and got me every day for lunch so that we always had someone to eat with. It wasn't that either of us didn't have any other friends; it was just that, since the incident, Chuck had been the easiest to be around.

In our year of training, we typically had one week of classes, followed by a week of hands-on training. Right now, we were all out on assignments or tasks, depending on which area we were heading into after graduation. Chuck was down in the hospital, working with the doctors who were trying to create a drug that would heal bones in hours rather than weeks. Mary was in the garage, working with a team of mechanics on building a new plane that engineering had been cooking up for months. Lucas was probably down there with her, yelling in her face that she was reading his plans all wrong. Engineering and mechanics had a rough relationship.

Charlotte was at the Orphanage, working on a bomb that could fit in a locket and get past security. I'd tried to convince her that, if we could make it, so could the bad guys, but she just responded that we should try to make it before them.

Jane was in New York, working under another agent whom she would join after graduation in a company they believed had ties with black-market weapon dealers in Africa. Elizabeth was helping with security for some politician heading to Canada, and Austen was, of course, in the Chief's office, following him around and taking notes, preparing for the day he would take over. That was it for my year of '01s.

Except for Darcy.

Since the incident and final statement, Darcy and I hadn't so much as stolen a look in each other's direction. Not a single word had been exchanged or note passed. As far as both of us were concerned, the other didn't exist unless someone else brought them up. Agent Asher, the teacher who told us our assignments for the week, had said that Darcy was going to Africa. I didn't pay much attention beyond that, and probably since she was an assassin in training, nothing about her assignment was given to the rest of our year.

Agent Maria was in front of Chuck and me, and she held open the door to the cafeteria. We walked through and made our way to the lunch line.

The room closely resembled a prison mess hall. There was no other use for this room besides eating, making it pointless to decorate it in a way that would make you want to stay. Agents typically had more urgent places to be.

I shoved my tablet under my armpit and picked up my tray. Behind the counter, retired agents served us our food. Retired agents who chose to stay at the Orphanage and work as staff were held in the highest regard. They did jobs like make meals, clean the facilities, and maintain the grounds. And if we were attacked, they would be our first line of defense if our security system shut down. In return for their continued support, they got full use of the facilities, which included things like pools, saunas, other things old people seemed to like, and any training room. Retired agents also got half the year off, which made for some killer holidays (with, hopefully, no actual killing).

That's what Collin had wanted to do when he retired. He wanted to be a groundskeeper, mowing the lawn every day and cleaning the gutters. He also liked the idea of traveling whenever he wanted and not taking orders. But now, that future was gone for him.

"Hello, Bennet," Leah said from behind the counter. Leah had been retired for almost twenty years now. She had worked in the kitchen for those twenty years, and every lunch, she fought her way to serving the vegetables. She was a nice lady who seemed to know every person here, which I guess isn't that impressive, considering we trained most of our lives to remember bucketloads of information.

"Hello, Leah," I responded lightly. "You are looking as lovely as ever." Collin's and my relationship with Leah consisted of us sweet-talking her into giving us as few green beans as possible. We both hated them. She could see right through us, but she always smiled and gave us a little less, making up for it by giving us more broccoli. You can't win at everything.

"Oh, Bennet," she laughed. "Stop making such a fuss and shove the beans down your throat. And how are you doing, Chuck? Anything to report from the torture chamber below?"

Chuck lifted his tray closer to the counter to make it easier for Leah to put the beans on his plate. "The hospital is going well. Luckily, Agent Ella came back with a broken humerus, giving us a test subject for our new drug."

Leah chuckled. "Lucky for you doctors. Not so lucky for Ella."

We smiled, told her to have a good day, and moved on down the line, collecting the rest of our lunch of chicken and rice.

Chuck and I sat at an empty table and dug into our meals. I reached over and grabbed a cup from the stack in the middle and poured myself a glass of water from the jug on the table. Chuck talked about how the doctors had spilled a whole test tray of drugs they were working on, and how the head doctor, Agent Caleb, was so mad he had flipped a table.

We moved on to talk about my morning and then landed on the classic conversation of superheroes as I choked down my green beans. This time we were discussing whether Chuck could stop all the accidents in the hospital if he had the superpowers of Mr. Fantastic. While Chuck was trying to explain why he would make an excellent Mr. Fantastic, we heard yelling behind us.

"What's going on?" I asked, starting to turn around.

"Don't bother looking," Chuck responded, uninterested. "It's just

Maria and Mason at it again."

Maria and Mason were the most annoy couple around the Orphanage. Maria was loud, meaning that if the two of them were arguing, everybody at the Orphanage could hear. Mason was able to outdo Maria's loudness with his stubbornness. The two of them shouldn't have made a good couple, but they managed to make it work. When they weren't arguing, they were head over heels for each other. They held hands everywhere they went, and Maria would sit on Mason's desk and watch him work when he was an earpiece in the office. I hated working in the office when they were in there. It was very distracting when they would start making out right in the middle of the office.

I laughed. "Mason is probably mad because it's his night to choose what they do for date night, and she doesn't want to watch *Bill and Ted* for the tenth time. Those two are so predictable it's—"

Bang!

The earth-shattering noise echoed off of every wall.

Dropping my glass, I leaped from my seat and booked it out of the cafeteria.

CHAPTER
7

The red-velvet couch beneath me was old and dusty. I tried my best to sink into it and relax, but I couldn't. It looked like it belonged in an old-folks home. In fact, everything in the little room looked old. Even the books on the shelf above the fireplace looked like they belonged in a grandparent's library. So did the paintings on the maroon walls, all of people playing musical instruments.

I was sitting in the Orphanage's only therapy office. When they'd found me, two hours after I'd run out of the cafeteria, they had brought me straight here. This wasn't the first time this had happened.

I hoped Baker wasn't too mad at me for abandoning him. Someone else would have taken my post as his earpiece shortly after I ran off. We can never leave an agent out in the field alone.

A part of my brain danced around the idea that, because I ran away, Baker wasn't going to make it home from his assignment. That would be two people in one year I would have lost. No one would ever want me as their earpiece. I wasn't even sure if I would want me for an earpiece, considering what a flight risk I was becoming.

After Collin died, I'd been in this therapy office every day for a week after the final-statement reading. They kept asking me to talk about what was happening in my head. After five days of not saying anything, I finally snapped and screamed until I could no longer scream. I slept for three days after that, and then the Chief sent me on vacation, hoping some sun would help me cool off. I went to Hawaii to drink smoothies, and then I came right back to class.

I straightened up at the returning memories of screaming at Agent Stephen, the therapist, who was staring at me from behind his desk. He was a thin man, and at the age of seventy-nine, one of the longest-lasting agents. Agent Stephen was obviously in great shape, but everyone could tell by the way he hunched his shoulders and the slight shake in his hands that he was slowing down. That and his marathon time was getting longer, but frankly, at his age, it was still impressive that he would run one every other month with the training ten-year-olds.

"Why did you run?" Agent Stephen was tired of waiting around. He knew I wasn't going to be the first to break the silence.

It wasn't that I was super masculine in the traditional sense. I wasn't one of those guys that had problems sharing my feelings. It was quite the opposite, in fact. My problem was that I had too many feelings. Apparently, I felt so strongly about different things that I didn't know how to express them and kept them bottled up until they exploded.

To make matters worse, my tears would fall throughout the day without my permission. I would be brushing my teeth, and the mirror would set me off. Austen would put something on Collin's empty bed, triggering a steady stream down my cheeks. The worst was when people would call me the wrong name in the hallway, forgetting for a moment which of us was dead.

I took a deep breath and replied sheepishly, "There was a loud noise."

Agent Stephen wrote on his yellow legal pad. "And do you know what that noise was?"

"No." The oppressive room seemed to press down on me, flooding my head with images I didn't want there, images of textbooks lying abandoned on the ground and blood trickling down a poor girl's face.

Many people see colors as warm or pleasing to the eye, but for me, colors were just noise, another thing to notice. The Orphanage did have some paintings on the gray walls, but they were mostly ocean scenes, and the blues almost seemed to blend in with the gray. Five beds in one room with gray walls: That was what home felt like to me, not this maroon office with its glowing fireplace and paintings of people playing instruments. I wondered what had made Agent Stephen decorate his office this way. Did other agents who came in here find it suffocating or was it just me? Maybe I did need to be in here.

"What was the last thing that you and Chuck were talking about?" he inquired.

What does this have to do with the noise? I wondered. Maybe he wanted me to figure out what the noise was. I thought hard about what had been happening when the Earth had felt as if it might explode again.

"Chuck was telling me that he probably wouldn't look good in Mr. Fantastic's superhero suit."

"Good, good. And what was happening at the table next to you?" Agent Stephen knew I should be able to answer that question. After all, we were trained to be observant in all situations.

I closed my eyes and pictured the room just before I had gotten up and run away. I saw the counter where Leah was serving green beans. I noticed three agents coming through the main cafeteria doors. Behind me, there was a group of fourteen-year-olds talking about their recent skydiving challenge. Behind Chuck were five agents huddled together over their meals, discussing something that seemed important. Around the room, others were moving about, collecting their food or heading to talk to someone.

My eyes popped open in sudden realization. "It was Maria," I exclaimed. "The sound came from Maria."

Agent Stephen nodded in encouragement. "Very good. Now you know who made the sound, but what *was* the sound?"

"She was talking to Mason about their date night. Everyone knows they've been dating for the past five months. She, she…" I trailed off.

"Agent Bennet, it wasn't a bomb," Agent Stephen told me, pity filling his voice. "There was no bomb in the cafeteria. The bomb was three months ago. That is in the past. Now think. What did you hear in the cafeteria?"

I took a deep breath and held it for a couple of seconds before slowly letting it out. My eyes brimmed over with tears that streamed down my face. "It wasn't my brother's bomb. It was Maria throwing a tray at Mason. I am safe, and Collin is dead. That happened three months ago."

Agent Stephen sighed. "Very good. You can't let this trigger win in your life. If you want to graduate, I suggest you come up with a trick to avoid running from every loud noise you hear. The Chief will never let you back in the field if this continues. Even to work behind a desk, you can't jump every time someone puts their coffee cup down too hard."

I could hear the pain in his voice. He wasn't trying to be cruel. I needed to get this under control. It made other agents worry, especially field agents. If I wanted to work with agents other than Baker, I was going to have to stop jumping at every little sound around me.

"But how am I supposed to do this?" I asked. "Last time I was in here, I yelled and screamed until I was out of energy. It worked then, but now I need answers. Every time I look at myself, I see my brother. I'm sure my brother's friends see him when they look at me. Sometimes they forget and call me by his name. I see him, but I can't feel him. When he first left, it was all I could do to tear my attention away from his voice in my head. As time moved on, his voice slowly started to disappear, and I don't know what I will do when it's gone. I miss him so much. I feel like I am dying every time I wake up in the morning and roll over, only to see his empty bed." I took a deep breath in between what had turned into sobs. "Collin was so strong. If the roles were reversed, and I was gone instead of him, he would just get up in the morning and follow orders. He would be on the mats wrestling Austen or sneaking off with Darcy. But I'm weak. I jump at every noise and cry at my own reflection. Chuck has been patient with me, but I know he misses the old Bennet, the one who would play boardgames after we finished our homework and joke about smuggling pudding out of the cafeteria. I'm so weak that I can hardly keep myself standing upright most of the time."

Agent Stephen had put his notebook and pen down and was listening intently. He nodded a couple of times and seemed to be getting his thoughts in order. "I do not believe you to be weak, Bennet. I believe we all have our own strengths, and it is for you to figure out what your strengths are. You need to acknowledge that in yourself. Until then, I would say your strength is how strongly you loved your brother, how much you care for your best friend, Chuck, and also how honest you can be. Thank you for sharing that."

"No problem," I breathed out, trying to catch my breath after my rant.

"As for Collin's friends," he continued, "it is not your job to worry about what they think. You can certainly be there for them when they need you to comfort them, but at the end of the day, you are Bennet, not Collin. You are allowed to miss your brother, but you are not allowed to let it consume you. And lastly, you are going to get out of bed every morning and do your job, like you have trained your whole life to do. You are an agent, and as you know, agents die all the time. If every time you lose someone you end up back here, then you are not what the Orphanage needs. So, I suggest that, if you can't get out of bed for yourself, get out of bed for Collin, because if he were here today in the cafeteria, he wouldn't have recognized you."

Again, he spoke the truth, even though it was painful to hear. He was the only person who hadn't tiptoed around my emotions since the incident. I knew he wasn't trying to purposefully hurt me, and so I tried my best to interpret what he was saying as advice. The gentle tone in which he spoke helped with that.

I looked at the floor, unable to make eye contact with Agent Stephen. "Do you think I should retire and leave this place?" I hadn't told anyone what was in the letter that Collin had written to me. No one knew that I thought every day about those words and whether or not I should listen to him. This office was the perfect place to find out someone else's opinion on the topic.

"I think you should do what makes you happy. It is not your responsibility to make your brother happy. He isn't here. So, the final question is, what do you feel called to do?"

"I want to be strong," I admitted, as the truth dawned on me. "I want to be strong like Collin."

I was done here. Agent Stephen couldn't make me stay. My body shook like electricity was running through it. Getting up, I walked across the room, opened the door, and left with a plan of my own.

I was going to run toward the noise.

CHAPTER 8

THE ORPHANAGE
MARCH 13
7:00 P.M.

I wasn't crazy. I wasn't going to be one of those people who ran head-first into an idea without running it past my best friend. Sure, Agent Stephen was a trained therapist and had spent years out in the field as an agent, but there are some things that only your friend can advise you on.

Passing by the boys' rooms on the left and the girls' rooms on the right, I paused. This was home. This floor belonged to training agents, ages eleven to eighteen, while the nursery was two floors below us, and ages five to ten were one floor down. We ran around in these hall-ways, playing insane games that we made up, coming up with a list of complex rules more insane than the game itself. It was a place where we could act like kids for a few minutes—at least until an agent came in to settle us down and tell us to behave.

Once we graduated, we would head over to the main housing area on the far side of the Orphanage. There, you no longer had to share a room with four other people, but just one. Most of the time, your roommate was probably off on an assignment, which meant you got the room to yourself. I figured if Collin were still around, we would have shared a room after we graduated. It would have been awesome. We would have had a minifridge full of snacks and hosted movie nights. It could have been our own space, for just us brothers.

We still had a few months of school left this year and then one more year before we graduated. School here was basically like any regular public school, except your education began the moment you arrived as a baby, and you graduated high school at the age of nine and moved on to university-level courses at ten. As well as teaching us math and as many languages as we could manage, the teachers would sprinkle in some martial arts training and the elegant technique of shooting a gun. We were probably some of the only six-year-olds who knew how to take apart, clean, and reassemble a gun blindfolded.

Not everyone continued with combat training. People like Chuck and me, who weren't specializing in fieldwork, stopped taking those classes at thirteen when we focused on a specific area. Our year still came together for basic classes like Espionage 101, but when it came to dissecting people, cars, or computers, we would split up. There were so many levels to our training that school could look different for almost everyone, depending on what the Orphanage wanted the individual to become.

Finally reaching my room, I burst through the door, giving no warning to anyone on the other side. Lucas, Austen, and Chuck were all there. It was an easy day of work with no major earth-shattering events, giving them an excuse to just laze around. Austen and Lucas were in front of the mirror, examining Austen's new black eye, which he'd probably gotten while combat training with Chief Benjamin. Chuck was sitting on his bed with a textbook open, but he clearly was not paying any attention to it, laughing instead as Lucas poked at Austen's eye. I could tell Austen was about ready to throw Lucas to the floor, so I waited.

A moment later, Lucas was on the floor with Austen on top, joining Chuck in laughter. Lucas looked up from the floor and noticed me. "Hey, how was the shrink's office?"

I prayed my face didn't give me away as I responded with, "A lot of 'and how does that make you feel?'"

Lucas laughed, and Austen looked puzzled. Austen was the more serious of the five—four—of us. I think the Chief had tried his best to remove whatever joy and laughter Austen had in him and replace it with a sense of responsibility.

"Agent Stephen has never asked me that," Austen stated. He went for monthly sessions to ensure that his mental health was in top-notch condition for when he became the Chief.

"It's a joke, Austen. Laugh a little." That was comical, coming out of my mouth, since it took everything in me these days to force a smile onto my face. I made my way toward Chuck's bed and plopped down. He snatched his textbook away before I could sit on it.

Austen got off of Lucas and got to work on the mat beside his bed, doing push-ups and other exhausting exercises. This was his regular after-dinner routine when we didn't have anything else going on. I had been gone so long this afternoon that I had missed dinner. I knew there would be leftovers in the fridge I could get to if I wanted any. I also had a bag of chips under my bed from a field trip to Chicago last Thursday.

The five—four—of us had been roommates since birth, so we were all used to each other's strange habits. We were used to Lucas's heavy breathing at night and to Chuck's pacing when he studied for tests. Lucas, Chuck, and I were used to Austen and Collin wrestling on the floor to see who was better. We all had our own thing, like how—since girls and boys weren't allowed in opposite rooms until we graduated—sometimes Darcy would hang out in the doorway after she and Collin had been on a date. They would stand there for hours talking, not paying attention to anyone else.

We all got along, thankfully, other than the odd fight over someone being too loud or not cleaning their toothpaste out of the sink. Pranks were a big thing in our room, and with Lucas being an engineer, they typically got way out of hand. One time he rigged Collin's bed to flip up the moment he lay down. In return, Collin attached some climbing ropes to the ceiling and waited right above the doorway for Lucas.

He gave Lucas a good scare when he landed unexpectedly on top of him. Luckily, he got it on camera.

Chuck looked up at me and asked, "Want a comic book?" He opened his nightstand and pulled out a couple. He opened up a new *Spider-Man*, and I reached for an old *Hawkeye* that I enjoyed.

We sat in silence for a little while, with me waiting for the right moment to speak. The only noise was the turning of pages and the occasional sound from Austen doing his exercises. Lucas had made his way to the '03 boys' dorm room, because they were organizing a massive game of sardines. Between a hiding space as big as the Orphanage and players whose job it was to be invisible, the game usually lasted an hour or two.

I was nervous, even though Chuck was my best friend. I finished my first comic book and reached for a second one, the conversation from Agent Stephen's office fresh in my mind. It was crazy, what I wanted to do, but I knew I had to say it out loud, or else I would sit at my desk as an earpiece for the rest of my life, regretting it.

Without glancing up from my comic book, I took a deep breath and let the words come smoothly out of me. "I'm going to become a field agent."

"Sorry, what?" Chuck questioned, looking up bewildered from his own comic book.

Taking another deep breath, I prepared myself again, knowing it wouldn't be the last time I would have to say this. "I'm going to switch career paths and train to be a field."

Austen was still off in his corner, too focused on his workout to take notice. I kept my voice down, because I wasn't prepared for sensible Austen to come over and tell me off just yet.

Chuck just shook his head at me like I had gone insane. "One more time?"

"You heard me, Chuck. I don't want to be an earpiece anymore. I *can't* be an earpiece anymore. I want to be a field agent."

"But… why? No offense, but you aren't exactly the most athletic person in this room—or even the second-most, for that matter. You can barely hit the target on the shooting range. Five months ago, when we had to go for a brush-up, you rigged up a robot to fire the gun and hit the target for you. You passed the written test last year for basic maneuvers on how to ditch someone tailing you, but when the practical test came along, you sat in the mall's food court and ate ice cream for two hours before Agent Andrew said you failed. This is not a good idea, Bennet."

I knew he was right. There were reasons I had become an earpiece, and my love for computers wasn't exactly at the top of the list, though it would probably be second. I had no hand-eye coordination—or any coordination, really. How can I put this delicately? I was like the kid on a soccer team that the coach would yell at to stop picking flowers and kick the ball. I wasn't the type of kid that wanted to solve my problems with my fist. I was scared of fighting. Collin had tried to help me get over it, but by the time I was thirteen, I was way better at breaking into someone's email than punching them in the face; it hurt my hand too much. So, the Orphanage gave up their dream of field-agent twins and put me in the computer labs.

"I don't want to be the one behind the computer screen watching other people in the line of fire. I want to be out there helping people and making a difference."

Chuck looked at me with his big brown eyes. "You do make a difference, and if you don't feel it now, when we graduate and become agents, you will get more assignments and more agents than just Baker to work with."

"Chuck, I need a change. Something that I choose and that isn't forced upon me."

Chuck gave a sigh, signaling that he was giving up. I could see the pain behind his eyes as he connected the dots and figured out that this had to do with my brother. Everything now seemed to connect to him. "First, no one is stupid enough to take you on to help train you and allow you to come on an assignment with them. Second, our teachers aren't going to allow you to change course when they have worked so hard to make you what you are. Third, the Chief isn't going to let you switch now, when you are so close to graduating."

"Thanks for the encouragement," I said sarcastically.

"No problem," he retorted. "So, how are you going to do this, you stubborn gun-slayer?"

I let out a chuckle. "I need to find someone who will take me on and train me, because I can't just jump into classes. They'd kill me during practice. Hopefully, if I find someone to help me out, then maybe I could convince the Chief to let me switch career paths. I mean, I can always ask. What's the worst that could happen?"

"Considering no one has ever switched career paths since the beginning of the American Orphanage, I'd say the worst is the Chief says no, and everyone finds out and teases you for a couple of months. It's not like the world is going to end or anything. Who are you thinking of asking to train you?" Chuck wondered.

"I don't know," I said, thinking out loud. "I'm not close with many field agents besides Baker, and he'd probably just laugh if I asked him. Who would give up their free time to train me?" I picked up the comic book and returned my attention to it, hoping that an answer would come to me tomorrow.

Chuck followed my lead and picked up his comic book as well. "Let's face it, no graduated agent is going to take you under their wing," he added before he started reading.

He was right. Only an idiot would take me on now, and Baker would probably say no. Maybe this was as far as my idea would go. Maybe my idea of becoming a field agent like Collin would remain a fantasy. No graduated agent would ever agree to train me.

No *graduated* agent.

"Chuck, that's it!" I exclaimed.

"What did I miss?" he asked, not looking up from his comic, clearly not wanting to encourage me.

"No *graduated* agent would take me on, but what if I asked

someone who isn't graduated?"

"Who do you have in mind?" I could see curiosity written across his face. As much as he didn't want to be a part of this, he was my best friend, and knowing him, he wouldn't be able to help but get involved.

"Someone who hasn't talked to me in over three months."

CHAPTER 9

Darcy was in the dimly lit weapons room. I hesitated at the door, then slowly entered. "Can I ask you something?" I asked.

Darcy and I hadn't really spoken since the reading of Collin's final statement, just polite words while passing in the hallways. I didn't know what to say to her. I mean, how do you say, "sorry that I lived and your boyfriend died"? The idea that she blamed me for his death made me give her a wide berth. She had always been a cold person. Considering her job title, no one blamed her for that, but she'd usually been nice enough to me while she and Collin were a thing.

My guess was that, since I looked exactly like him, I was too much of a reminder of all that we had lost. That was basically why I broke all the mirrors in my dorm room the day after his death. Chuck, Austen, and Lucas didn't say a word when I threw the mirrors to the ground. They just let me continue until they were all gone. I assumed it was because no one had ever seen me act out in anger—*I* had never seen me act out in anger—and so most of them tiptoed around me when it came to things like my brother. The janitors cleaned up the mess right away and put new mirrors up while I was on my break in Hawaii.

"What?" Darcy didn't look up from her workstation. Her hands were moving, but her body was perfectly still. I couldn't see what she was doing, but it sounded like she was sharpening knives. Typical.

I didn't know how to ask my question. What if she said no? What if she laughed and told the others and still said no? What if she said yes? No matter what happened, I didn't know if I was prepared for the answer.

I stared at the wall rack, which was filled with every gun you could think of. I could probably name most of them and take apart and put back together about ten. I would've bet Darcy knew how to take apart and put together all of them blindfolded.

Classes in this room had always bored me. Cleaning knives and polishing whatever gadgets an agent had recently brought back from an assignment wasn't my idea of learning. This room reminded me more of a dungeon—a torture chamber—than a place to teach students. The low ceiling and lack of windows made me feel claustrophobic.

"Train me," I blurted out nervously.

"I'm sorry," Darcy replied. "I'm still waiting for a question."

Of course, she would make this difficult. "Can you please train me?" I mumbled, looking at the cobblestone floor.

Her movements never faltered. She kept mechanically sharpening her knife. "Train you for what?"

I took a deep breath. "Train me to be a field agent like my brother."

Darcy flashed up from the chair, knife in hand, and stood perfectly still except for her blonde ponytail, swishing behind her. "You want me to *what?*"

I eyed the knife in her hand. Though I knew Darcy well enough, I didn't trust her. She was an assassin, after all. Thankfully, she didn't have a reason for killing me at this point.

"Train me to be a field agent like my brother. I can't just sit behind a computer till I'm forty and then retire to teach new recruits how to do my job."

Darcy took a step forward, away from her chair and desk, the knife twirling in her hand. She wasn't exactly looking at me; it was more like she was looking past me. "Your brother seemed to think that you would spend the rest of your life behind a computer, so if you feel like honoring him in some stupid way, stay where you belong." She turned to head back to her desk as if the conversation was over.

"*No!*" I shouted. I was getting emotional, but I couldn't help it; Darcy scared me. "I can't sit behind a computer anymore. I want to do what Collin did. I want to be able to help people out in the world. I can't just let everything Collin did die in that explosion. I have to try to keep him alive somehow." I was either sweating or crying by this point; I couldn't tell. This would have been much easier to do through an email.

She looked directly at me this time. Raising her knife slowly, until it was pointing straight at my face, she started to walk toward me. "Let me get this straight. You have spent your whole life focusing on being an earpiece, something that you love and happen to be very good at. And now, so close to graduation, you want to switch career paths to become a field agent in memory of your *dead* brother. Do I have that right?"

"Yep," I squeaked.

"And to top that off, you have zero hand-eye coordination, you get sweaty when you are overwhelmed, and you can't even kill a spider, let alone a human being with your bare hands."

So, it was sweat and not tears. Great. "That sounds about right."

"You're an idiot."

"So, you'll do it?"

Darcy lowered the knife to her side, walked back to her workstation, and picked up the four knives she had already sharpened. "No," was all she said before she turned, ponytail swishing, and walked out of the weapons room.

I slumped down on the chair she'd been sitting in. Why hadn't she said yes? What had I done wrong?

I toyed with the knives that were still on the table. Collin would have said the right things. He always knew how to get what he wanted. One time he talked Chuck and me into giving him all of our chocolate pudding for a week. We clued in when Mary and Charlotte sat with us at dinner and told us that we were not over regulation weight from the chocolate pudding we'd been eating but rather from Collin stepping on the back of the scale while we weren't paying attention.

Standing up, I picked up one of the knives and tried twirling it in my hand like Darcy was doing earlier. She made it look so smooth and easy.

"Ouch!" I'd grabbed the wrong end of the knife. A tiny bit of blood oozed out of a thin cut. This field agent thing was going to be harder than I thought.

Darcy was right. I knew this was a terrible idea. But it was my only chance at a piece of joy, a chance to feel closer to Collin. I had spent my whole life here avoiding becoming a field agent, and now I was running head-first into the idea. Collin had always been there to help me pass the hard classes that bored me to no end, like martial-arts training or outdoor education, while I helped him pass computer coding or documentation class. We were in perfect balance. The best team. But now I was missing my other half—the half who knew how to do everything that seemed to matter.

"Oh, Collin, what am I doing?" That was probably the wrong question to ask my dead brother. Anything I did at the Orphanage involved a computer. Maybe I had to be more like him. "Collin, what would you do?"

Picking up three knives from the table, I left the weapons room and made my way toward the training room I hoped Darcy was in. I had to prove myself worthy of a title as great as field agent. This was my chance.

CHAPTER 10

The training room only had a few people in it this late at night. There were four different sections. One corner housed the mats and equipment for practicing hand-to-hand combat; that was Collin's favorite, and my least favorite. In another corner were five targets that could be used for arrows, knives, axes, or anything else that you could throw. The third corner had weight-training equipment. Nothing fancy, because we had an actual room for weights and such, but enough for a quick workout. There were no treadmills. If you wanted to run, you could either go to the main training room near the graduated agents' housing or go to the track. The last corner had a whiteboard and a couple of desks with chairs for teaching purposes. It was also home to the first-aid kit and a fridge full of ice packs.

Like everything else at the Orphanage, the walls were all different shades of gray. There were no windows. Most rooms at the Orphanage had few windows or none at all. We didn't want to risk a drone seeing what was going on inside. Not that a drone could get anywhere near without malfunctioning.

To the outside world, the Orphanage looked like a fancy hospital for people who needed special care. A high wall surrounded the entire property. We were pretty far from civilization, so anyone driving out to us came on purpose. If they did, they couldn't get past the gatehouse, because they were told that they needed an appointment to enter. If they tried calling the number on the card they were given, they would get either a busy signal or an answering machine. Needless to say, no one ever got an appointment.

Darcy was on the training mats, hitting a dummy with a wooden pole. Her perfect blonde ponytail swished back and forth as she moved gracefully around the dummy, almost like a dance. It fascinated me how she could stand perfectly still at attention at one moment, as rigid as a statue, then move with the lightness of a bird the next moment. She was in total control of her body.

I took a deep breath and gathered every ounce of courage I had before I opened my mouth to speak to probably the scariest person I knew. My voice boomed in the room. "I wasn't done talking to you." The knives I still held had become slippery.

Darcy paused with the pole frozen in the air, inches from the dummy's head.

The few others in the training room turned to see what was going on, including a group of '05 boys who stopped throwing axes at the targets to see what was happening on the mats. It wasn't every day an earpiece shouted at an assassin.

I took a step toward Darcy as she dropped the wooden pole and turned to face me, a cold expression on her face. I was probably pushing my luck with her. The only people who spoke to her with authority were our teachers or the Chief or someone higher up at the Orphanage. Anyone in the regular world who spoke to her in a demanding way most likely didn't live to see tomorrow.

Darcy was average height for a girl, which meant she was almost a head shorter than me. Despite that, with her training, she could take me down if I said the wrong thing. I had to be very careful and craft my next sentence with extreme caution.

"I can do this. Please just let me prove it," I begged, my voice losing the confident sound it had had just a moment before.

"You aren't going to let this go, are you?" she asked.

"Nope."

Closing her eyes and taking a deep breath to calm herself, she asked, "Why do *I* have to train you? Why are you asking *me?*"

I paused to think, then replied, "Because I know you're not afraid to hurt me."

She debated this new information. She knew I was right. I could feel the pent-up anger she had toward me.

"Let's make a deal," I proposed. I didn't need to outfight Darcy, I just needed to outsmart her. There was no way I could beat her if we played by her rules, so I needed to make sure we were playing by my rules.

Darcy looked suspicious. "What kind of a deal?" She didn't have time to beat around the bush. She wanted to get rid of me as fast as possible.

I looked around the room. The boys by the targets had put their axes on the ground and were not even trying to hide the fact they were staring at us. They were probably hoping I would get a beating.

Raising the knives in my hand, I replied, "Give me three chances to get a bullseye. If I hit it, you'll train me."

"Three chances?"

"Yes. That's all I'm asking for."

"And then I have to train you to become a field agent?"

I nodded.

Frowning, clearly weighing the pros and cons of the situation, she started toward the area that housed the targets. I followed her. The boys moved away and sat on the floor nearby as spectators. Others that were in the gym also paused their workouts to watch.

Pausing forty feet away from the targets, she turned, grabbed one of the knives from my hand, spun, and threw it. It hit the board dead center. She went to retrieve it. On her way back, she started to speak. "To lay out what this will look like, if you—with zero coordination and lack of strength—manage to hit a bullseye with one of the knives,

I will agree to train you. Now, that does not mean you will get permission from our teachers or Chief Benjamin. If somehow you are able to make the same deal with them as you are with me, and manage to convince them to let you change career paths, then I will train you. That is also *if* they agree to let *me* train you, instead of a graduated agent.

"Training you means that you do everything I say. It's stupid of you to come to me, because I'm an assassin, not a regular field agent. My approach to all of this is kill first and ask no questions, so you'd better get used to that."

She paused, handing me the knife she had brought back from the target. "When you fail," she said, leaning in close for only me to hear, "you will leave all of this behind and go back to sitting behind your computer. You will never speak of becoming a field agent again. You won't even think of being a field agent. Do I make myself clear?" She stared me down with those piercing blue eyes.

I smiled in spite of myself. I couldn't believe I had managed to get her to agree to my deal. I thought I would have to do a lot more convincing. Technically, I still had to talk to the Chief and my teachers, but by hitting the middle of the target, I would be halfway to honoring Collin's memory. I could be a field agent like him and never have to sit behind a desk and watch other people risk their lives. I would never again have to carry the pain of losing someone, because it would be me who would be lost if something ever happened.

"Yes," I answered, grabbing the knife from Darcy.

She stepped out of my way, and I lined myself up with the target.

Folding her arms, she smiled and leaned against the wall. "Why do you want this so badly?"

I knew why. I couldn't lose Collin. But she didn't need to know that. "Why do you care?" I asked. "You already made the deal."

"You're an idiot."

"Can I throw the knives, or are you backing out?"

"Go ahead," she purred. In her mind, she had already won. There was no way I could possibly win. She had nothing to lose, and I had the rest of my life on the line.

Deep breath in, deep breath out.

Putting two of the knives on the ground, I held the third in my right hand and pulled back my arm. I gave a couple of gentle sways, trying to focus on aiming. Thinking I was lined up and had a good grip, I flung my arm forward and released the knife. It swung through the air and made its way toward the target. I watched in anticipation, praying for it to make contact.

The knife didn't even reach the target before it hit the floor. I heard some snickers from the boys sitting off to the side. I didn't bother to give them a look. I had a plan.

Reaching for the second knife, I positioned myself again to throw. This time I focused my efforts on using more strength so that I could actually hit the board. When we had practiced this in our brush-up on combat training class, since I wasn't becoming a field agent, we had stood a lot closer to the target. I could hit the target in those instances, but never a bullseye.

An agent using the weights walked over to get a better view. Everyone was curious to see what would happen.

Believing I was lined up and ready to go, I flung the knife toward the target. I let out a groan when the knife flew past the board and hit the wall behind.

"First, not enough strength," Darcy sneered. "Now, too much."

Ignoring her, I grabbed the third and final knife. Silence filled the room as I took aim. I tried my best to appear like I was putting some effort into my stance.

Then, letting out a scream, I charged the board. I ran as fast and as safely as I could with a knife in my hand. Getting closer to the target, I reached the knife out and focused on the center of the board. I came to a halt and stabbed the target, hitting dead center.

I had done what was in the deal. Darcy and I agreed that she would train me if I hit the middle of the target with one of the knives. We'd never specified how the knife had to get there. We'd never said I couldn't run right up to the target.

Smiling, I turned around and looked at Darcy in triumph. Her expression was one of shock—something that didn't cross her face often. I tried to prepare myself for what was next, unsure if she would uphold her end of the bargain or if she was about to explode. All around, the people who had been watching looked at one another in confusion.

Darcy gathered her composure and simply said, "Smart. Get the Chief on board and permission for me to train you, and I'll uphold my end of the deal. If you listen to what I say and work hard, you'll graduate a field agent."

CHAPTER 11

"And she agreed? Even after you cheated?" Chuck whispered. He was sitting on his bed, and me on mine. We were sharing a bag of chips. I had come back and told him everything that went down between Darcy and me.

"She smiled when she realized what I had done," I told Chuck, putting a chip in my mouth before offering him the bag. "I think she thought it was clever."

He took a handful and put some in his mouth. "I still can't believe it. This is unheard of. No one switches career paths."

It had been a long day. Austen was already asleep, and Lucas was taking a shower. I had come back from the training room a little while ago. I hadn't stayed long after Darcy said she would help me, for fear she would change her mind. Also, my anxiety couldn't handle anything else on this upside-down day.

Chuck had still been reading his comics when I'd come back to the room and was interested to hear what I had to say.

"Do you think you're rushing into this?" Chuck asked. "I mean, you only came up with this idea today, in a therapy session of all places."

I didn't want to answer that. I didn't want to think too hard about that or anything. For the last few months, all I had been doing was thinking, and it hurt. I wanted to move forward, and this was the best way for me to do it.

Instead of answering his questions, I changed the subject. "I think the more important question is, what's up with your hair?"

Chuck sighed in defeat. He walked on eggshells around me, always trying not to make me hurt more than I already was. I felt bad that he did that, but I also appreciated it, because I never had to worry about him saying something random and triggering a reaction from me.

He seemed to weigh his options. Should he push the matter further, or should he move on?

He decided to move on. A smile crept across his face. "It wasn't working with my hospital cap, so I got Austen to help me get rid of it while you were off with Darcy. I think I'll keep it short. Besides, I want my main feature to be my beautiful chocolatey eyes, not my crazy hair."

We both let out a quiet laugh, ignoring all the unspoken words between us.

I put the unfinished bag of chips under my bed and rolled toward the light on the dresser between us. We both said goodnight, and then I clicked it off.

The room was almost pitch-black. The only light was coming from the bathroom, where I could still hear the water running from Lucas's shower. I heard Austen murmur something unintelligible in his sleep and Chuck shifting, trying to get comfortable in his bed. I knew these noises. These were the familiar sounds of my life, a routine for the past sixteen years, the only difference being the absence of Collin.

His nighttime ritual no longer added to the constant noises and movement in our lives. The bed next to mine was empty and would stay empty until the Orphanage decided to replace Collin with someone from another Orphanage to ensure five boys graduated in our year. What a horrible day that would be, to not only turn to look at my brother's bed without him in it but to see a completely different body there.

I lay on my back, staring up at nothing, recalling the events of the day. My heart ached as my emotions caught up with me. A tear escaped my eye and ran slowly down my cheek and into my ear. I wiped it away and rolled over to face Collin's bed.

On one wall, there were three beds: Chuck's, mine in the middle, and then Collin's. On the other wall were Lucas's and Austen's beds. It had been like that since we were old enough to be out of cribs. We each had a dresser beside our bed full of our stuff—not that we had a lot of stuff. I kept reminding myself that, even though a huge piece was missing, this was still my home.

Lucas was out of the shower now. I heard the door to the bathroom open and shut. He went straight to his bed and crawled in. I tried to close my eyes and let sleep overcome me, but my brain decided to work overtime.

Where had my strength to talk to Darcy come from? I hadn't formed complete sentences around her since the day before the incident. I hadn't even made eye contact with her before today, so the courage I had managed to gather was completely foreign to me. Maybe I'd figured she would be the only person crazy enough to help me. Maybe, since we shared a connection with Collin, I'd figured she would soften her hard exterior for me. Or maybe, I'd thought that me looking exactly like her dead boyfriend would scare her into helping me.

That last one was crazy. Nothing scared Darcy.

I wondered whether or not she hated me for losing her boyfriend, just as I hated myself for losing my brother.

What would Collin say if he could see me now, trying to become a field agent like him? A whole part of me was missing, and I was trying to replace it by becoming him. I wondered if Agent Stephen knew what I was thinking. I hoped not, because he would probably advise that I come to therapy for the rest of my life. But I couldn't live without Collin. Every day it felt like I forgot some piece about him, and I needed to do whatever I could to save him in my mind.

No matter what I told myself about training to be a field agent, no matter how many people told me I was terrible or that this was a bad idea, I had to keep fighting. I knew this was what I needed, that this was the change that would finally keep me from drowning in my broken heart.

I shifted in my bed, turned onto my back, and closed my eyes again. Holding on to the idea that I was doing what was best for me and for Collin, I fell asleep.

THE ORPHANAGE
MARCH 14
6:55 A.M.

Sitting outside Chief Benjamin's office, I went over in my head what I was going to say to him. I'd woken up early—at the same time as Austen—anxious about what I had to do. I needed to get it over with, like ripping off a Band-Aid. I had to ask permission to change careers now, or else I feared I would never do it. My foot shook in anticipation.

Chief Benjamin had a morning routine, making it easy for me to find him. He wasn't exactly a terrifying person, but he was the Chief. He had power over everything in the American Orphanage. What he said was basically the law. Everything needed to have his signature, or it couldn't happen. He knew every secret there was to this place and probably the other Orphanages, as well. Every month, the Chiefs of all five Orphanages got together for a meeting. No one but those five Chiefs knew what happened behind those doors.

He had become Chief when he was thirty-four. He was now fifty-two but didn't look a day older than when he'd started except for a couple of gray hairs. He was in excellent shape. He would probably retire when he reached his sixties, which would make Austen, who would be in his mid-twenties, the youngest Chief in American Orphanage history. Until then, Austen's schooling wasn't over, and he would continue shadowing the Chief.

To avoid tapping my hands as well as my leg, I put my hands into my hoodie pockets.

I got this, I told myself. *I tell agents what to do all the time as an earpiece. Why should face-to-face be any different?*

I couldn't tell if my pep talk was working, but at least it gave me something to do. Sure, I did tell agents what to do, but that was typically a life-and-death situation. This did feel like that, except I was my own earpiece. I was pretty sure that the Chief didn't have training agents ordering him around. Who *knew* how he was going to react to me being so forward?

My ears perked up and my thoughts stopped when I heard movement behind his door. Then it opened, and Chief Benjamin and his assistant, Agent River, came out. They walked right past me without even glancing in my direction and made their way down the hallway.

For a shocked moment, I sat completely still, watching my chance disappear. Then, shaking my head, I jumped up and followed them. I knew they knew I was behind them, but they paid no attention to me.

I caught up to them at the office, where the other earpieces and I often worked. This morning, about a third of the desks were occupied by agents. There were one hundred stations to work at, and that was only in this office. I've also worked in my bedroom with a laptop and a headset, but that was only for easy assignments with Baker.

"Peggy would be great for this assignment," I overheard River tell the Chief. "But if you don't want her, I have two backup options. I've also put together a team for the Morocco assignment that you need to double-check. They will most likely be there for a minimum of two months, so keep that in mind when you approve it. Oh, hi, Bennet," River said, looking over her shoulder at me for the first time.

River knew everybody at the Orphanage by name. She also had a master list of the other Orphanages and always knew who to call for help, though I didn't know if she knew anything about the Russian Orphanage. I was too scared to ask and probably didn't want to know the full answer.

"Hello, Agent River, hello, Chief Benjamin." I tried to muster every ounce of whatever formal and respectful speech I could. I couldn't screw this up because I said something disrespectful to the Chief.

"Hello, Bennet," the Chief responded, not looking up from the paperwork that River had handed him.

"Chief, I have an important question to ask. It is something that means a lot to me, and I need your permission to go forward with it." I rubbed my sweaty palms against my pants.

"Go ahead, Bennet. Make it quick. I have a briefing to get to." He glanced at me for a moment before returning to the papers in his hand.

River gave him a slight nudge from behind and cleared her throat. The Chief looked up at her, and I could see her making eyes at him, as if telling him to give me his full attention. That was what I liked about River. Even though she was small and had a quiet voice, she was very good at making sure the Chief wasn't distracted. The Chief had a policy of showing us the same respect that we showed him, but sometimes he forgot, in which case River would step up to remind him.

"I'm sorry, Bennet," the Chief said. "You have my full attention."

I tried to forget the fear I was feeling and looked for the courage that I'd had the day before with Darcy. Having the Chief and River stare at me was very different than having a training agent's curious eyes watching me.

"I would like to switch career paths," I began.

Chief Benjamin looked at me, confused. I knew he'd never had this request before. What the Orphanage told you to do, you did, not the other way around.

I continued, "I would like to stop training as an earpiece and train to become a field agent. I understand I would need someone to train me in addition to my teachers. I have already taken the necessary steps to find that someone. Training Agent Darcy has agreed to help me." This was going a lot better than I thought. Compared to how I'd handled it last night with Darcy, mumbling my way through explaining what I wanted to do, I was doing great. Apparently, my preparation while waiting for him was paying off.

"Do you want more assignments where you work on location rather than at the Orphanage as an earpiece?" he asked, trying to take control of the conversation. Probably none of his own training before becoming Chief had prepared him for this.

"No, Chief," I told him. "I feel like I have more to offer working as a field than as an earpiece."

Looking back at River and then back at me, Chief Benjamin asked, slightly baffled, "You want to throw away years of earpiece training to become a field agent?"

"Yes, Chief," I answered. I had no idea what he would ask next or how this was going to go down. I thought this might be a sinking ship, but I still prayed that, by some miracle, he would say yes.

Looking back at his paperwork, he replied, "Fine."

"Seriously? Just like that?" I asked, shocked, forgetting to be as respectful as possible to the man who had just granted me my wish.

"Do you want to continue questioning your Chief?" he asked in annoyance. "Now get out of here, and I'll get River to send word to your teachers. You've got a lot of hard work ahead of you."

"Thank you, Chief." I returned to my polite manner, standing as straight as I could. Giving him a nod, I turned and walked away.

I couldn't believe that had worked! It had actually been easier than convincing Darcy to help me. He wasn't even going to make me go talk to my teachers; he was going to do that himself—well, he was going to get River to do it. They were probably going to be very annoyed and confused, mostly because I showed no promise of becoming a successful field agent.

Then, behind me, I overheard the Chief and River talking.

"Chief, was that wise?" River asked. "He is an excellent earpiece, and he is so close to graduating. He'll never pass as a field agent."

"Let him have his fun," the Chief responded. "He'll either go back to his computer or quit. I'm tired of him walking around this Orphanage like a zombie. At least this will keep him distracted for a while."

With the Chief's last words ringing in my ears, I quickened my pace and walked right out of the office and toward my new future as a field agent.

The classroom was familiar, but at the same time, completely different. In this classroom, the focus wasn't on coding or the skill of talking your agent through a building that only you had the blueprints to. No posters outlined how to build a computer or the basics of coding. The walls were the normal gray that the rest of the Orphanage sported. It had ten chairs and ten desks. There was a television at the front of the room as well as a whiteboard. It was strictly business.

I was sitting in my first class of the day, extra early, waiting patiently for my first field-agent training session to begin. Chief Benjamin had made me finish my specialized fieldwork week and any paperwork I had to deal with before anything switched for me.

No more earpiece duties sitting behind a desk in the office for me. No more following agents on security cameras and erasing footage. No more watching the danger and not actually being in it. I was so excited that my leg vibrated under my desk.

It's not like I didn't know anything. I had taken plenty of classes about being a field agent while growing up, but this was much more focused. It was easy to learn the theory of being a field agent, but here I would have to put that theory into practice. I would be lucky if I could even hit the target in shooting practice later that day.

We were all taught basic self-defense maneuvers growing up. Sadly, for me, the term was misleading. I could never actually defend myself against anyone and was usually pinned against the mat within a couple of seconds. I could count on one hand how many fights I had actually won growing up. Hopefully, the only reason I was terrible back then was that I didn't care enough about being in the field to learn any of it. My teachers and Darcy had their work cut out for them, but I was willing to put in everything I had.

Darcy entered the classroom. She gave me a sharp look and walked toward me. Reaching my desk, she stopped, towering over me, and said, "You're in my spot."

I looked around the room at all the empty chairs. There were nine other spaces, and only Austen, Jane, and Elizabeth would be joining us.

"Are you wanting me to move?" I asked a bit cheekily. I smiled, hoping she would laugh or something.

She didn't. "That would probably be a good idea."

I gathered my notebook and pen, stood up, and sat one desk to the left. Darcy sat gracefully in my old seat, placed her notebook and pen on the table, and folded her hands on her desk, sitting perfectly still.

As I settled into my new seat, Jane and Elizabeth arrived, whispering to each other about something. Following them was Austen. When he looked up from his notebook, he noticed me. Word had spread about me switching career paths, so nobody was surprised to see me sitting here.

The problem with this place was that there were no secrets among the trainees. If you ended up in the hospital, everybody knew. If you started dating someone, everybody knew. If you broke up, everybody knew. One way or another, everybody seemed to know everything about everyone's personal business. Which was ironic for a place whose sole purpose was to keep secrets. Needless to say, I'd been the hot topic around the Orphanage for the past couple of days.

Austen, Darcy, Jane, Elizabeth, and Collin had taken these types of classes together for the past few years. Now I was replacing Collin. I assumed it would be weird for them to see someone who looked like Collin but clearly wasn't Collin sitting in their class. Same looks, different mind and personality.

Even though Jane specialized as a financial analyst, she still had to come to these classes because she was technically a field agent. She needed to be prepared in case something went down in some boring office building. She also took some special math classes that the rest of the '01s didn't, just like Chuck had a specialized class in the hospital, and I used to have classes on being an earpiece. The specialized classes often had training agents from different years in them. There had been a couple of '00s and two '02s in my hacking class.

"Good morning," Agent Asher said, hobbling into the classroom and heading straight to the whiteboard. To my surprise, he had a beard. I couldn't believe I hadn't noticed it before. When had he grown that?

"Training Agent Bennet," he said, "the Chief told me that you have switched into my classes. I will show no mercy when it comes to your training. You are so far behind that an '07 would be better than you at this point. I believe that you will excel in your written exams, but when it comes to the practical work, I'm expecting you to explode."

I tried not to wince at the irony of him using that last word.

He continued. "Being an agent is convincing people that you belong somewhere that you don't. Now, convince me that you belong here."

That was the only time he or any teacher would address me about this change. That was my only warning. I knew I would have to put in many more hours than the rest of my friends. I was prepared to work hard—I thought.

He started writing on the whiteboard, and everyone around me started copying what he wrote. I picked up my pen and followed their lead.

Turning to us, Agent Asher ripped off his convincing beard, about an inch long. "The art of disguise," he started, "is what we will be focusing on for the next week. We have touched on it briefly in past years, but this week we will master changing into a new disguise and applying fake facial hair, makeup, and wigs. You girls will turn into men, and you boys will transform yourselves into women. Some boys giggle at the thought of applying makeup, but this may be your greatest tool when you need to cover up a bruise when heading to a gala or add a bruise to earn sympathy points. There are some agents—but not many—who specialize in what we call 'stage makeup,' meaning that they are experts in disguise and can apply a whole new face and accessories in minutes."

I wrote as fast as my hand could move. I needed to get down every word he said, not wanting to fall even more behind than I already was.

Agent Asher was only one of many teachers. One group of teachers taught ages five to ten, and another taught ages eleven to eighteen. There was also a group of agents that worked with all the babies that came in, staying with them until they were five.

The teacher's ages depended on when they'd retired. Agent Asher was in his forties. He retired to the classroom after losing his left leg in a ski chase two years ago. The doctors wanted to give him a bionic leg with the help of some engineers, but he'd decided that his time as a field agent was up and would rather order around training agents. He settled with the simple metal leg that most amputees wore.

"Everybody up," Asher commanded. "We are heading to the closet."

"Try using some black eye shadow to blend the purple," Austen suggested.

I grabbed another brush and stuck it in the black, then looked back into the mirror. "I feel slightly ridiculous," I said.

Austen and I were paired up while the girls were all together. We were trying to create fake bruises, and the girls were doing a way better job. Agent Asher had made it look way too easy to apply makeup. In reality, it was incredibly difficult.

"We're going to work on disguises for the next week, from the start to the end of the school day. This will be second nature to you by the end of the week. At least, it better be," Asher barked. He made a disgusted face when he saw how horrific my fake bruise was.

I had already formed a plan to practice this the next morning before class. I vowed not to be the worst at this.

"I think yours looks better than mine," Austen commented, turning to face me.

I had to agree with him. I wanted to say that he looked like a raccoon, but that would have been offensive to raccoons. His eye was practically black. The purple he'd originally applied was hidden underneath all the other eye shadow he had applied. I tried using my finger to blend the makeup like Agent Asher had shown us, but I couldn't fix it.

"I think your eye is a lost cause," I joked.

"Why are you doing this?" Austen asked.

I knew he wasn't talking about the fake bruise. He hadn't asked me anything about switching career paths at all last week.

I didn't know what to tell him. I knew it wouldn't be the last time someone would ask me, and I needed to have a quick and easy answer. I just hadn't been able to think of a convincing one yet.

"Maybe you should use green eye shadow around the edges instead of yellow. It might show up better," I offered instead.

He turned back to face the mirror again. "I don't understand makeup," he said in defeat. "The girls are killing it."

We both glanced over where they were working. Elizabeth, Jane, and Darcy were laughing as they covered Jane's knuckles in bruises. How on Earth I was going to create bruises on my knuckles when I couldn't even create a black eye was beyond me.

"I needed a change," I told Austen.

He nodded, knowing I was answering his previous question.

Austen was a good guy. He never pushed things that weren't his to know. He was incredibly respectful of other people. I think it had something to do with the fact that the Chief had taught him to be respectful to fellow agents, so that when the time came, they would show respect back two-fold.

The Orphanage had found Austen in an actual orphanage in a small town in Japan. At age five, he showed exceptional leadership and organization skills. He was able to work under pressure and keep an even temper. Apparently, the nursery teachers thought there was something wrong with him because he never seemed to cry. It turned out the agents higher up liked that quality and picked him to become the next Chief.

Grabbing a makeup-removing cloth, I started to wipe away the mess I'd made on my face. A fresh start and no rushing this time was what I needed. Working on making a tiny bruise on my right cheek, I started exactly how Agent Asher had said, using a little bit of red makeup as a base. Next, I applied a little purple, and then yellow around the edges. I took a look in the mirror and thought it was starting to look a little bit more convincing. Thinking back to what we were instructed, I applied the black that we had used too much of last time. I put a little around the edges where the yellow touched the purple. I finished by using my finger to blend it all together.

Looking at Austen, I asked, "What do you think?"

"Unbelievable," he said. "You're here for one day, and you're already better at the lesson than I am." I could tell he was trying to keep it as a joke, but in his eyes, I could see the panic at the idea of being bad at something. His eye was completely black by this point.

"Less black, more purple. Black is only for tiny additions, not the whole bruise," I responded, turning to the mirror with a smile. Maybe I could fake my way into becoming a field agent.

Darcy showed up behind me with a fake bruise covering her upper arm. She sat on the ledge in front of the mirror I was facing. Grabbing my chin, she turned me to examine my tiny bruise.

"Cute, but let's see if we can make that into a real bruise tonight. Be in the training room by seven." With that, she hopped off the counter and left me to my own fear as I imagined what kind of training she would be honoring me with that night.

CHAPTER 13

I lay on the mat, trying to convince myself to get up yet again. Darcy and I had been training for three hours, and the bruise that she had promised me had most likely formed by now, as well as multiple others. She really had her work cut out for her.

Thankfully, for the first two hours, we'd practiced on the air and then moved to a dummy, but for the last hour, I'd been trying—and mostly failing—to dodge Darcy's blows.

"Again!" she yelled.

I got to my feet again and prepared to defend myself. She was at one end of the mat, and I was in the middle. I stuck both fists up in front of me. Coming at me, she dropped into a slide, knocking me off my feet. Before I could recover, she flipped around and smoothly slid her leg over me, sitting on my chest. As she pulled her arm back to strike my sore face, I used as much force as I could to flip her off and spun myself around in order to be on top of her. I sensed a moment of hesitation on her part; she was clearly a little shocked that I'd managed to get her on her back. I sat on her stomach and pulled my right arm back in the same motion she'd used a moment before, intending to land a blow to her face.

I tried not to hesitate at the thought of punching Darcy, but it didn't matter. She used her core strength to lift her head and shoulders off the ground and headbutt me. As I jerked back, she freed herself from under me and kicked me in the chest with both feet. I flew back and lay there for a second, trying to catch my breath.

I was exhausted.

"Stop!" I said in a panic, blocking my face with my hands, as she landed on my chest again. "I need a break."

"No breaks in life-or-death situations," she hissed, slapping me rather gently across the face in a mocking matter.

I lay back in defeat.

Darcy got off of me and headed over to the side to grab some water. I couldn't move. Every bone, muscle, and cell hurt. I didn't know if I would ever be able to use my legs again. How did Collin train like this every day? His whole body must have been calloused from rubbing on the mats and getting hit over and over again.

"Again!" Darcy shouted, putting down her water.

I stared at her for a second, still unable to move. It's funny how you can live with someone your whole life, take classes with them, and not really know them. "We've been doing this forever. Everything hurts, and I can barely breathe. Aren't you tired of hitting me?" I mumbled through swollen lips.

"One, I don't think I'll ever get tired of hitting you," she responded, standing basically at attention. Her posture was perfect, whereas mine typically looked like that of a middle-aged man living in his mother's basement, hovering over a videogame.

"Two," she continued, "being a field agent isn't about complaining about your circumstances; it's about adapting to them."

"What is that supposed to mean?" I asked, slightly confused. I had never heard the Orphanage teach that.

She sighed, annoyed, and said, "Imagine you are in Estonia on an assignment. It's freezing cold, snowing, and no shelter in sight. Now, if you stand there and complain about being cold, you aren't going to get warm. You need to keep moving. Come up with a plan. Are there trees around you? Start a fire. Wiggle your toes and jump up and down to keep your blood going. You have a job to do, and if you complain, nothing is going to get done. You need to adapt to your circumstances. If things change, you change."

I let that sink in. It made sense. I compared her lesson to what had felt like the last day of my life, when Collin had noticed the clock getting closer to zero. He didn't keep trying to stop the clock. He pulled the fire alarm and got everyone out. He'd changed the plan in order to complete his goal.

Then I thought about how I'd switched to becoming a field agent. That had not been in the plan the Orphanage had had for me, but at the end of the day, as long as I worked hard, I would still graduate and work at the Orphanage. I was adapting to my circumstances. In theory, I knew how to do this; I just needed to apply it to the field.

I got up off the ground and prepared myself again for Darcy's attack. I spread my feet shoulder-width apart for better balance and bent my knees slightly. I tried to lower my center of gravity and kept my fist up to protect my face.

She didn't move. "You're too prepared," she said, tilting her head.

I lowered my fist and straightened. "I'm too prepared?" I said, flabbergasted. "Aren't I always supposed to be prepared?"

"Come here," she said, using her hands to summon me toward her.

"No," I said, terrified.

"Don't you trust me?"

"No," I said again, shocked she would even ask.

She smiled and cocked her hip, relaxing her stiff exterior. "Smart man," she said before taking off and running at me. She jumped in the air and somehow twisted herself around my body, causing me to lose my balance and go down. My neck was going to be sore tomorrow.

"Come on," she laughed. "You trained in combat for how many years? And you are still terrible."

I had gotten used to looking up at her from the mat. "Why do you think I became an earpiece?"

"Because you didn't want to be here, but you still wanted to be close to Collin. You know, no one is forcing you to stay at the Orphanage. Everyone was sort of expecting you to leave after your breakdown."

Her words stung. How could she read me so well? I had never really clicked here at the Orphanage. Sure, I was good with computers, but I could do that anywhere, not just here. I had stayed here while growing up because Collin was here. I'd never shared those thoughts with Collin, or Chuck, or anyone else, although Collin had guessed at them in the letter he'd written me. So how did Darcy know?

"Can't we just go for a run?" I asked, breathless from hitting the mat, trying to avoid responding to Darcy's previous observation.

"Bennet, I already know you can run around a track all day. In fact, you are an excellent runner. But what are you going to do when someone catches you?"

It was a good question. I knew that this was all important stuff. I just prayed somehow my weak little body could manage to get it, to make it look as graceful as Darcy did.

"Come over to the punching bag." She motioned toward the bag. "Let's work on the strength behind your punches and then call it a night."

We walked across the room, and she positioned herself behind the punching bag, holding it. I stood opposite her and got into a ready stance. I hit the bag, alternating fists. I tried to use all my strength, but it made no difference. Darcy barely had to hold on to the bag to keep it from moving.

I knew that on top of the extra homework from my disguise class, I would also need to work on building up my strength. I was a weakling; that's what typically happened to people at the Orphanage who didn't need muscles for their jobs. We all ended up only working out or running enough to maintain our mandatory weight and muscle mass. If you were working in the field, you needed more muscle than someone working as a doctor. Collin's shoulders had been huge compared to mine, but it hadn't bothered me growing up. Now that

R. S. TWELLS

I needed the strength that Collin once had, it bothered me a lot. Why hadn't I ever gone with him when he asked if I wanted to be his partner in workouts? Why had I always just gone running around the track with Chuck?

I had a lot of late nights ahead of me.

We trained in silence for a while. I worked hard, using my whole body to throw the punches, but I could feel myself falling apart. Every single one of my bones seemed to cry out in pain each time I hit the bag. After Darcy excused me, I would go straight to my room, shower, and then collapse in my bed. I knew I would have no problem falling asleep. Tonight, I would have no time to fill Chuck in on my crazy day of makeup bruises and real bruises.

Darcy broke the silence. "You've probably gotten this a lot from other people, but I need an answer for myself if I'm going to continue with you. Why do you want this? Why do you want to become a field agent?"

Sure, some people had asked, like Austen, but I'd never given them a great answer. I didn't know what to tell Darcy. I didn't know what she would believe.

I gave her my usual response. "I needed a change."

She sighed and looked at me, her blonde ponytail hanging to the side as she tilted her head. "That's not it. But I'll get an answer out of you eventually."

Darcy had her own demons to worry about. I wished she would just leave mine alone.

"Alright," she said, after an uncomfortable amount of silence. "That's it for today."

She moved away from the punching bag and toward her water bottle. I joined her, sat down on the bench next to my water bottle, and took a drink.

Mid-sip, I noticed (from the corner of my eye) Darcy swinging her fist toward my face. I flinched, and she grabbed my water bottle. "Mine's empty," she said and finished mine. Lowering the bottle, she asked, "Why are you so scared of me?"

"Do I have to answer that?" I grabbed my water bottle back from her.

"Yes, you idiot. It can't be just because I'm an assassin. Charlotte, Mary, Elizabeth, and Jane share a room with me, and they aren't scared of me. We grew up together, so why are you scared of me?"

"Well, it's *partially* because you're an assassin."

"What's the other part?"

"You're a girl," I said, embarrassed.

She laughed. "Well, I found a hole in your training. I'll add 'talking to girls' to the list of things I need to teach you. Every day this week, we'll be training in here from seven until eleven. I expect you to do some training on your own as well. Now, get some rest."

She walked out of the room, leaving me in a pool of my own sweat, barely able to move.

CHAPTER 14

The rest of the week went pretty routinely. Well, pretty routinely for a new routine. I would wake up at six in the morning to go for a five-kilometer run and work out in the gym for thirty minutes— something my muscles were not used to. I would then go shower, eat breakfast, and study the previous day's lesson for another hour before heading to class.

This week we only had the one class about disguises, with no joint classes with anyone else from our year. I would sit in class until lunch, eat, and then head back to class and stay there until five.

In our study of disguises, we learned how to apply a fake beard, which was handy since it was something I could not grow just yet. We also learned how to change small features of our outfits in order to appear different. After class came dinner, and then I got a tiny break before heading to the training room to practice with Darcy.

Needless to say, this new routine exhausted me.

It was Friday night, the end of the school week. Darcy still wanted to train this weekend, five hours on both days. On Monday, the specialized-fieldwork week for our year started, meaning our training sessions would have to be put on hold. Unfortunately, due to my lack of field knowledge, no field agent would agree to take me with them.

Chief Benjamin said it would be best if I stayed at the Orphanage and trained there, joining some of the younger years in their classes. I tried to look on the positive side of not getting an assignment. I would get time to master what I had learned in class and catch up on the massive amount I had missed over the past couple of years. It was the last week of specialized fieldwork, so I wasn't missing much.

All the '01s were eating dinner together in the cafeteria. I was trying not to fall asleep in my mashed potatoes and gravy before my lesson with Darcy that night. Next to me, as usual, sat Chuck. Unlike usual, across from me sat Darcy. For the past three months, Darcy had always sat at the far end of the table when our year ate meals together. This was the first time she'd sat close to me. I could tell everybody noticed, but no one said a word. They probably figured we were bonding over training. It was more like her fist was bonding with my face. At least I was learning something.

We still hadn't gotten around to having a real conversation. We never talked much, except in training sessions, where she would instruct me how to kick, punch, and roll, or go over the lesson from class. She'd taught me some survival skills as well, things I sort of knew but had never had to apply to myself. Darcy was making sure that those skills were engraved in my brain. After she came back from her assignment next week, we would work on other things, like ditching a tail and jumping out of an airplane. I could honestly say I was not looking forward to purposely jumping out of a plane, but I couldn't tell anyone, because I didn't want to give anyone an excuse to shove me behind a desk again.

I turned my attention to my plate of food and tried my best to scoop up some peas and force them toward my mouth. I knew I needed the extra food with all of the training Darcy was putting me through.

"I say we challenge the '02s to a game of 'cops and robbers' Saturday night," Lucas told the group.

Most of them nodded along, agreeing, but I noticed Mary pushing her food around as if she was figuring out a problem. I tried to come up with something to say to her. I watched as her brow tightened, and she pushed her peas into her mashed potatoes. Maybe I could say something about her peas drowning in gravy? No, that sounded dumb.

Before I got a chance to speak to her, Charlotte turned to grab her attention. "You in for 'cops and robbers' against the '02s, Mary?"

Mary, shaken out of her own little world, replied, "Are we the cops or the robbers?"

"The robbers, of course," Austen responded. "We were the cops last time."

Over the years, we've all gotten along well as a group. Some have bonded more than others. I preferred the guys, because I had an easier time talking to them. The girls were great, and I really respected how they worked in their given areas within the Orphanage; I just never built any bridges to form close relationships with them. After all, with a best friend like Chuck, what more did I need?

We discussed our plans for the game. We all knew that Chuck, Mary, Lucas, Charlotte, and I would be caught first if we didn't have a great plan. I tried my best to join in. In the end, I took mental notes of what the others came up with, in case I could transfer it over to any of my homework assignments. Lucas gave the most and loudest input. Sadly, half of his ideas were too elaborate for teenage agents to carry out.

In the end, Mary was supposed to hide in the computer lab underneath a loose floorboard I had discovered three weeks ago, Lucas was supposed to strap himself to the underside of a vehicle in the garage, Chuck was to hide in the '02s dorm room as a joke, and I was supposed to hide in the closet among all the disguises for assignments. Unfortunately for anyone who found Charlotte, she would be hiding with a water balloon full of cornstarch and water; she liked to make things interesting. Austen, Jane, Elizabeth, and Darcy would constantly be moving around, always switching their locations between the nursery bathroom, the janitor's closet by the office, the pool, and the lounge in the graduated agents' tower.

We had an excellent plan to win. They had two hours to find us, and then it would be game over, and victory would be ours.

We returned to eating, and Charlotte occasionally flung her peas onto other people's plates. This was quite normal for Charlotte; we were all used to her. Charlotte had fiery red hair and enough freckles to play connect-the-dots. She was rather wild and preferred to run around the Orphanage in her socks, claiming they let her slide through the hallways for maximum efficiency.

All of us were unique in some way. Austen was typically serious, though he tried not to be, as though he'd grown up with the stereotypical Asian parents who wanted him to excel at school and sit up straight at the dinner table. Instead, he'd grown up with the Chief riding his back and the pressure of eventually running the Orphanage weighing him down. Sometimes I felt bad for all the responsibility they had flung onto him at such a young age.

Mary was sweet, with shoulder-length black hair. She seemed like an old soul since her favorite pastime was knitting while drinking tea. Well, that and building anything on wheels in the garage.

Lucas was what the older female agents called a "blond cutie." I didn't know exactly what that meant, but it might have had something to do with his rosy baby cheeks. He also had ADHD, which helped him move a million miles an hour. He always made everything interesting, or he was sleeping someplace he shouldn't be sleeping.

I loved looking around the table at these people I considered to be family. They weren't blood, but they were all I had left. The nine of us had experienced crazy things together that had bonded us for life. We had been through horrible training classes and some fun ones, like the time we got to go to an amusement park and spot pickpockets.

Elizabeth was also in our little family. She was rather mousy in shape and face. She had dark hair and eyes and was rather pale. It wouldn't have surprised me if, in the future, Elizabeth orchestrated the takedown of some corrupt government system. She had a passion for politics. Right now, she wanted to work in security. I could picture the Orphanage sending her to run for public office on her days off. Funnily enough, she always talked about working with the new babies that were brought into the nursery once she graduated.

Last was Jane. She was tall, dark, and gorgeous, and I think the most I said to her after she grew boobs was, "Yes, I can fix your computer." It was pretty pathetic, but she was a real-life Princess Jasmine in the looks department.

Collin was better at the making-friends thing than I was. He was also better at the talking thing. I had always just stood beside him and nodded along to what he was saying. I used to think of him as my wingman, but he was actually more of a security blanket. Hopefully, Darcy could help me fix my lack of social skills. You'd think the Orphanage would have fixed them for me, but I guess once I was behind a computer, they didn't care.

I smiled around the table at the memories these people had given me, and at the idea of more to come with the game of "cops and robbers." The warmth from my smile spread to the rest of my body. It was like the cold that had surrounded my heart since Collin left was slowly melting away. Maybe I could focus on this family I still had instead of the one I'd lost.

"Why are you smiling like an idiot?" Darcy whispered, kicking me under the table.

My smile faded as she tore me away from my thoughts. Before I could answer her, Chief Benjamin came up beside our table, followed by a boy about my age who was carrying a dinner tray. I didn't recognize him, meaning he wasn't from the American Orphanage.

"Good evening," the Chief said to our table.

We all sat a bit straighter. "Good evening, Chief," we all said back.

"This is Oliver," the Chief said, patting the boy on the shoulder. "He has transferred from the British Agency and will now finish his studies here. His dad is a good friend of mine. I expect you all to treat him as if he has been here from the beginning."

"Yes, Chief," we responded. No one dared move. We all gave our attention to the Chief, but I could feel everyone subtlety shift their attention in my direction.

This boy in front of me was Collin's replacement. He would sleep where Collin had slept, workout where Collin had worked out, and sit where Collin had sat. He would eat at the table with us and be our friend and form new bonds with the people at this Orphanage.

I cringed at the idea of him taking over Collin's position. How dare he replace someone who was irreplaceable? It was bad enough that there was an empty bed beside mine. Now a stranger would be sleeping in it and disrupting our routines. I already hated him, and he hadn't said a single word.

This wasn't the first time the school had gotten a transfer student. One time, an '05 got cancer and died quite quickly. It was weird to lose an agent to some mundane disease. Their replacement was from India. Another time, a '98 thought he had created a new form of a jet pack. He decided to try it off of the roof, and unfortunately, it didn't work. India, again, sent a replacement.

"Hello," Oliver said to our table in his snotty British accent.

"Hello, Oliver," we all said back.

Oliver sat down at the table beside Darcy. He was too close for comfort. I didn't want to stare at him, so I looked back at my mountain of potatoes. My muscles were no longer tired but now on full alert.

"Oh, and Bennet," the Chief added, "could you please give Oliver a tour of the Orphanage and show him where his bed is?"

I held in my internal scream. It shook every nerve in my body, and I prayed that it didn't show on my face.

"Yes, Chief," I said—the only thing I would be allowed to say.

The Chief turned and walked away, as his business here was done. He left us with this stranger and expected us to be his friend.

Oliver got to work eating his food without forcing conversation.

For a group of agents, when it came to our home turf, we were terrible at remembering our training. Everyone at the table was basically watching him from the corner of their eyes. No one said anything. I felt a little bad that no one started up a conversation or asked how his trip was. I tried to put myself in his shoes, being the new person, and this whole situation being a bit awkward. Considering I would be stuck showing him around, I tried to think of something that would break the ice.

I decided I should try and make a good first impression. I would bury my initial feelings and do my best to like him. I would try to consider this my first test as a field agent. Out in the field, I would always have to put on a show and pretend to be someone different. Right now, I would pretend to be someone who liked the new kid.

I noticed that he held his fork at an odd angle, and that helped give me an idea of what to say to him. "Why do you hold your fork all weird?" I said, then winced. I was off to a terrible start on my first impression.

"Why do you hold your fork like an idiot?" he sneered without looking up from his tray of food.

Darcy let out a quick snicker.

So maybe he wasn't the best at first impressions either. I tried to give him the benefit of the doubt.

I ignored Darcy and said to Oliver, "You're holding it upside down, while *I* use it to spear and scoop things. So, who's the idiot now?" I scooped up some peas to prove my point. As I opened my mouth and brought my fork closer, all the peas fell off.

"Yes, who indeed?" Oliver said.

"Someone didn't pay attention in etiquette class," Darcy muttered at me.

Oliver was smooth. He never wavered in his position, and he continued to eat. I'd try, but I could tell I wasn't going to like him. He looked like someone had pulled him right out of one of those ridiculous fake action movies where the main character wears a white shirt with a black leather jacket and has perfect black hair. Do girls actually like that sort of thing?

"Hey, new kid," Lucas spoke from the other end of the table. "You in for a game of 'cops and robbers' against the '02s tomorrow night? We're the robbers."

Oliver smiled, swallowed his food, and said, "Always."

Lucas filled Oliver in on the plan. Austen and Jane joined in, coming up with a role for Oliver. Talk of the next day's game went on for the rest of the meal.

I didn't join in. Instead, I sat there and dreaded the time I would have to spend with Oliver showing him around. Even worse would be taking him to our room and helping him unpack right next to me. I didn't want any of his things contaminating my area, let alone Collin's area. This was going to be a rough couple of weeks, trying to get used to this intruder.

I glanced up from the potatoes I was still pushing around and noticed Darcy looking at me. She hadn't said a word since the conversation had turned back to the game. I wondered what was going through her head. Maybe she'd been reminded of how Collin was gone. Maybe the pain of losing someone she loved was too much to bear. Maybe she wouldn't want to train me anymore, since I reminded her every day of everything she lost. I was over-reacting and tried to calm myself down. This new-student thing was going to put a damper on a lot around here.

I finished the rest of my meal and noticed that Oliver was also done his. Grabbing my tray, I stood up and asked him, "You ready for that tour now?"

"Lead the way." He motioned for me to go ahead.

We both took our trays to the dirty-dish counter and dropped them off. I led Oliver out of the cafeteria and began the tour.

CHAPTER 15

I couldn't believe I had to spend what little free time I had when I wasn't sleeping showing the new kid around. We barely got new kids around here. Something that was supposed to be fun and exciting was absolute torture. Why couldn't Austen have given Oliver the tour?

Oliver followed me through the hallways of the Orphanage. I showed him the office, the weapons room, the garage, the hospital, all of the classrooms, and the different training rooms. We made little conversation as we wandered the halls. I mostly told him about the building and the special features it held, like the walls that would close in if there was an intruder or the darts dipped in a sleeping formula that would fling across a room if someone wasn't supposed to be there. There were many interesting facts on my tour, but all Oliver would do was nod his head. He wasn't much for talking, it seemed, or maybe he was just soaking it all in.

I finished by showing him where the Chief's office and a couple of other important people's offices were; then decided I was done with the tour. He was an agent, after all. He could snoop around later.

We made our way to the dorm rooms, and I explained the different living arrangements. "The nursery is two floors down, the five to ten-year-olds are one floor down, and this level is ages eleven to eighteen. After you graduate, you head to a different building, where you get one roommate instead of four."

"It's very gray in here," Oliver finally said.

"What color is the British Agency?" I asked, walking a bit faster. Just the sound of his accent annoyed me.

"Brown," he said, keeping up with me. "What with all its old architecture, it's really rather beautiful. This is just so… square." He scrunched up his face in disgust, looking at a painting of a boat on the ocean.

The '01s had taken a trip to the British Agency when we were seven and stayed there overnight. I didn't want to agree with him, but his Agency definitely had more character. It felt like an old mansion that had stayed in the family for generations. We stayed there because our teachers had wanted us to learn about the security system at Buckingham Palace with some hands-on experience. The year after, I broke into the palace's security cameras and accidentally set off their fire alarms.

"This is our room." I opened the door and walked in.

Oliver's suitcase was already on Collin's bed, or what was now his bed. I told him where everyone slept as he started to unpack.

"You've got quite a few Orphanages talking. Even the British Agency is spreading rumors of you," he said, interrupting my explanation about Lucas getting up in the middle of the night if he had an idea that he needed to write down. "You know, what with your switching career paths. That is unheard of. What the Agency tells you to do, you do. Or for you, what the Orphanage tells you to do, you do."

I rolled my eyes. I had heard all of this from plenty of people around here. This was not something that I wanted to get into with him. I didn't know him, nor did I want to get to know him. I just wanted to head to the gym, where Darcy would be waiting for me. Today we were going to practice climbing and rappelling on the rock wall.

"And what were you told to do?" I asked, trying to shift the focus off of me. I sat down on my bed while he started putting his clothes in his dresser.

"Following in my father's footsteps and all." He sounded like he was almost mocking himself. "I'm training to be a field agent like him."

"Did they tell you that you had to come here, or did you volunteer?" I was curious. I didn't know how switching Orphanages worked, because the American Orphanage never gave up agents unless they had graduated.

He shrugged and said, "It was time for a change. Wanted to learn more about America by firsthand experience. When they approached me, I said yes."

I had to give it to him; he had this way of acting like nothing was a big deal. It made him seem cool. Between his coolness in the way he acted and dressed and his incredible British accent, he would be what everyone would talk about for the next while. At least the spotlight would be off of me and what some people were calling my "mental breakdown."

Noticing the time, I started to get changed for my training session with Darcy. I was hoping all of my work this week lifting weights would pay off. I had no idea what to expect. Would I just be climbing up and down the wall a million times, or would I also be climbing other things? Darcy never really prepared me for our lessons. She just kind of threw me into the deep end and hoped I didn't drown.

"I have to get going," I told Oliver. "If you have any questions, I can answer them later."

Without looking up from his suitcase, he said, "I've read almost every document the British Agency has on this place. Trust me, I know all I need to know."

Yep, I definitely wasn't going to get along with this guy.

I opened the door and made my way to meet Darcy. I thought about nothing but Oliver the whole way there, fuming that the Orphanage had given me no warning about him coming here. Was everyone else okay with this?

I tried to feel nothing but hate toward the new guy, but something else bubbled up in my stomach. Oliver represented everything I had lost. I didn't hate Oliver so much as I hated myself.

There must have been something else I could have done that day when Collin left me. All we did was joke around on the radio. I had read and reread the transcripts every day for a month after he died. My last words to him weren't anything meaningful or funny. They weren't sharing a heartfelt memory of laughter. I had told him to get back to the van, and he'd never made it.

We had been together our whole lives, and now I was the one who had to go on alone. There had always been the possibility that one day he could die out in the field, but I'd figured that day was far off and almost impossible. I'd never let the idea bother me, because it was crazy. I was always supposed to be the annoying person in his ear, telling him what to do.

Why couldn't it have been me instead of him? He would have had an easier time moving on. He would have had Darcy and his job. He knew I didn't have my job to focus on. He'd told me to leave. He knew I couldn't make it here without him.

A few tears rolled down my face. I made it to the training room. Darcy would be waiting for me inside. I sat down on the floor outside for a couple of minutes, trying to regain my composure.

"Why are you doing this, Bennet?" a voice asked me.

I looked up, surprised. It was Darcy. The hard mask permanently attached to her face was gone. She looked upset.

"What?" I said, confused.

"Why are you becoming a field agent? And don't tell me it's because you need a change."

I sat there, unsure of how to respond. The tears were still wet on my face. She knew I'd been crying, and she probably guessed it was because of Oliver taking Collin's spot. I wondered if she knew how hard it had been for me to show him around. I wondered if she thought I deserved that pain for losing her boyfriend.

She sat down on the floor next to me. "You don't have to tell me the truth yet. Hold on to why you're doing this and let it drive you to be better."

We sat there in silence together. Her presence was actually comforting for once.

"Now come." She stood up after a few minutes. "We're going to climb the wall a couple of times before we head outside and climb the building."

She was absolutely crazy.

"Alright, coach," I said, trying to forget my pain.

I stood up and followed her to get a harness. Strapping it on, I looked over to Darcy, who hadn't made eye contact with me.

I watched as silent tears rolled down her cheeks.

The '01s and '02s were gathered in the language classroom. There were posters on the walls promoting languages from around the world. I could recognize five of them: English, French, German, Mandarin, and Japanese. With everything changing, I wished I'd taken Russian more seriously, because as a field agent, it was one of the main four languages to know, along with English, French, and Mandarin. If you knew Spanish and Hindi as well, you were more likely to be chosen for a mission. I guess my lack of languages put me lower on the list, but I could add coding too. I liked to think of coding as its own language. The most embarrassing language that I knew was Elvish. I got Collin to learn it with me when I first read *The Lord of the Rings*. We got good enough that we were able to pass notes back and forth in Elvish.

Darcy knew more than ten languages. She picked them up at a young age. She was the kind of kid who knew what would be important later on in life and learned it while she was young.

Everyone was excited as we clarified the ground rules for our game of "cops and robbers."

Austen climbed on top of a table and spoke to the whole room. "Alright, for this game, we are going with the classic rules of the

Orphanage. Once a cop tags a robber, the robber has to come back here, and once the cops find all ten robbers, the game is over. If the robbers aren't found in two hours, the robbers win. Now, anything goes, meaning you can use trackers and radios, hack into cameras, climb through the ceiling—basically anything we've learned in class is fair game. Once the buzzer goes, the robbers have five minutes to spread out. After that, game on."

The '01s quickly got into a team huddle to finalize our plan for the game.

"Come on, Bennet," Lucas began. "We need you to get into the cameras and keep tabs on the other team. You're the only earpiece we've got."

I knew he was right. They needed me to be an earpiece, but I didn't want to be that guy anymore. I wanted to be treated like any other field agent and wander around during the game. It was going to be hard for our team to win without that advantage, but it just wasn't me anymore. I refused to hide with a butt-load of tech strapped to me.

Thankfully, Darcy spoke up for me. "Bennet's a field now, Lucas. Treat him as one."

"Alright," Austen said, trying to keep the peace, "we will stick with the original plan. That just means we need to apply more of our schooling and keep out of view of the cameras, or stay hidden if that's what you're supposed to do."

"Every inch of this place is covered in cameras," Chuck said, pointing out the obvious.

"Then stay hidden," Lucas responded, annoyed. He was only a *little* competitive.

The tension was high on our team. We hadn't had a win since Collin left. Now that our numbers were even with the addition of Oliver, maybe we had a better chance. Though I didn't really like him on our team, the idea of beating the '02s was enticing.

Lucas, Mary, Chuck, Charlotte, and I would have to move quickly to ensure we got out of view before the '02s set up cameras. Nancy and

Agnes were both skilled earpieces and worked really well together. We had our work cut out for us. Hopefully, our secret weapon, Oliver, would prove fruitful.

Since it was only his second day, none of us knew much about him. Chuck and I had tried searching the Orphanage's database for any information on him. There wasn't much besides his dad being a field agent and his little sister training to be a decrypter. He had a pretty impressive background. Even though I couldn't stand him, I was glad for the advantage of the cops not knowing anything about how he played or worked in the field.

We agreed that we would make no attempts to communicate with each other and would stay out of each other's hiding areas in hopes we wouldn't mistakenly lead a cop to anyone.

Austen hopped back up onto the table. "Everyone note the time. Game will end at 2200."

We all looked at our watches. It was 7:54 p.m. In one minute, we robbers would be set loose, and at eight o'clock, the cops would come looking for us. Everyone was excited to have some easy fun. For the briefest of moments, we were kids. Sure, we were kids with tasers and night-vision goggles, but we were having fun and running free.

The Orphanage actually encouraged these games. They hoped they would be learning opportunities. It was a good stress-release. Back when I was the earpiece, I felt like a scientist, tracking everyone like mice. I actually enjoyed it. Now I was taking it more seriously. I had to prove myself to not be the weakest link.

Our watches struck 7:55, and we robbers charged out of the room, sprinting down the hallway toward our designated areas.

I broke off from the pack and made my way up two flights of stairs and through another hallway. I passed one of the weapons rooms, and a couple of agents moved out of my way as I rounded the corner. I found the door to the closet and threw it open with two minutes to spare.

No one was inside, meaning I didn't have to worry about anyone getting in my way or me in theirs. I walked down rows of clothing racks, trying to find the perfect spot. In the back corner were the makeup tables, and on the left wall was the accessory corner. This room had so many options that anyone could pick out something they liked.

I reached the rack full of ballgowns, found one of the biggest dresses with the most tulle, and climbed into the hoop skirt to hide. From the outside, the dress should look undisturbed. I curled up in a tight ball on the floor. I wouldn't have to worry about falling asleep, because I was incredibly uncomfortable.

I looked at my watch. Eight o'clock. The cops would be on the move, trying to find us. I would have no idea if any of my friends were caught. I would have to stay here and wait to see what happened. My team would be totally blind and clueless throughout this whole game.

I knew I would be able to hear the door open if someone came in because it was a squeaky door that no one had bothered to fix—one of the reasons we'd picked this place for me to hide. I'd have some warning if some agent or an '02 came in. The problem was I wouldn't be able to know the difference, so hopefully no agent was going on an assignment where they needed a giant purple ballgown.

I pulled my cell phone from my back pocket and opened up a game, putting the volume on silent. I went to work trying to get further in *Candy Crush*. I knew it was an older game, but I couldn't help myself. It was addicting. I was already at level seventy-two and rising.

Thirty minutes had passed, and I was incredibly bored. I thought I should have agreed to be the earpiece for our team, because then, at least, I would have had something to do and someone to talk to during the game. We had never played this way before. We had always had contact with each other. Thankfully, Austen, who was always our team leader, hadn't seemed too upset by it. Before I grew bored, I'd been grateful he was giving me a chance at being a field.

I got up from my hiding place, thinking I could just jump into a clothing rack if someone came into the room and wandered around. I fumbled through the clothes and grabbed a couple of sweaters that I wanted for myself. Folding them up, I put them off to the side of the room so no one would take them. Agent Daisy was in charge of the closet and would restock it when supplies were low, and she would ensure that we had proper sizes of different things. I never felt bad for occasionally coming in here and finding something new for myself.

The clothes in here had been on some incredible assignments. If they could talk, they would probably tell tales of staking out politicians for months and going undercover as some Mexican drug lord. There were styles from every decade and country. There was a rack dedicated to winter gear and a rack right beside it dedicated to bathing suits. Agent Daisy made sure every agent was well covered for any possible circumstance.

I rummaged through the suit rack, looking for something to make me feel James Bond-ish. Pulling out a nice jacket, I faced the full-length mirror to see how I looked. Posing as if I were holding a gun in my hand, I smoothly said to myself, "The name's Bennet, Agent Bennet." It would have sounded cooler if I'd had a last name. The Orphanage didn't believe in last names; only the year we were born.

Trying to waste more time, I headed over to the makeup mirrors, thinking I could work on my disguise techniques. Sitting down in front of the mirrors, which were surrounded by lights, I picked up one of the many makeup brushes and got to work. I had studied plenty during the week and read everything that was available in the library about disguise. I felt rather confident in my new abilities.

As I began working on my scar, I wondered who from my team had been found, if any. My guess was Charlotte had been found, and I was sorry for whoever found her, though most likely she'd made herself known when she spotted the first '02 just so she could drop the water balloon on them. I was hoping Chuck wasn't found yet.

He was bad with the stress and anxiety that went with this game. He would probably spend the rest of his career working in the hospital here in the safety of the Orphanage.

My scar was coming along nicely, and no one had come into the closet yet. The Orphanage was huge, and the '02s probably expected us to pick a better hiding place than behind some dresses. They were most likely leaving this section of the Orphanage till last. They had their work cut out for them checking all the hiding places in the garage.

For fun, I grabbed a long blond wig off a stand to the right of the mirror. There were other fun wigs, like a short purple one, and even a bald cap. Pulling on the blond wig, I attempted my best Darcy expression, though her hair was always up in a ponytail, and if I tried to do that, it would look awful. Swishing my head back and forth, I felt the long hair gently brush past my face. It was weird feeling the hair touch my neck, and I understood why Darcy always had hers tied up.

"Blond isn't really your color. Maybe if your skin was a bit darker, you could go for a beach vibe," said a female voice off to the side.

I cursed under my breath for letting myself get distracted and not noticing the door squeak open. I quickly turned my head to see if I had been caught by surprise by a cop, which would have been a terrible start to my field-agent career.

Agent Daisy was holding several colorful Indian saris on hangers in one hand. "You playing 'cops and robbers'?" she asked.

I breathed out a sigh of relief, knowing that I was still in the game. "Yeah, I am," I told her. "It's the '01s versus the '02s. The '01s are the robbers."

"So, why are you spending your time hiding in the closet instead of out there playing the game? I thought you wanted to be a field? Fields run around during these games—or at least they did when I used to play." She headed over to a rack and hung up the clothing. I watched her walk over to a different rack full of sweaters, thinking about what she had said. She selected a gray sweatshirt and put it on over her tank top.

"My team doesn't trust me to run around and not get caught. I don't know if I trust myself to not get caught," I confessed to Agent Daisy. I stared back at myself in the mirror, still wearing the ridiculous wig.

Daisy walked toward me and sat in the chair next to mine. Her wavy brown hair was stuck a little under her sweatshirt, and she reached back to pull it free. Picking up a makeup brush and some powder that was three shades darker than my skin tone, she started applying it to my face. "Well, maybe you don't have to be yourself," she said with a smirk.

CHAPTER 17

THE ORPHANAGE
MARCH 24
9:00 P.M.

My hands shook as I walked down the hallway toward the cafeteria. A million eyes had to be staring at me. But when I glanced around to double-check, everyone was focused on his or her own business, paying no attention to the stranger roaming the halls of the secret facility.

I quietly breathed, releasing any anxiety that swam around in my head, knowing that I was no longer playing the game as Bennet. I was playing as a field agent.

Agent Daisy had said to play the game as someone else, and that was what I was doing. She'd helped me apply my new face and pick out the new outfit I was now wearing. If anyone asked, I wasn't Bennet, I was Alex, a visiting teacher from the British Agency here to freshen up his American Sign Language. Good thing I had a pretty good fake British accent.

I was happy that I was able to use what I had learned in field-agent classes. It had taken twenty minutes to make me look tanned and apply a fake nose that was pointier than mine. Agent Daisy had given me a shaggy black wig and dark-brown contacts. I had a completely new look.

Daisy was really excited about this look and had a hard time controlling herself. She'd wanted to dress me up in a sailor's uniform, but I said the point of this disguise was to not draw attention to myself, so instead she gave me a padded bodysuit to make me look older and more muscular. It was rather uncomfortable, though it was fun to look in the mirror and look like I had the body of a superhero. Daisy also grabbed me a navy turtleneck sweater and a pair of dark-wash jeans. The final touch was a flat cap that my curly wig stuck out beneath.

When the masterpiece of my new look was done, Daisy sent me out into the Orphanage to play the game like a normal field agent. I was excited and terrified. This was what I considered my first assignment. It was also nice to stare into the mirror for three seconds and not see a reflection I had once shared with my brother.

Now, calmly walking through the hallways, I was on the lookout for any '02s. I was curious to see if they would know it was me. Now, thinking about it, I wasn't sure if anyone had used a disguise in this game before; usually, kids would run around or just hide. I was proud that I'd had the guts to try something new, even if it took some convincing.

Reaching the cafeteria, I made my way toward the drink station and started to make myself a cup of tea. I needed something to do, and I was in the mood for an evening treat. When I finished making my tea, I made my way over to a table and promptly opened a book that Daisy had given me to make me look busy. It was from the wardrobe room and was about the art of hats. It wasn't exactly a page-turner, but I tried my best to look distracted while scoping out the room for any cops.

We had an hour left of this game, an hour to stay hidden behind my muscular bodysuit and flat cap. I was jumping back and forth between *I can totally do this* and *You might as well give yourself up*. My inner critic was the worst. I wouldn't be surprised if Nancy and Agnes had already spotted me on camera and sent people to get me. Daisy had tried to convince me that with my fake nose and long black hair blocking both sides of my face, there was no way facial recognition would be able to detect me. Agent Daisy had so much faith in her and my abilities that she would have bet money on my team winning.

I stared at an interesting hat in the book with a flowerpot on top of it while I wondered where the rest of my team was. I hadn't spotted anyone while I strolled the hallways on my way here. Were they all caught? Were they hiding away from the dreaded cameras? I had no way of knowing. I couldn't give them or myself away and go looking for them. Besides, Austen had given us our orders, and though I wasn't following mine, I wasn't going to mess up anyone else.

I tried to casually glance around the room, carefully raising my eyes from the book, but not my head. No '02s were in the room that I could see. Grabbing my phone from my pocket, I brought it up and turned the camera to face me, pointing it over my shoulder. Turning as if to crack my back, I used the phone to glance behind me and saw that I was in the clear.

I was perfectly bored after thirty minutes of reading the book, and with a surge of bravery, made the executive decision to wander the hallways. Since the game was practically over, I thought I might as well risk it. No one had approached me yet, and my chances seemed good.

Knowing it was now or never, I stood up, taking the book and my cup of tea with me, and headed out of the cafeteria and into the rest of the playing field. I didn't know where to go yet. I knew their base was the language room where we'd started the game. I would avoid that area until the game was over.

I could head up to the offices and play around on some of the computers. The only problem with that would be if someone came over and asked who I was, and I couldn't have that. Still, if I made my way to a computer, I could access the cameras and see what was going on…

I shook my head. I was no longer an earpiece but a field agent. So, where would a field agent go?

I decided on the weapons room. I thought I could easily keep my face hidden there. At least I wouldn't be cowering in the closet the whole game, even if my plan wasn't the most exciting.

I walked with purpose toward the elevator and was about to hit the button to head to the weapons room when someone shoved their hand in to stop the door from closing.

It was Agent Baker. He must have just gotten back from his assignment, because the last I'd heard he was off driving in Atlanta.

This was where my cover would be blown. Nancy and Agnes would be watching the elevators, and they would notice the strange way Baker would be interacting with me. They would turn on the microphone to see what was going on, and I would be doomed.

I swayed on the balls of my feet. Baker hadn't paid any attention to me yet and was studying his folder. I tried to calm myself and act normal. I was, after all, a field agent and would have to do this countless more times in the future. He hadn't even talked to me yet.

"Dinner sucked," Baker finally said for pointless conversation, shuffling through the papers in his folder.

I cursed in my head and prepared myself to give him my best British accent. Daisy and I had quickly practiced before I had ventured off.

"Just got here," I quietly responded, trying to sound posh. "Only needed a cup of tea," I finished, lifting my cup only slightly.

"You visiting?" he asked.

Thinking of my cover story, I told him, "Only for the weekend. I'm just here to brush up on my American Sign Language. Languages are my specialty."

"Hmm." He nodded.

We waited in silence for the elevator to beep, indicating that we had arrived at the correct floor.

The doors slid open. "Enjoy your stay," Baker said to me and walked away.

"Thanks," I called after him as I stepped out in his wake, unsure why he was being polite to me, because as Bennet, I never got such a nice farewell from him. Maybe he just didn't like to give the time of day to training agents. I might have to try harder with him after all the effort he had put into helping me when no one else would allow me to be their earpiece after the incident.

Heading in a different direction than Baker, I rounded the corner and bumped into someone. They dropped what they were holding on to the floor, and I, unfortunately, spilled my tea all over myself. My sweater had a stain running down the front.

I reached down to pick up what the other person had dropped, and fear struck my heart when I saw it was a radio.

"Hey, thanks," Toby, an '02, said, holding out his hand to me—fake me—to take back his radio.

Shocked, I passed it back to him and muttered, "No problem." I swallowed hard and prayed that my nose wasn't sliding off or that my hat and wig hadn't shifted. The seconds seemed to slow down while I waited to see what Toby would do or say. All he had to do was tag me, and that would be it for me. But if I could fool Baker, then hopefully my disguise would work on Toby.

"Sorry about your drink," Toby apologized, making a move to help me but clearly preoccupied with something else.

I tried to brush off the spilled tea like it was no big deal, wanting him to leave me alone. "Don't worry about it."

"Any updates?" he asked into his radio, walking past me and continuing on with the game.

I tried to listen to the response, but he was walking too fast, and if I followed him, it would look suspicious. Trying to celebrate the fact that I had succeeded in being a field for once, I walked through the door of the weapons room and headed to a desk in the back corner by the wall lined with camouflaged weapons. These were some of the coolest weapons that the Orphanage had cooked up. There were laser pens and shoes with guns in the heels. Other objects included lipsticks with tasers and tie-clips with poison hidden inside. Collin once got to use gum that was actually an explosive.

Hiding in the back of the weapons room and not at all interested in the hats of the '60s, I thought about my interaction with Toby. I'd have to tell him that he needed to be more aware of his surroundings and more polite when spilling someone's tea, even if he was in a hurry. He was a good guy, just over-excited usually, and very competitive. He and Lucas got along very well when they weren't arguing over who had won whatever game they were playing.

The game of "cops and robbers" was almost over. It was no wonder Toby had been in such a hurry. I was so close to having survived my first two hours of pretending to be a field in hiding, and I was rather enjoying it. Things were a lot different on this side of the board.

Glancing up from my book and sad that I had no more tea, I looked around the room. I was here trying to kill time, and what better way to kill time than by brushing up on some of my weapons skills? Leaving the book and the empty cup behind, I walked over to the far wall, which was covered in guns, and pulled the smallest one off the wall to start taking it apart to clean it. I fumbled with the different pieces and wasn't very confident in what I was doing. I knew sooner or later, either from Darcy or one of my teachers, I would be tested in taking apart and putting back together many weapons, all while blindfolded.

I was feeling good after my last two interactions. My undercover identity of Alex, a dark-haired agent from the British Agency here to study American Sign Language, was going great. I continued with my task while doing visual sweeps of the room.

Five seconds, four seconds, three seconds, two seconds, one.

I watched my watch count down to the game's ending and my team's victory. I had made it when no one had really believed that I could and had tried to hide me away. I was curious to see who else hadn't been caught. Everyone would be making their way back to the classroom.

Putting the gun I had just finished cleaning back on the wall, I left my empty cup of tea and book behind, too excited at what I had accomplished to worry about putting them away. I made my way back to meet everyone else. Running through the hallways, I ignored the elevators and took the stairs, wanting to move as fast as I could. It took me a while since the weapons room was practically on the opposite side of the facilities from the language classroom.

Panting, I slowed down when I reached the correct hallway. Five steps away from the door, I stopped and leaned against the wall, not wanting everyone to see me out of breath. I could hear what was going on inside the classroom. It seemed that everyone was already back.

"We won!" Austen cheered. "You didn't find Bennet."

A cheer from the '01s filled the room, celebrating the victory. I stayed outside in the hallway, frozen at how unreal this all was.

Finding my strength, I went into the classroom and saw Lucas celebrating on top of a table, the rest of the team cheering from the ground. The '02s were sitting around their surveillance setup. Lee, a tall, skinny '02 with an annoying habit of always being right when it came to practically anything, had stuff stuck in his hair, probably from Charlotte dropping the cornstarch and water-filled balloon on him. When people started to notice me standing in the doorway, the room fell silent, curious who this stranger was.

"Can I help you?" ever-polite Austen asked, hopping off the desk he was sitting on and making his way toward me.

Clearly, my disguise was still working, and I froze, not sure what to do. Should I just take off my disguise and announce who I was, or should I keep going with my role?

I decided to go with the latter and see how much fun I could have with this. I only hoped that Oliver wouldn't give me away, since he probably knew everyone from the British Agency.

I crossed my arms over my chest and looked at everyone in the room. "What are you doing in here?" I tried my best to sound angry.

Austen looked back at the rest of the gang before turning toward me. "Agent Asher gave us permission to use this classroom for our game tonight since he wasn't using it. May I ask who you are?"

I had to think on my feet. "I'm Agent Asher's replacement for the coming week, and I need the classroom to prepare myself. You'd better find someplace else to play your game."

Slowly, the group started to stand up and face me, showing me respect, as we would any guest teacher who came here. I was having a good time playing this up, but I had no idea how to end the joke.

Then I heard footsteps coming from down the hall. "Just here to collect papers to grade. I'm not here to kick you out," Agent Asher said from behind me and started to make his way toward his desk, which Toby quickly moved away from. "Who won?"

I prayed that no one noticed the fear that crossed my face. Pretending to be another person was hard. No one said anything. I knew it would be Austen who would speak up and start questioning Agent Asher about his surprise guest teacher the class hadn't been informed about.

Agent Asher hobbled over to his desk and opened the top drawer, grabbing what he'd come for. He looked up at everyone in the room, still waiting for an answer. His eyes fell on me. He didn't let any expression of confusion or shock cross his face at seeing a stranger standing in his room.

"Who are you?" Agent Asher cut right to the point. He didn't like surprises, and a stranger standing in his classroom was probably the last thing he wanted to deal with on a Saturday night.

"Umm," I managed to get out. I tried to find the creativity I'd had when I was talking to Austen, but nothing came to me.

Agent Asher walked toward me, eyes narrowed. The room was still silent while he looked me up and down. I wondered if anyone thought I really was from the British Agency, or if they thought I was an intruder—not that anyone had ever broken into the Orphanage before. A half-smile formed on Agent Asher's face, and I could tell he was figuring it all out.

"Well done, Bennet. That's one way to win 'cops and robbers.'" He nodded a few times, then looked back at the rest of the room to see their faces filled with shock. Half of them were excited that they'd won, and the other half were confused at how they'd lost.

He reached up and ripped the wig off my head, along with the hat. Waving it in the air, he walked out of the room. I was left there still wearing a tea-stained sweater and a face full of makeup, feeling both foolish and happy for having fooled everyone else.

"Let's hear it for Bennet!" Lucas shouted, and my friends began cheering and celebrating a much-deserved win after so many months of losing.

I stumbled toward my celebrating friends to join them. "What happened with the rest of the game?" I asked Austen, who was still looking at me with a smile and shaking his head in disbelief at what I had pulled off.

Austen moved closer to my ear so I could hear him. "Charlotte and Chuck were caught after fifteen minutes. Oliver had no clue where all the secrets and cameras are in this place, so it's our fault he wasn't properly prepped. He got caught after thirty minutes. Darcy and I tried a new tactic, which didn't prove productive, and we were caught next. Then Lucas was found when the vehicle he was hiding in randomly needed an inspection. He had to come out, and they found him on the cameras. Next was Mary, who sneezed just as Toby entered the room she was in. Jane and Elizabeth were the last to be found," Austen continued, brushing away Lucas, who had come to scream in his ear in excitement. "That just left you, and no one found you."

I was dumbfounded. I was the only survivor. That had never happened in all the years I had played. Sometimes I and a couple of others would survive but never just me. I decided to enjoy the victory and celebrate the fact that maybe, just maybe, switching to becoming a field agent wouldn't be the biggest mistake of my life. At the very least, I'd learned that my art of disguise was indeed a gift, and Agent Asher would be proud of me and what I had learned from his class last week.

"Well," I confessed to those who could hear me, "Toby actually found me." I nodded toward him, and he looked up, confused, and then it hit him what had happened. The rest of his team looked at him curiously.

"You were the person I bumped into in the hallway with the spilled tea," he said, annoyed, understanding that his team could be the victors right now if only he had known it was me. His team was clearly disappointed in him. Nancy even reached up and smacked him on the back of his head.

"Ice cream in the cafeteria in honor of Bennet!" Lucas shouted.

Everyone gave up on their disappointment or celebration and followed Lucas out of the classroom toward a well-deserved reward. I followed behind, noticing Darcy glancing at me before she turned back to rejoicing with Elizabeth.

CHAPTER 18

This week was anything but normal for me. The high I got from "cops and robbers" carried over throughout the week. I felt like I was running on adrenaline. First thing Monday morning, while the rest of my year was doing their specialized-fieldwork week, I joined the '03s in their lessons. When I walked into the classroom, they applauded me. I was confused at first and then realized that they were congratulating me on my success in Saturday night's game. A couple of them even asked me to go into detail about how I had formed my disguise.

It was like people were now starting to accept me as a field agent. That simple act of clapping gave me the confidence I needed to join a class of students who were actually far above me in their field knowledge. This proved true in the lesson for the day, which would be taking place in the cafeteria, perfecting our "walk and drop." A "walk and drop" was exchanging a package with someone when you walked past them, or leaving a note for a person sitting next to you, without anyone else noticing. It was something you needed to do quite smoothly. Alli, who spent last year undercover in a ballet school in Russia, was able to make it look effortless, and I tried to study her specific movements.

I tried not to dwell on the fact that they'd stuck me with a younger age group. I focused on the fact that they were putting me in classes that would help me in the field instead.

Agent Peter, our teacher, told us that one of the keys to a successful "walk and drop" was to not make eye contact or move your head in the direction of your target. Your whole body had to be focused on something else in a different direction, preferably off in the distance. I tried to keep my focus on Agent River, grabbing coffee and juggling six different folders. My hands got very sweaty with nerves, and I managed to drop the package on the floor, alerting everyone to what I was doing and earning a failing mark for the day.

I spent the rest of the week in class with the '03s, getting my butt kicked. We worked hard and long in many areas, practicing at the shooting range for an hour every day and then spending the next hour cleaning our weapons and organizing bullets. Finally, on Friday, I managed to hit the target dummy in the head. It was only once, but it was enough to make me celebrate.

Agent Peter also made us work all day on Wednesday speaking only in German, which was rather easy for me, because that was one of the first languages I mastered. Agent Peter moved at a quick pace and never liked to dwell on one topic for too long. It was good to keep moving. I tried to bury the tiny piece of me that missed sitting down in front of a computer and hacking into phone records and looping security footage. This was a new challenge before me, and quitting wasn't an option. I hadn't felt so distracted since Collin died, and having no time to think during the day and then going to bed exhausted was a perfect escape from the past few months.

On what little time off I had during this week, when I wasn't catching up on homework or training with whoever would practice with me on the mats, I managed to ask a couple of people to work with me on specific tasks. I was hoping that, when Darcy got back from her assignment, I could surprise her with a few things I'd learned without her.

First, I asked Chuck to go over a couple of first-aid things with me.

Monday night in our dorm room, he spread out a bunch of medical supplies on our beds and proceeded to show me some simple techniques that would be helpful in the field. We all had basic first-aid training, but back when I was an earpiece, I'd figured if I was desperate and had to help an agent over the headset, I could just quickly Google the answer or ask someone at a neighboring desk for help. I had a bad habit of ignoring my teachers and only learning what I needed to pass a test, if the subject didn't interest me. Now I was mad at my past self for not taking every single class seriously. Collin had always taken every class seriously—even computer class, where he'd basically only known how to start up a computer and set up a fake Facebook account.

After Chuck showed me how to make a splint out of two sticks and use my shirt to tie it in place, I got Austen to work with me in the training room. I saw a hint of a smile when I asked him to train with me in the boxing ring; I think it reminded him of the old days when he and Collin would practice in the morning. Austen went easy on me, and Tuesday night, he showed me how to disarm someone who was holding a gun to my face.

Even though he was going easy on me, my body still ached, and I constantly wondered if I would ever wake up and not feel sore. I tried to tell myself I had only been training to be a field for a month, and my body was still adjusting to the change. I knew this was going to be a long journey, especially if I wanted to graduate next year with my friends. I couldn't imagine watching everyone else graduate and move on without me. It was hard to remember that what I was trying to do had never been done before. No one really knew what this was going to look like for me. We were all just trying our best.

Wednesday night, Mary taught me how to hot-wire a car. She was a little mad when I ripped out the wires. She assured me that it would be a quick fix, before we moved to a different car to try again. She asked me to be more careful with this one, since it was a car she was building herself. It was a monster of an SUV; you could have fit our whole year in it. Mary was very patient, even when I got frustrated and asked why I couldn't use one of the devices the Orphanage created to stick on the side of vehicles and start them automatically. Mary calmly explained that sometimes, out in the field, things don't go as planned, and I wouldn't always have all the tools that I needed. At the end of the night, Mary managed to get my time to twenty minutes from the moment I started to break into a car to the moment I was able to start it and drive away.

I also managed to get Baker to teach me how to drive a standard. It was a lot easier than I thought it would be. He took me around the airstrip the Orphanage had in the back. He taught me how to use the emergency brake to spin the car around and helped me get over my fear of going too fast by slamming his foot on top of my foot. I didn't appreciate the harsh teaching technique, but it was fun to be outside instead of stuck behind a book.

On Friday, in geography class with the '03s, we were learning about the fastest routes to take in France. I was trying so hard to keep my eyes open when Rob, an '03 who was particularly skilled in the kitchen, came back from the bathroom and mentioned Darcy was back from her assignment, having finished early. I finished my own work as fast as I could, hoping Agent Peter would let me out of class early to go see Darcy. I couldn't wait to train with her and show her that I had added five more pounds to my weight-training routine.

He wouldn't let me go, but at least we only had twenty minutes left of the class by the time I had finished. Sitting and listening to the rest of Agent Peter's rant about the pros and cons of taking the subway— or metro, as it's called in France—I watched as time ticked down. We were finally dismissed. I gathered my books and walked with the rest of the year back to our dorm rooms to get rid of our books before heading to dinner.

I listened as Rob and another '03, Marie, got into a heated discussion about the secret passageways under the city of Paris. The '03s were named after the Jason Bourne series, and they took that to heart. They were kind of cocky when it came to their field-agent skills and had all decided at a young age to specialize in specific areas of fieldwork. They all worked very hard to prove themselves after watching the movie together when they were seven. Alli was a fantastic dancer, if that wasn't already clear from her time at a Russian ballet school, Marie decided to study politics, Rob was quite the chef, and the others had their own weird and useful skills. The whole year had unique but useful talents that the Orphanage hoped to be able to put to use one day.

We made it back to the dorm rooms, and their dorms being first, I continued past them to get to my room, wondering if anyone would be in there. Lucas was in the workshop today, Chuck was in the hospital, and Austen was glued to the Chief's side.

On the girls' side, only Mary had been around all week, working endlessly on a new aircraft that a team Lucas was a part of had created. The two of them working together was never a good idea, because it usually ended up with Lucas telling Mary that she was killing his dream and Mary telling Lucas that his dreams were unrealistic.

Thinking about Mary and Lucas and what their day might have looked like, and looking forward to finding Darcy, I finished putting my books under my bed and headed back into the hallway. Shutting my door, I noticed that the girls' door across the hall was slightly open. I decided to knock to see if whoever was in there wanted me to shut the door or if they wanted to come to dinner with me.

Reaching to knock, I paused, hearing voices inside the room. I didn't want to eavesdrop—or at least, I didn't want to be caught eavesdropping—but I couldn't help myself. Standing still, I listened. I tried to tell myself that this was good training in surveillance to help combat the feeling that what I was doing was rude.

"I don't know, Mary," I heard Darcy say through the crack. "I never really thought about it. Elizabeth and Jane have done it. I just figured it was something I had more time to figure out."

"I'm sorry, Darcy," Mary responded. "This isn't something that I have to deal with. I'm not sure what to say."

"This would be one less thing to worry about out in the field," Darcy said.

I tried to decipher what they were saying. It didn't make any sense to me. I kept listening.

Darcy continued. "I mean, when I was with Collin, it wasn't serious or anything, and we didn't talk about the rest of our lives, but I didn't really consider this."

My ears perked up at the mention of my brother. Most of the conversation about Collin had died down a couple of weeks after his death. Darcy and I seemed to be avoiding talking about him at this point in our training, and I was just as glad he didn't come up because of the pain that would follow.

"Agent Lydia brought it up on our assignment. She was the one who mentioned that it would be one less thing to worry about, and I sort of agreed with her. At the British Agency, they pride themselves in family history, but here, everyone is alone."

I'd never heard Darcy talk like this before.

"Let's face it, Darcy," Mary said softly, "if the Orphanage tells you to do it, you will, won't you?"

"If they ask, I will. If they leave it up to me, I don't know what I'll do."

Darcy was upset, and I felt like I needed to make her feel better. If Collin were here, he would be all over this and comforting her. Leaning against the doorframe, I ran through different scenarios in my head of what could go wrong if I knocked.

"What would Collin say if he were here?" Mary asked.

Darcy paused a moment to think, which gave me a moment to think. What *would* Collin say if he were here? What would he say about me becoming a field agent, about me not following his orders, and about me bottling up everything? There was no point in focusing on any of that because, at the end of the day, Collin wasn't here. All that mattered was what I had to say about it.

I made my choice and decided I would knock. I could always play it off as me needing to talk to Darcy or ask them if they wanted to walk to dinner together as I'd originally intended.

Facing the door, I raised my hand to knock—then the door swung open, and a fist punched me in the nose. Pain shot through my head, and blood poured down my face and into my mouth, filling my mouth with a horrible taste. Shocked, I looked up to see Darcy standing in the doorway, furious.

Racking my brain, I tried to come up with an excuse. I failed.

Mary came up to stand behind Darcy, a little confused and also annoyed, cluing in that I must have been eavesdropping on their private conversation.

Darcy stood up straight and reached to tighten her ponytail before saying, rather calmly, "I'll see you after dinner on the roof for training."

Pushing past me, she and Mary made their way toward the cafeteria to join with the rest of the dinner crowd. Blood was dripping onto my shirt now and was sticky and itchy on my skin.

"Oh, and Bennet," Darcy said, turning her head to talk to me as she kept walking down the hall. "I would put some ice on that." Smiling, she tapped her nose twice before disappearing around the corner with Mary.

CHAPTER 19

"Why are you eating alone?" Mary asked.

I looked up from my plate of spaghetti and into Mary's brown eyes. She was standing over me, which wasn't a difficult task, since I was trying my best to be as small as possible.

Embarrassed, I replied, "I'm avoiding Darcy, and frankly you, and hoping no one sees that my nose is gushing blood." My nose was no longer bleeding; I was just being overdramatic.

Mary smiled and set her tray down next to me. I looked across the room and noticed the rest of our year sitting at a table together. None of them looked concerned that two people were missing. The cafeteria was decently full. Agent Leah and the other cooks were behind the counter, serving the proper portions to each person. Most of the training agents were celebrating the weekend and enjoying the extra free time since they didn't have a ton of homework to catch up on like me.

"I'm sorry I was eavesdropping on you and Darcy," I told Mary, spinning some spaghetti onto my fork and shoving it into my mouth.

"Sorry you got caught?" she asked mockingly. Mary had a light tone to her. She would have made an excellent kindergarten teacher if she'd been raised in the outside world and not in a gray institute designed to create soldiers on a game board. "Besides," she continued, "it's Darcy you should be apologizing to. It was her secret that you overheard."

I thought about that while we both ate in silence, only the sounds of quiet conversations and forks hitting plates floating around the room. Mary was right. I would have to apologize to Darcy, though it would be a lot easier to pretend it had never happened and let her take her anger out on me during our training session tonight. Who knew what she had planned for us up on the roof?

Stabbing a meatball, I decided I might as well try asking Mary about the conversation. "I know I was listening to you and Darcy, but honestly, I didn't understand anything. What was she talking about when she said, 'One less thing to worry about out in the field'? And why did she bring up Collin?"

Mary let out a long breath, clearly debating what to say next. She looked at me, biting her lip like she was trying to hold something in. "And this is why I will never be allowed out in the field. I am trying to keep this a secret, but I think you might be able to talk to Darcy about this. I mean, you and her probably talk about losing Collin all the time, especially now that you guys are training together."

I felt a stab in my gut at that. I had spent so much time and effort avoiding bringing up the subject of my brother with Darcy, and I'd thought I was doing the right thing. Mary didn't know that Darcy and I never talked about anything important, Collin included. We had one goal being together, and that was training me. The idea of talking about Collin with Darcy sent chills up my spine and an unhealthy dose of anxiety to my stomach.

"Oh, man, Darcy is going to kill me," Mary said. "I can't imagine being in her position, even though lots of female agents have to deal with this—"

"Mary," I interrupted "Sorry, but... just spit it out."

"Ahh." It sounded like a quiet scream of pain. "The Orphanage is putting pressure on Darcy to get sterilized to avoid complications out in the field."

I sat there, stunned. This was not what I'd expected. Now I finally understood the part in Mary and Darcy's conversation about what Collin would have said if he were here. It was a strange and uncomfortable topic. I stared at Mary. She was busy slurping up a stray spaghetti noodle.

"Darcy is only sixteen. Why does it matter if she gets the surgery now or in a couple years? Does she really need it?" I asked. "We're just kids."

"Sure, you could call us kids, but we never really got to be kids. If the Orphanage told Darcy to pretend to be twenty years old, then she would be twenty. We are whatever the Orphanage needs us to be. Sometimes that works out for people here, like how I get to work with engines, and sometimes they take it all away from you."

I silently wished there was something I could do to help.

"You cannot talk to anyone else about this, only Darcy," Mary reminded me.

"Okay," I promised.

Knowing I would never understand how Darcy was actually feeling, I thought that maybe I shouldn't bring it up with her during our training session. I prayed Mary could reach out to Darcy, if that was what Darcy needed.

I wondered if Darcy would have talked to Collin about it if he were still here, and I wondered what he would have said. It would have been an uncomfortable conversation to have at the age of sixteen. Throw in a job as a secret agent, and things got a lot more complicated. Some of us dreamed about families and the future, but the Orphanage had taken that all away from us when they took us from wherever they found us. Our dreams were now the ones the Orphanage had for us, and our futures were the ones the Orphanage trained us for. No one complained about it; it was just what happened when you grew up the way we did.

We continued eating dinner, talking about Mary's project, and her hopes for the car she was slowly building. Time passed quickly while I shared all I was learning and how sore my body was after these few weeks of intensive training. The conversation flowed smoothly, surprisingly, because usually in the past, whenever I'd talked to the opposite gender, I'd had Collin by my side. It was a shock, after he died, learning how much I had relied on him for such simple, mundane things.

I noticed Chuck glance in our direction over his shoulder. He was probably wondering why I wasn't sitting with him. It would be easy enough to fill him in later, as long as he wasn't working late. Turning back to look at Mary, I let out a laugh as she finished her story about how she'd thrown a screwdriver at Lucas for trying to order her around after she turned down his idea for a rocket launcher on a skateboard.

"What is this going to accomplish?" I demanded, looking over the edge of the building. We were twelve stories up, which looked a lot higher when you looked straight down. The trees looked like shrubs, and the grass looked like anything but soft.

I had met Darcy up on the roof after dinner with no clue of what we were about to do. Well, I had since found out, and I wasn't impressed.

"I am making you do this, because if you fall, you're dead. Just like in the field. If you mess up, you're dead." Darcy didn't look too impressed either, but when did she ever look at me with a tender expression? I was the person she referred to as an idiot all the time.

I climbed up onto the edge of the roof and sat down, my feet dangling over the side. Taking a deep breath, I lay down on my stomach and reached out for a pole projecting off the side of the building. Grabbing the pole, I transferred my weight and rolled off the roof, swinging through the open air. The goal Darcy had laid before me, after I had stupidly bragged about the extra five pounds I had pushed this week in the weight room, was to hang from the pole until she was happy and said I could come back onto the roof. Like the idiot I was, I didn't argue. I prayed the pole would hold my weight.

A smirk crossed Darcy's face as she watched me swinging from the pole with nothing underneath me. "How you doing, champ?" she asked, sarcastically.

"Been better," I grunted, focusing on not dying. My arm muscles were always sore, and under the strain of my weight, they ached and begged me to let go. Beads of sweat formed on my forehead. This was not an ideal evening to be doing this. There was a light rain, and I had to focus on my hands not slipping accidentally from the bar.

I let go with one hand and wiped it on my shorts, trying to get the sweat and rainwater off of it, then clutched the pole again. "How long are you going to make me dangle here?" I prayed the answer would only be a couple of minutes.

She thought for a moment. "Until I feel better." She sat down on the rocks that covered the roof and made herself comfortable, as though we were going to be here awhile.

I debated in my head if she was referring to her conversation with Mary and her potential future, or if she was still mad at me for eavesdropping. My guess was probably both. My nose still throbbed from where her fist had made contact with it.

I dared to ask a question, hoping she wouldn't lash out by making the pole wobble or throw rocks at me. "Are you mad at me for eavesdropping?"

"Yes," she admitted. "But I am madder at myself for not catching you sooner. Sorry about your nose. I acted out of anger, and—here's a lesson—an agent should never do that. An agent should always make the smart move instead of letting their emotions lead them. Though if it happens again, I'll probably do the same thing."

I let the silence come back, not wanting to distract myself from what I was doing. It hadn't even been a minute, and I didn't know how long I could last. I knew my discomfort was written all over my face.

"Do you want to talk about it?" I stammered.

She put her arms behind her and leaned back. "I don't know."

A strained laugh came out of me at the idea of Darcy not knowing something. To me, it seemed she always spoke her mind and did what she wanted. Unless the Orphanage told her what to do or what to say, she was unstoppable. Maybe I had built her up too much in my head, but to me, Darcy was fearless and practically perfect. I'd been kind of glad Collin had been with someone like that, even though she scared me.

"Well," I tried to joke, "I'm just hanging here if you want to talk."

"I thought our thing was that we didn't talk?" Darcy sneered, annoyance crossing her face.

She was right about that. We didn't talk. I wasn't sure if it was my choice or her choice or if it was a mutual thing. So far, it had worked in our strange relationship. Right now, though, we were at a fork in the road. Either we would go one way and start talking, or we would continue to only have a shallow relationship where we were around each other's lives but never truly participating in them.

I chose the first option. Maybe it was time for a change. Maybe this was what we needed. We were the two people closest to Collin, so why shouldn't we be close to each other?

"I'm sorry I killed Collin," I whispered, my chest tightening. I decided to start at the beginning and apologize, because the main reason I'd avoided her was that I had killed her boyfriend and was afraid she would want to kill me. I carried the weight of that knowledge with me wherever I went.

Pain shot across her face, and she leaned toward me, resting her arms on her crossed knees. "You're kidding me, Bennet. Collin was not your fault. You know that, right?"

Looking Darcy in the eye, I told her the truth. "No."

Darcy, the strongest person I knew, fell apart before my eyes, and it pained me no end. "Bennet, I read the transcripts and all the paperwork from that day. It was not your fault. You told him to get out, and he didn't listen. You did what you could as an earpiece. The Orphanage should have sent someone more experienced on that assignment, but I don't blame them either. Things like this happen in our line of work, and you need to be okay with that, or else it is going to tear you apart from the inside out."

I was choking, partly from the strain on my arms and partly from the truth that Darcy spoke. It felt like I'd been released from a prison I had locked myself in since December, since the explosion. I'd had no idea that I had been searching for her forgiveness. I'd believed part of me would always carry the blame for the incident. Now so much of me was being freed by the knowledge that Darcy didn't blame me.

"Hopefully one day it won't feel like my fault," I told her, hoping that one day I could look myself in the mirror without feeling guilty. "But now that you have that out, do you feel better? Can I get back onto the roof?"

"People are more than the one problem you see, Bennet," Darcy said, her face sad. "People are complex and can have many issues going on at once. Come over for a break." She motioned with her hand for me to come join her on the safety of the roof.

Moving as carefully and quickly as I could, I got myself back onto the roof and rolled onto the stones, lying with my arms over my head. My whole body felt like jelly. I cherished every second of my break, not knowing if Darcy was going to make me hang on the pole again.

I had been hanging for roughly two of the longest minutes of my life, and it was getting darker and darker outside. Luckily, the roof had some lights on it. The rain was starting to pick up, and my T-shirt was almost soaked through. I turned my head toward Darcy, who was sitting cross-legged in the rain.

Figuring this training session was now turning into some strange form of counseling, I realized that maybe she wouldn't let us go back inside until we had worked out our issues.

"I know losing your brother killed you, Bennet," Darcy went on, "but it killed me, too. Can you imagine how I felt when I didn't get a letter from Collin like you did? Why did you ignore me? Why couldn't we have gone through it together? I know we've never been super close, and frankly, the only reason we hung out at all was because Collin forced us to, but we could have been there for each other. You were so absorbed in your own feelings you didn't even look at me the day of Collin's final statement. I was dying, and you only cared about yourself." Her hair was glued to her face, drenched by the rain.

The weight returned to my chest, and I choked on a sob. Tears mingled with the rain on my face. Thankfully, I wasn't the only one crying. Darcy's head was bowed, and her shoulders heaved.

"I thought you hated me," I said. "I thought the best option was to avoid you in case you felt like killing me."

A strange, wild laugh came from Darcy's lips. I sat up, startled—and then I started laughing too. I couldn't help it; her laughter was contagious. We laughed and laughed at the idea of Darcy killing me and at the past months of us misunderstanding each other's intentions.

"Are we good? Can we go back inside?" I finally asked.

Her laugh abruptly stopped. "We are far from good. Back on the pole," she ordered.

Forcing myself up, I made my way back to the edge of the roof. I shook my arms out before reaching for the pole. I left the ledge, my legs gently swaying in the open air. I racked my brain for what else could be bothering her. I thought of her saying that people were more than the one problem you see. So, what didn't I see?

"Mary told me about the Orphanage pressuring you to have surgery."

Darcy wiped her face. "Leave it alone, Bennet."

She wasn't going to let me off the pole, so I decided to poke the bear some more. "Come on, Darcy, pretend I'm Collin." Even the idea of me pretending to be Collin stirred something in my gut. Wasn't I already playing pretend by trying to be a field agent?

"Not a good idea," she said.

"Fine," I replied. "Then talk to me as Bennet, someone who cares about you."

"You won't understand it. This is a girl thing. The truth is, I don't like closing doors on things I'm not sure about."

"So, you want kids?" I didn't know what else to ask. That was basically the only reason I could see why she wouldn't want to go through with the surgery. Kids weren't exactly running around the Orphanage. Well, they *were*, but they were handpicked for a purpose. The Orphanage wasn't known for being a breeding ground for agents.

"No. It's just… five years ago I didn't picture my life being here, training you and losing someone I loved. Why should I shut out possibilities that future Darcy might want? If future me decides this is one hundred percent what she wants, then fine. Or if the Orphanage steps in and tells me I *have* to go through with the surgery, then obviously, I will. Until then, I see no reason why this is even a topic we need to talk about."

I wanted to fish further and figure out what she really wanted. She was so used to being told what to do that she didn't know what she actually wanted. Maybe if I kept bothering her, she would eventually figure it out. Maybe she could eventually find the strength to say it out loud. The problem was that it wouldn't solve anything if the Orphanage said she couldn't do it. We lived in a world normal people could only dream about, but both of us had dreams of living in a normal world.

"Do you want to get married?" I asked the dumbest questions, which no sixteen-year-old could possibly know the answer to. "Not to me, but just in general."

"Who knows? Maybe one day I'll want a family or at least a husband," she told me. "But this conversation stays between us. This is all just daydreaming."

I couldn't picture Darcy cooking in a kitchen, waiting for a husband to come home from work, and talking about mortgages and what color to paint the bathroom. A little hurt that she didn't consider her friends here to be her family, I let the first thing I thought of come out of my mouth. "I can't picture you as some housewife," I said, like the idiot I was.

I looked over to where Darcy was sitting silently. She was turned to one side, looking out into the forest. For the briefest of moments, it seemed as if her face fell a little at my mocking of her future.

Kids weren't something I thought about. I never pictured myself as a father. To me, my future had always consisted of Collin and me running around the world and Chuck and myself endlessly fighting over which superhero we would like to be. I guess things change. Darcy was right about one thing, though. Five years ago, I would not have pictured myself here, hanging from a pole in the rain.

"You let the team down," she said, moving on.

"What? Where is this coming from?"

"I'm serious, Bennet," she said. "During the game of 'cops and robbers,' you could have made sure the whole team survived, not just you. You are a fantastic earpiece, and you didn't use that to your advantage. What kind of field will you be if you don't even use the skills that you have?"

She was the one who was supporting me in my goal, and she'd decided now was the proper time to tell me what she was really thinking. She'd thought it was a bad idea at the beginning, but she'd still held up her end of the bargain, and I had come a long way already. Anger and hurt flew through me.

"You were the one backing me up and telling Lucas off for wanting me to play the game with tech strapped to me!"

"Because I was hoping that you would open your eyes and realize you could be both a field *and* an earpiece. Stop being such an idiot."

"Stop calling me that! I'm going to be a field! Darcy, you agreed to support me in this!" I was shouting at her, frustrated that she was trying to put me back behind a desk.

"Bennet, if you live behind that mask of yours for the rest of your life, you may impress people, but you will never truly be with people. Friendship isn't about trying to show off; it's about connecting."

That startled me. "So, we're actually friends?" My grip shifted on the pole.

"Is that all you got out of that? Of course, we're friends, you idiot. We just suck at it." She got up from the roof and walked over to the door that led back into the building. Opening the door, she yelled back at me, "Hang there for another thirty seconds. We're done for the night."

Our talk had taken so many turns that I had whiplash. Her comment about me being both an earpiece and field would follow me for a long time. For now, I knew I needed to focus on my goal. If I took my eye off the prize of becoming a field, I feared I would slip back into my hole and fall apart again. I couldn't afford to do that.

Swaying on the pole, I cursed under my breath, praying for time to go by faster. I could have easily ignored Darcy and climbed back onto the roof, but a part of me believed that she would have found out and punished me in some way at our next training session. I finished out my orders in the rain, dangling over the side of the building.

CHAPTER 20

THE ORPHANAGE
APRIL 10
10:25 A.M.

Practically falling asleep in class, I used my hands to hold up my head. Trying to keep my eyes open was another story. My new technique was to drink an excessive amount of water so that I always needed to pee. I figured, if I always had to pee, I wouldn't fall asleep during class.

All the '01s were in class with Agent Asher, learning about the oil in the world and the ever-rising prices of gas. As thrilling as this conversation may sound, I was more focused on my seat buddy for the class. I had been the last one to make it to class and was forced to sit next to Oliver. Every inch of me hated him, even though I told myself not to. I couldn't help it. He was kind of a jerk.

I'm not sure if it was training from the British Agency, or if he was trying out some sort of role, or if, perhaps, he moved here because no one liked him back home. The last one wouldn't surprise me in the least. He had a thing for always needing to be the center of attention whenever he was in a group setting. He would always try to steer the conversation, and it felt like he needed to get the last word in and constantly had to be right. Maybe those annoying traits were more annoying to me because of my secret dislike for him since day one. Maybe I was looking for a reason to hate him. That made sense, but deep down, I really didn't care. It had become a hobby to secretly hate him every time I saw him.

The previous Saturday afternoon, as I was heading to the lounge to watch a movie with a group of guys, I heard Oliver and his upper-class accent around a corner. Not wanting to have to force myself to smile as he passed, I jumped through the nearest door. Unfortunately, I wasn't paying attention, and it was a ladies' bathroom. Luckily no one was in there. As I was about to exit, after I thought Oliver would have passed by, Darcy opened the door. She gave me a funny smile and moved out of my way, with a motion of her arm gesturing me to go first. Embarrassed, I kept my head down and made my way briskly to the lounge, hoping Darcy would never bring it up.

Oliver had been here for almost three weeks now and was a part of life. I knew his routine for the morning and nighttime. He would wake up with Austen in the morning, and together they would go work out. I hated that, because that was what Austen and Collin used to do. At nighttime, he would study in his bed and catch up on home-work. Every Monday and Wednesday night, he would call home. They were interesting conversations to listen to because only his dad and sister were aware of the organization and what they did. His mom had married into this life, and it was kept a secret from her to help keep her safe. The British Agency had strange rules and traditions. It would have been so much cleaner if they had modeled their Agency after our Orphanage, leaving no room for messy relationships.

The thing that bothered me the most about Oliver was how quickly everyone else in our year accepted him. He always sat with us when we ate as a group; he participated in movie nights and board-game nights. It seemed that, as Oliver moved in, the last of Collin moved out. Even where Collin once slept, not a trace of him was left. Oliver had put his clothes in the dresser and pictures of his family by his bed. He had even brought a blanket that his mother made him.

Even though the British Agency had strange traditions, I was slightly envious of how Oliver had grown up. He seemed to have a personal life outside of all of this. His space in our room looked completely out of place among our gray blankets and the matching lamps above our beds. We had no pictures decorating our room or personal objects that carried sentimental value. The only thing I had of sentimental value was the letter that Collin had written to me. I kept it under my bed in an old *Spider-Man* comic book.

"And that is why oil prices are going to continue to rise," Agent Asher finished.

I had completely zoned out and had missed the last half of what he had said. Hopefully, Chuck had taken good notes, and I could copy off of him later. I couldn't afford to zone out in class; I already had so little time as it was, every second of my day needed to count if I was ever going to catch up.

Specialized-fieldwork weeks were over for the rest of the school year. That was fine with me. When I was an earpiece, I had purpose during those weeks. Specialized-fieldwork weeks were a special thing for this year of schooling, where we got to get more hands-on practice in our career areas. I spent those weeks in the office as an agent's earpiece. Before the incident, most agents would be happy to have me, but after the incident, only Baker would take me on. We got reviewed by the agent we worked with for the week, and they pointed out ways we could improve. Now that I was training to be a field, I was stuck training with younger ages because no agent was crazy enough to take me with them on an assignment. Thankfully we were moving on to other things. There was too much to get done before the end of the year to send us on unnecessary assignments. The American Orphanage tried to hold school like a normal public school, running from September to the end of June. During July and August, it was our job to stay on top of our studies, but we got lots more time for games and fooling around. Sometimes, if we were lucky, a couple of retired agents would volunteer to take us somewhere.

One summer, when we were thirteen, Agent Abigail and Agent Titus, two retired agents in their seventies who had been together for the past twenty years, took us to Disneyland. It was funny to picture twelve trained killers riding the teacups.

Another option during the summer months was to put your name on a list to get assignments. Collin and I usually spent half our summer doing assignments together and the other half goofing off. I didn't know what this summer would look like.

June felt like it was just around the corner, and this being our second-last year of training, we had a final project out in the field. The Chief would split the ten of us into teams and give us our assignments. Only four teams in the Orphanage's history had ever failed. They were kept back another year, which was considered very harmful to their chances of getting interesting future assignments. With something like that on your record, you were more likely to be given boring assignments like tailing someone rather than fun stuff like exposing a possible drug den.

I was nervous that no one would want me on their team—or worse, that I would be the reason our team would have to repeat this year of schooling. None of them deserved that. It added to the pressure of needing to work harder in all of my classes. Maybe Chuck could give me some sort of shot that would help me stay awake.

"Come on, Bennet," Chuck said with a grin. "Let's go to the cafeteria and grab you some coffee before our next class. I'm pretty sure that, even if learning about the Canadian pipeline didn't put you to sleep, Agent Naomi will definitely put you to sleep talking about proper etiquette in Egyptian culture."

It was like he'd read my mind. Grabbing my books, I pushed back my chair and stood up. My thighs ached from the marathon run I'd done the day before. Zipping up my sweater all the way to my neck for extra warmth, I followed Chuck out of the classroom.

"How's it going with Darcy lately?" he asked.

"Could be worse," I told him. "She hasn't made me bleed in a week, so I can't complain."

Chuck laughed. "I can't believe she stabbed you with a knife. How are your stitches?"

I tugged at my sleeve, trying to raise it to see the stitches on my left arm, but gave up when it started to hurt. I was being a baby about the situation. It wasn't like she'd stabbed me with a big knife. It was more like a small-to-medium knife.

"They're holding," I told my doctor, who had been fixing me after every training accident I'd been through with Darcy.

We passed by all the classrooms and reached the staircase, choosing it over the elevator. We ran up the stairs two by two until we got to the third floor. We walked side by side through the cafeteria doors and toward the drink station.

Throughout our time here, our strides had become so in-step that we didn't have to worry about slowing down or speeding up for each other. Without knowing it, we walked the same speed, even though Chuck had longer legs than me. We were totally in sync.

I put my books on the counter and reached for a generic gray mug. Instead of coffee, I reached for a tea bag and poured hot water over it. Grabbing the milk and sugar, I added a bit of each to my tea. Chuck was all done making his coffee and was leaning against the drink station, sipping his hot drink.

He started to say something, smiling, then seemed to think better of it and stopped himself.

I looked at him questioningly and asked, "What?" His smile was making me smile. I wanted to know what he was thinking, but he really didn't look like he wanted to tell me, like he knew a funny secret he'd almost forgotten I wasn't supposed to hear.

"Nothing, Bennet, seriously," Chuck said. He was trying to backtrack, but he was still unable to get rid of his smile. It made him look like he was in pain.

Not wanting to drop it, I pushed further. "Come on, Chuck. What's so funny?"

Biting his lip, he asked, "Are you sure you want to know?"

"No, I'm just asking 'cause I'm bored," I answered sarcastically. "Come on and tell me already." I was preparing myself for something good.

"Do you remember that time you, me, and Collin came down here after dark, and he pushed you into the drink station, and you accidentally broke the water tap? The water kept running, we couldn't turn it off, and it practically flooded the cafeteria before you ran and told someone what had happened. We were forced to spend the next morning mopping up the whole floor before breakfast started." Chuck grinned at the memory.

I'd focused on my breathing when he mentioned Collin's name. The two of us had kept anything that would remind me of Collin off-limits. We never talked about Collin, and I was grateful for that. But I knew that it couldn't last forever. If the roles were reversed, I would have wanted Collin to be able to reminisce about me.

Forcing myself to smile, I looked at Chuck. He was waiting for a response. "But we didn't go to get help until all three of us were soaking wet from trying to stop the water," I reminded him.

"Oh, yeah," he laughed, seemingly glad I hadn't shut him out for bringing up my brother.

We both leaned against the counter in silence. This was foreign territory, and neither of us knew where to go from here. We could walk back to class, but there was something keeping us here. It was almost like we had to clear the air, or we would leave this moment forever and never return. This was what Darcy had been talking about that night on the roof. This was what we tried to work on.

I ran my fingers through my hair, slightly stressed, grasping for the words to say. Thankfully, Chuck broke the silence first.

"Bennet," he practically breathed, "are you aware that this is the first time we have talked about Collin since he died? I don't mean to sound insensitive, but Collin was my friend too."

"I know," I choked, fighting back tears and holding my head down so that he wouldn't see my face.

"I've tiptoed around you for months, and you've never asked me how I'm doing," he said. "I always have to put aside my problems and whatever is going on with me, and focus on you and your feelings because your brother died. Agents die, Bennet. We have to move on."

I stood in shock, unable to believe he had just said that to me. It was refreshing to hear such honesty, and also a punch in the gut. I gripped the side of the counter for support.

First Darcy, and now Chuck. Who was next? Baker?

"I'm sorry, Bennet. I took that too far." He set his mug on the counter and turned to face me like he was going to hug me and try to make everything better.

He had to stop making things better for me. Our friendship had become one-sided, with Chuck always taking care of me. At first, that was what I needed, like at the final-statement reading, and slowly it had become an unhealthy habit for us. We were stuck in a rut, and now it was my choice: Would I get us out of it, or would I continue using Chuck and never have a friendship that went both ways?

"No, no, Chuck, you're right," I found the strength to say. I looked him in the eyes, wanting him to know that I was serious. "I've been a terrible friend to you. I want you to be honest with me and tell me what's going on, because even though you may think my problem is huge, your worst is still your worst, and you need to tell me about it. I know I am bad about it, but I need to be able to talk about memories of Collin, and I think talking about them with you will be the easiest. So, thank you."

Chuck nodded and picked up his mug and books. "We're going to be late," he told me, trying to smile.

I forced a smile on my face as well, picked up my books and tea, and walked beside my best friend.

We walked back to class slower, not wanting to spill our drinks, and took the elevator to avoid wobbling with our cups on the stairs. Hopefully, we would make it back to Agent Naomi's etiquette class before she started. I hoped she wouldn't call us out for being rude for not bringing a drink for everyone in the class. I never knew what was going on with her. She almost floated around the classroom while she taught, her arms out, gesturing in every direction. She was crazy, but at least she knew her stuff.

I thought more about what Chuck and I had worked through, not wanting to go back to how things were but rather moving forward. I was slowly leaving Collin in my past and moving on, mending relationships I had unconsciously hurt, and figuring out who I needed to be now that I was apart from him. It hurt a lot, but it was something that needed to happen if I was ever going to truly live.

CHAPTER 21

"Goodnight, Bennet," Darcy said, taking off her boxing gloves. She smirked. "I'd put some ice on that."

Darcy and I had spent the evening boxing. I think I only got two punches in while my face probably resembled a brown banana.

"You have to admit," I said, lying on the floor, defeated, "I'm getting better."

"Your desperate punch to my thigh while you were falling to the ground doesn't count as improvement, but you are staying up longer. So, yes, you're improving." She tightened her ponytail and then wiped the sweat from her brow with the back of her hand.

She turned to leave, and I shouted from the floor, "Goodnight, Darcy!"

Our friendship had started to grow since our conversation on the roof. It was the little things that mattered. One day, when I was working on homework in the lounge, Darcy came and sat with me. We worked in silence, and it was actually nice. We had gone back to eating together more often, and we also chose each other as partners more often for class assignments and training. It was good to hang out more than just when she was training me. We had a long way to go, but I had a feeling that the friendship that Collin had longed for us to have would one day happen. It was sad that it took his death to bring us together.

I was getting so used to Darcy's scariness that it had become normal. Well, normal for her. Other people, like Baker, still scared me. Maybe after enough time hanging out with Darcy, my fear of intense people and authority figures would go away, and I would become more confident around others. Darcy often told me that I needed to act like other people didn't intimidate me, and then one day, I would simply believe it. Until then, I would keep giving people like Baker a wide berth.

Still lying where Darcy had left me, I mustered what strength I had left and lifted myself off the floor. The training room we were using was empty and oddly peaceful. Finding an empty place at the Orphanage was rather difficult, since people were always moving, and groundkeepers always seemed to be repairing something or checking on security equipment.

Being alone with my thoughts was something that had been difficult for so long, and now all of my thoughts seemed to revolve around becoming a field. This moment of silence, with no one around to see what I was doing, was an opportunity to be alone for a few minutes.

The training room had a rack of audio equipment for people who liked music with their workouts. I walked over and turned on the radio, hoping for something light and happy. I could have gotten my phone or even used my computer to hack into the speakers in the training room, but the simplicity of turning on a radio just seemed so fitting for that moment. It was something that new Bennet would do, whereas the old Bennet would have taken any opportunity to hide behind a computer. I was starting to lose the need to always have a computer in front of me to solve my problems. It was freeing to be able to use my own hands to complete a project, even if that project was lifting weights or cleaning a gun.

Once the music started to come through the speakers, I waited for the beat and started to move my feet, praying no one else would decide to come to train this late at night. I was pleased when something I didn't recognize came on. It allowed me to make something up rather than preplan to lyrics I already knew. The joy of the unknown was new and welcoming.

Making my way to the punching bag, I punched to the beat of the music. I was getting good at this. It had started to become therapeutic for me, taking out whatever emotions I had on this unsuspecting bag. The music was getting to me, and everything around faded and disappeared until all that mattered was the punches that I threw.

Swinging my leg, I kicked the bag with all the force I could gather. I could feel myself getting stronger, better, smoother, and I liked it. Even though Darcy still kicked my butt at everything, I loved the new power I felt when I came to the training room.

Every day, I studied anything and everything I could that would help further my goal of becoming a field agent. One day when Agent Asher had given us a break from class, I asked if I could sit in on an '02s class and got to study the art of knocking someone out in public without people noticing.

The hard part wasn't the learning, because in theory, I knew most of it. It was putting it into practice. I had spent years helping Collin and other agents from behind a desk, telling them what to do.

Jumping back and forth between my feet, I pretended I was a professional boxer, imagining that the punching bag was my competition. In this situation, I was winning, unlike when I would fight with Darcy and constantly lose. The music urged me on as I gave my opponent two right punches and then a swift kick with my leg. He had no chance of hitting me back, and our match was drawing to a close. I gave him one final blow to what I imagined would be his face, knocking him out and claiming victory.

Turning in circles with my arms in the air, I started cheering, celebrating my win. Halfway through my celebration, I heard a gentle, "Mm-hmm."

Startled, I put my hands down and spun toward the entrance of the training room to see Agent Asher standing in the doorway.

"Agent Asher," I said, embarrassed of what he had just witnessed. I stood up straight, hoping to act at least a little bit professional in front of someone who was in charge of whether I passed or failed.

"Turn the music off, Bennet. I can't hear myself think over that." He motioned with his cane toward the radio.

Quickly walking to the radio, I pressed the off button and again stood up straight, facing my teacher.

Giving me a disapproving look, he told me, "Do you know what time it is? Head off to bed."

Confused, I spoke before I could think. "But we've never had a bedtime."

"I suggest you get to bed now, Bennet," Agent Asher commanded. He wasn't even caught off guard by any of the new bruises on my face. Most of the agents around here were used to seeing me injured in some form or another.

Nodding my head and not wanting to question him again, I walked past him and out the door, still baffled as to why I was being sent to bed. Usually, we could stay up as late as we wanted. We could stay up all night as long as it didn't affect our schoolwork. Yes, a couple of times we had been sent to bed during emergency situations, but I hadn't heard of anything going on, and I didn't dare ask.

I headed straight to my dorm room, not wanting to get yelled at by Agent Asher. My footsteps echoed through the still hallways, cutting through the silence. After the freedom and joy of my strange dance session, my sore muscles caught up with me. I decided against heading to the kitchen to get some ice for it. I would just get Chuck to look at it in the morning.

Walking down the hallway that led into the dorm area, I passed by a couple of '05 girls. I stepped out of their way and stared after them while they disappeared around the corner, walking in the opposite direction from their rooms. Were *they* going to be sent back to bed? Why was *I* sent to bed? It was close to midnight by this point, and tomorrow was a school day, but none of that usually mattered.

When I opened the door to the room, I found everyone already in bed and asleep. Lucas was even snoring a little. I quietly slipped in, trying not to let in any light from the hallway. Getting ready for bed as fast and quietly as possible, I put on my pajamas and pulled the covers up to my neck, enjoying the cozy feeling of being warm.

Listening to everyone's gentle breathing, I faded away into sleep.

Hands abruptly pulled me out of my peaceful sleep, covering my mouth, making it impossible for me to say anything. The coziness of my blanket was gone, and panic started to set in as I realized that this wasn't a dream. Opening my eyes to darkness, I tried to see where Chuck or Lucas or Austen were, or even Oliver. I couldn't make out much in the room except that there were many bodies in here that shouldn't be. I looked at the closest person to me and could just make out that he was wearing a black hood.

Next to me, I heard Chuck grunting, and worry set in. I knew he was the last of us to be able to fight back. I heard someone shout out in pain but couldn't tell who it was. It didn't sound like Oliver, but it came from his direction. Maybe he'd been lucky enough to get a punch in. I would've hated to get saved by Oliver, but right then, I was so desperate I would've accepted anyone's help.

The only noise was the shuffling of feet on the tiled floor, the movement of bodies, and the occasional grunt. With a stranger's hands on my body, holding my arms, head, and legs down, I struggled to gasp for breath and make noise.

I felt like a failure after studying for all these years. I had been caught completely off guard. How could this have happened? Who was in the Orphanage wreaking havoc? Questions flooded my mind. The whole situation seemed impossible. Were we under attack?

It seemed I wasn't the only one failing after all of our years of studying. Silence came from Oliver's direction, and I feared that he'd been knocked out after the fight I imagined he'd put up. On the other side, Chuck had also fallen silent. A slight sense of pride came over me with the realization that I had outlasted a couple of people in my room. I couldn't hear Lucas or Austen, so I felt that I might, in fact, be our room's only hope.

Still lying in my bed, unable to move from the intruder's grasps, I gathered air into my lungs, hoping I could at least let out a muffled scream, and someone in another room might hear it. But before I was able to let out a noise, one of the intruders put a sack over my head, cutting off what little vision I already had.

I stayed calm, not allowing this to distract me.

More hands grabbed at me, lifting me over someone's shoulder. Attempting to kick out, I noticed that they had tied my legs together. I thought back to my training with Darcy, but before I could put any knowledge I had into action, I felt myself drifting away, and my eyelids slowly slid closed.

CHAPTER 22

WHO KNOWS
UNSURE
I WISH I KNEW

I had given up on untying the ropes that held me to the chair. My legs were tied to the chair's legs, and my hands were bound behind my back. My wrists stung underneath the rope, raw from my attempts to break free.

The room was dark and damp, like an unfinished basement with no windows. A dim light shone beneath the door several paces in front of me. Above, I could almost see a light bulb. The whole room had a very classic interrogation-room vibe. It might have been pulled straight out of a movie. Maybe it was.

I had no idea how long I had been there. My stomach made a noise, letting me know it had been long enough for me to be hungry, almost uncomfortably so. My mouth was dry, longing for a drop of water. No one had come to see me since I'd been put here, and all of the questions running through my mind about my friends and the Orphanage were going unanswered.

I'd been unconscious when they first brought me here, having been knocked out by whatever drug was in the mask they threw over my head. I had woken up alone and confused, luckily without that terrible hood on. Trying my best, I'd kept my fear to a minimum and my breathing even, trying to think of anything I could do to make this situation go in my favor. Being in bed felt like hours ago, and I had to admit I was slightly bored and tired of sitting.

I hadn't attempted to call out or anything. I was worried they might barge into the room and beat me if I made a noise. I'd decided right away to be patient, but that was before my stomach started thinking about peanut butter. I had no idea how long I'd been asleep, so it could have been days or only hours. I hoped it had only been hours. Thankfully, I had gone to the bathroom before bed and didn't need to go. Yet.

The purpose behind this kidnapping was a huge mystery to me. I was no one important, after all. I decided to do the only thing I could do to get some answers.

"Ex-excuse me," I politely stammered, breaking through the silence. "I-I'm getting a little hungry in here. If I could get, I don't know, an apple, that would be awesome. Just letting you know."

My voice echoed off the walls. A few seconds later, the door slammed opened, and light flooded the room. I closed my eyes against the brightness, then opened them just a little. One man came into the room, shutting the door behind him and bringing the darkness back.

"Seriously?" I said, frustrated that the light had been taken away so quickly.

Before I could get more disappointed, the man flicked a switch, and the bulb above me came on. I had to squint my eyes again. The man towered over me with his average build and clean-shaven face. He had kind of a small head and big ears—not a flattering look.

With my eyes adjusting, I looked around the room, noticing the things I couldn't before. I wasn't sure if it had been made to look intimidating or if the items around the room were actually going to be used. There was a table off to my right that held all sorts of knives, and not the cleanest-looking ones either. On the wall were a handsaw and an ax. Someone could easily confuse this place with a workshop. Pliers and hammers and other things that you would find in a plumber's toolbox lay on the floor a little too close for comfort to my wooden-chair prison.

The man grabbed another wooden chair that had been against the wall and sat down in front of me. He pulled an apple from his pocket, took a bite of it, and motioned it toward me, as though he were asking if I wanted some. I gave a little smirk in response and shook my head slowly to say no. We were about to enter into a battle of wits—at least I hoped it was going to be a battle of wits, and that it didn't involve me getting stabbed with a screwdriver.

The man continued eating his apple, chomping loudly and obnoxiously, emphasizing the fact that he had food and I didn't. I tried not to let him get to me, but my stomach was quietly whimpering.

The man sat rather relaxed, with one leg crossed over the other. His shoes looked like he'd just gotten back from a major hike. His clothes, on the other hand, looked like he spent lots of money on brands that not a lot of people could afford. He looked warm and comfortable, whereas my clothes felt damp, and in fact, were pajamas. If I'd known I was going to be kidnapped, I would definitely have dressed differently.

He finished his apple and tossed it into a can by the table full of knives. I watched it land perfectly in the can, and then I turned my gaze back to his beady eyes and clean-shaven face.

The man adjusted his sweater and wiped his sticky hands on his pants. "So, am I starting or are you?" he asked.

"Wh-what?" I responded, trying to be confident and failing miserably. This was my first interrogation, and from what I had studied in my classes, usually the interrogator didn't ask who was going to be starting.

"Well, you asked for an apple, and I conveniently had one and offered it to you. You rudely declined. Are you going to demand anything else, or should I start?" He held onto the leg that was crossed over the other and leaned back in his chair, giving me space to respond.

"Um," I said, not knowing what to ask. "Maybe you should start." I wasn't a hundred percent sure what information I needed from him, and I figured maybe he would give some up either by accident or freely. I decided that, since this was his interrogation, maybe he should take the lead.

"So, Bennet—"

"How do you know my name?" I jumped in, already not sticking with my plan to let him do most of the talking.

The man smiled. "I know a lot about you and what you do. What I'm hoping is for you to fill in a couple of gaps in the information that my, let's say… company… has collected."

I attempted to shift in my chair, uncomfortable with what he had told me. The Orphanage was supposed to be a secret organization, doing things that the governments of the world couldn't. No one was supposed to know anything about us except people who were part of the Orphanage.

I didn't respond to him, and he continued, "Tell me, Bennet, how long have you been with the Orphanage?"

I had gotten ahead of myself when I jumped in and asked how he knew my name. I knew I had to keep my mouth shut now. It was a lot harder to control my tongue than I thought. Instead of answering his question, I decided to compromise and still allow myself to talk by asking a question of my own.

"Where are my friends?"

The man made a tsking noise, and planting both feet on the ground, leaned in. "This is an exchange of goods, Bennet. You tell me what I want to know, and I'll tell you what you want to know. You did say that I could start, after all. Let's try this again. How long have you been with the Orphanage?"

I was trapped. If I gave in, I was compromising the Orphanage, and if I didn't, it could mean the end of my friends and me. My training was telling me that I was supposed to kill him and anyone he was involved with, or at least get rid of the problem at hand. I was never supposed to give in to threats like this. I was supposed to give my life for the Orphanage before I gave up information, and that would mean giving up my friend's lives as well. That was what it meant to work for the Orphanage.

The man stood up, tired of waiting for me to respond, and walked over to the toolbox. "I gave you a chance to make this very simple. Obviously, letting you marinate in here didn't soften you, so let's try a different tactic." He dug in the toolbox for something.

My palms began to sweat, and I could feel my nerves taking over my body. I needed to keep control of myself. I prayed that my sweaty hands would make it easier to slip out of the ropes.

"Wh-what are you looking for?" I stammered, trying to distract him.

I heard the clanking of metal against metal as he picked up the toolbox and brought it over to the table, apparently not wanting to bend over to have to search for whatever it was he was looking for.

"Something to make you a little uncomfortable," the man told me rather calmly. I, on the other hand, was anything but calm.

I desperately looked around the room for an escape or a distraction while trying to seem nonchalant, but this space had been masterfully designed to offer someone in my position no hope.

"This will have to do," he said, picking up what looked like a giant hole puncher. He walked toward me and reached for my right ear. I tried to pull away, but he grabbed it.

"All you have to do is tell me how long you've been at the Orphanage. In fact, you can tell me anything you want about the Orphanage, and I won't give you a nice little hole in your ear. Can you do that for me?" he said.

It sounded easy enough. Tell him something minor, and I wouldn't be bleeding out of my ear. I could probably even come up with a lie. But all this time with Darcy kicking my butt had been training me for this moment. I could take this little bit of pain and not give up anything. I relaxed my body in preparation.

"I gave you a choice," he told me, squeezing his hand.

Pain shot through my ear, and I bit my lip, holding in any noise that might try to escape. Blood dripped onto my shoulder and down my neck. My ear throbbed with the new, unwanted hole.

"That's all?" I stupidly asked.

The man smirked. "I've got all the time I need, so get comfy if you can." He walked over to the table with all the knives and grabbed a small kitchen knife. "Where is the India Orphanage located?" he asked, returning with knife in hand.

"In India," I responded, smiling and ignoring the pain from my ear. I eyed the knife.

In response, my interrogator started cutting my pajama pants, exposing my right leg from the knee down. "I'll give you the option again, Bennet. Tell me anything about the Orphanage, and I won't shave a layer of your skin off." He towered menacingly over me.

"What's your company, and where are my friends?" I countered. It took everything in me to stand my ground—well, sit my ground. I could probably tell him the date that the Orphanage was created, and he would maybe grant me an answer. I knew this wouldn't end until he got everything he wanted, and then who knew what he had planned for me? I would stay strong and give him nothing, knowing I could possibly die in this chair.

The man dropped the knife, went around behind me, and shoved me in my chair as hard as he could. My knees slammed into the floor. My momentum tilted me forward, causing my face to hit the floor next. Intense pain struck me, like the kind when you stub your toe. I toppled over and landed on my side, still tied to the chair. Lying on the floor, I let the breath I'd been holding whoosh out of me.

"I was hoping we could come to an understanding, but it seems we haven't reached that point yet," the man said. He hauled the chair onto its legs again.

I was grateful to be back in an upright position. Blood had run across my face from my ear and into my mouth while I lay on my side. I spat out what I could, not liking the taste of it.

Picking up the knife, the man reached for my exposed leg and swiped the blade down from knee to ankle, like he was peeling the skin off of an apple.

I couldn't help but scream. It felt like what I imagined standing in a fire would feel like. I didn't dare look for fear that I might throw up. I could feel blood pouring onto my bare foot. My world became unfocused, but I struggled to keep my eyes on the man, not wanting to give up eye contact after my scream of pain. I was breathing heavily and let out a few pained grunts, trying to control myself.

"Let's let you marinate with that for a while and then see if you'll talk." The man threw the bloodied knife back on the table. He went to the exit, flicked off the light switch, and then opened the door.

Again, light flooded the room. I was unable to make out any details beyond the door before he slammed it shut again, leaving me in the dark.

I sat still, scared to move and send more pain through my body. At least the pain gave me something new to focus on besides my hunger and thirst. I wondered how long I would last before they would just kill me. I wouldn't give any information about the Orphanage to him, and hopefully, none of my friends would either.

It might be that the Orphanage would be down five boys for our graduating year.

CHAPTER 23

WHO KNOWS
UNSURE
WELL PAST DINNERTIME

Freezing-cold water abruptly splashed my face, waking me from my sleep. I had no idea when I had passed out or how long I had been unconscious. It felt like years had gone by since the horrible man had skinned my leg. My ear still throbbed, though I thought the bleeding had stopped, whereas my leg felt like it was engulfed in flames.

I shook my head, trying to wake myself up and also get rid of the water in my eyes. Panting from the shock of my rude awakening, I looked around the room, squinting in the light from the bulb above my head, which had been switched on again.

"Rise and shine, gorgeous," said my interrogator, placing the water jug he had used to wake me on the table. He grabbed the chair he'd sat in before and turned it around, sitting on it backward.

Groggy from sleep, I tried to pull myself together and not appear weak. I was starving and thirsty, and now I was also feeling the desire to use the bathroom, and not just for a hot shower and to brush my teeth. The last thing I wanted was to continue sitting in this chair.

"Good morning," I greeted, sounding more chipper than I actually was. "Or should I say afternoon? Or maybe night?"

The man smiled. "Nice try, but I do believe it's still my turn to ask questions."

I was tired of this. Bored, almost. I knew what the end result was, and I just wanted to get there. I couldn't tell if I was giving up or if I was being honest. I was stuck in this chair with no way of escaping, and I had no idea if the Orphanage was even trying to come get me. My only options were telling my interrogator everything he wanted to know, and then he would kill me, or tell him nothing, and he would still kill me.

A sudden peace came over me at the realization of what death meant. It meant I would be with Collin again. I wouldn't have to force myself out of bed every morning and convince myself that what I was fighting for was what I actually wanted. I could just close my eyes and never open them again. All this pain and uncertainty could be over, and I wouldn't feel like half a person anymore.

A burst of uncontrollable laughter escaped me, sitting there in my chair with my hands tied behind my back and a hole in my ear. Going from falling asleep in the warmth of my bed to suddenly being here was too much. The whole past couple of months had been too much, and now that I thought about it, what with how much I had been training and working toward something I had told myself I wanted, something I needed, this was probably the most relaxed I had been in a long time.

The man, annoyed by my outburst, stood up from his chair, walked over to me, and slapped me across the face. This only made me laugh harder. If I'd been observing myself, I would probably have thought I had cracked and lost it. I was not giving this man any information, so I figured I might as well enjoy my time here before I got to join my brother. The man's slap only moved my head slightly, and the pain that it should have caused me was nowhere to be found.

"Thank you," I told him, honestly grateful for my new clarity.

The man looked at me, confused, and asked, "For what?"

"I'm not going to give you anything, so I suggest you wrap this up quickly. Now, I would prefer it if you just shot me in the head, but I understand if you want this to go on a little longer. Might I suggest the ax on the wall over there?" I nodded in the ax's direction.

The man gave me an exasperated look, then paced back and forth in the small room, clearly debating how to move forward. I gave him his time to think, not wanting to rush him and also curious about what route he was about to take. I was excited and itching for the pain to be gone. Not just the pain in my leg or throbbing ear, but especially the pain in my heart.

Letting out a sigh, the man went to the table and picked up the knife he'd previously used on me. My eyes widened as I realized he wasn't going to take my suggestion and would instead start carving me up again. He dropped to the floor, put the knife to my right ankle, and sliced upwards.

I cried out, but no matter how loud I screamed, the man kept going. I squeezed my eyes shut, trying to block everything out. It got to the point where I couldn't tell if he was still skinning me alive or not, it hurt so badly.

After eons of pain, I was finally able to open my eyes.

The man stood with a gun in his hand, pointed right at me. He tilted his head as if questioning if I was going to crack or not.

"Pull the trigger," I cried out. "Or else you're going to be wasting your time." I stared him down, forcing the pain away, not an inch of fear in me.

He walked closer to me and put the gun to my head. "What a waste," he said and pulled the trigger.

I shut my eyes the moment I heard the click. When I noticed I could still feel my throbbing ear and my burning leg, I slowly opened them again.

The man had put down the gun that had only clicked, revealing it wasn't loaded in the first place, and picked the knife back up instead. A new fear set in, and I started breathing heavily. I thought I had escaped being tortured to death. Apparently, he had more pain in store for me. I knew I would have to patiently sit through it all until he finally gave up and killed me, and I had no idea how long that would take. Being skinned alive was not the way I had hoped to go.

The man walked behind me, knelt down, and started cutting something—my ropes! I prepared myself to make an epic escape. I wasn't going down without a fight. Either he was going to have to kill me, or I was going to have to kill him. I would focus on getting out of here and whatever lay on the other side of the door—after I had finished with my interrogator. The pain from my leg was going to hold me back, but I would have to push through.

I sat calmly as he finished cutting my hands free. He moved around the chair and started working on cutting free my right leg, and then my left leg.

My good leg.

I kicked him in the face with it and leaped up, ready to tower over him and kick him again.

He tumbled backward and yelled, "Damn it, Bennet, you passed. Quit it!"

Ignoring him, I stomped on his shin and heard a satisfying crack. Then I lunged for the knife that he had dropped. I got down on top of him and held the knife to his neck. "Who do you work for?" I demanded.

"The Orphanage. Now get off me!" he spat back.

"Liar," I said. I steeled myself to drive the knife into his throat. He would be the first person I'd killed. Nothing could stop me.

Well, nothing except maybe the door suddenly opening. People rushed in. One of them was Chief Benjamin, and I was confused all over again.

Dropping the knife, I stood and backed up against the far wall. Leaning against it with my mouth open, I watched as agents I recognized lifted my interrogator from the floor—without saying a word—and helped him out of the room. Clearly, I had done some serious damage to his leg. After he was gone, Agent Maria pushed a wheelchair into the room and rolled it over to me.

Shaking my head at her, I hobbled farther away from everyone, even though my body was screaming in pain and begging me to sit down.

"Bennet," the Chief said softly. "This was a test. Now please get in the wheelchair, and we will take you to the hospital to get you fixed up."

I knew, that right now, that was all the answer I was going to get as to what was going on. I trusted the Chief. Hobbling over to Agent Maria, I sat myself down in the wheelchair.

Chief Benjamin came over and patted me on my shoulder. "You did well, Bennet," he told me before leading the way out of the room.

CHAPTER 24

THE ORPHANAGE
STILL UNSURE
MAYBE NIGHTTIME

Agent Maria wheeled me through hallways dimly lit by lanterns that looked like they belonged in a mine and into an elevator. A couple of other agents piled in with us. They stood—and I sat—quietly while the elevator rose. When the door opened, I recognized the Orphanage hospital. Clearly, they'd been interrogating me in the Orphanage's basement.

As training agents, we knew there was a basement, but none of us had been allowed down there before. When we graduated, we would get our clearance into the lower levels. We knew that it housed information on every single agent, dead or alive, and prison cells for extra-special people that governments wanted to get rid of.

The elevator doors opened, and we all filed out. As the wheels of my chair turned, every slight bump sent lightning bolts of pain coursing through my body. The only thing keeping me going was my curiosity about what had happened to the rest of the guys. Well, that and the idea of all the drugs they were about to pump into my body to relieve me of my pain. My body felt as if it were going to spontaneously burst into flames.

The hospital was in an uproar. Doctors were running around with bandages and bedsheets while field agents and some of my teachers stood off to one side with notebooks. Doctor Caleb, the head of the hospital, was yelling at Doctor Theo, who was standing right next to me. Agent Maria had stopped pushing my chair and had gone to join the other agents off to the side. Doctor Theo took my chair and pushed me to a bed, where he was joined by two other doctors, who positioned themselves to lift me into the bed. I wasn't sure if they thought I was unable to get onto the bed myself physically or if they thought I had gone into shock and couldn't do it mentally.

The hospital was a giant room filled with beds. The normal gray of the Orphanage didn't touch this room. Instead, white decorated this area, leaving you with a sense that everything was cleaned and sterilized. Off to the back of the big room were double doors that led to operating rooms, X-ray rooms, storage closets, and other areas that Chuck would know about.

The bed was much more comfortable than the chair. My butt had gone numb from it. The pillow was nice under my sore head, and lying flat, I was finally able to stretch out. I pointed my toes with joy at freely being able to move, then had to bite my lip to prevent myself from screaming when that slight movement sent excruciating pain up my leg. In the thrill of knowing that I was going to be okay, I'd forgotten about my leg.

Doctor Theo was at my side in an instant, putting a needle into my arm and attaching a drip. I had no idea what he was pumping into my body, but I prayed it would knock me out.

Someone started cleaning the blood from my face and ear while I looked up at Theo and smiled. He was a nice guy who cared about his patients. One time, when I was eight, someone shot a squirrel on the lawn with a slingshot. Theo was studying with his friends nearby and went over to the squirrel and spent eight weeks nursing it back to health. I knew I was in good and gentle hands. He was working away on my right leg.

Grabbing a pair of scissors, Theo got to work cutting off my pajamas. I was a little uncomfortable being so exposed while he did this; thankfully, he worked quickly. After removing my top, he quickly wiped me down with a damp cloth and put a hospital gown on me, lifting me up gently so he could tie up the back. He carefully put me back down on the soft pillow and continued to clean me up. Next, he took the scissors and cut off my soiled bottoms before pulling the hospital gown down. Finished with that, Theo walked away from my bed, carrying my soiled pajamas with him, leaving me alone with my thoughts.

Lifting my now much-cleaner head, I attempted to look down at the rest of my body to scan my injuries. As I was double-checking my arms, Doctor Caleb came up to my bed with Agent Asher.

"What happened to this boy?" Caleb asked.

"Nothing terrible," I heard Asher reply. I had dropped my head back down. The pain from keeping it up was too much.

"Nothing terrible?" Caleb scoffed. "He's missing all the skin off his right leg. Do you know how long that's going to take to grow back?"

"You and I both know that you have skin in a can down here," Asher replied. Then he reached down and leaned against the bars of my bed, examining my injuries closer. "Honestly, Caleb, we thought he would crack the instant he needed to go to the bathroom. I'm impressed he just went in his chair, considering we marinated him for four days. I'm going to go check on the others. Oh, and good job, Bennet," he quickly told me before walking away and leaving Doctor Caleb at the end of my bed.

I tried to forget what Asher had just said. I didn't really want to think about the fact that I'd relieved myself in the chair I was sitting on when I didn't even remember doing that.

Since I didn't want to think about that, I thought about my friends instead and prayed they were doing okay. If this had been a test, then both the guys and the girls must have been taken. I knew Darcy and Austen would be fine. It was Chuck I wished hadn't had to go through this, and Mary. I didn't want to imagine someone like Mary getting tortured.

One time, when she was working on an airplane, she broke her arm when a safety door malfunctioned and slammed shut. Chuck and I were in the shop attached to the garage with Lucas, trying to work the 3D printer, when we heard her screams. Lucas and I were able to hot-wire the door and force it to open, releasing Mary's very bent arm. She was white as a ghost, and we had to carry her to the hospital. She had looked so small and helpless.

Thinking about my friends in pain caused me more pain. I didn't want any of them to be hurt—even Oliver, weirdly.

Caleb was still at the bottom of my bed, writing notes on a clipboard, and I was waiting for Theo to return with some wonderful drugs. I guessed what he'd already given me was just nutrients for my body. If Chuck were here, he could tell me exactly what was going on.

I tried to take a better look around the hospital. Everyone was still in a frenzy, probably trying to prepare for everyone else who was still to come. I relaxed when I saw Theo walking toward my bed, carrying a tray. Sadly, he didn't make it to my bed, because at that moment, a scream filled the air.

If it didn't hurt so much to move, I would have covered my ears. The high-pitched noise was coming from the bed beside me. I hadn't noticed anyone beside me until now. Someone was flailing around in the bed.

Doctors dropped what they were doing and rushed to the bed. Carefully turning my head, I tried to get a better look at who it could be. I could see dark-brown hair and a tiny body, and the only person that could be was Elizabeth. She was lying on her stomach and crying out in agony.

Embarrassed, I saw that Elizabeth wasn't wearing anything on her top half. I couldn't tell about her bottom half since she was covered with a blanket. Her back startled me. It wasn't her usual pale color; it was a mixture of floppy skin and red—*lots* of red.

Theo made it to my bed and got to work on my ear, giving me a shot of something first that froze it.

"Theo," I managed to say, "what happened to Elizabeth?"

Theo looked at me with sorrow in his eyes. I knew all this pain was a lot for him to carry, and he would do anything to make us all better. It was strange to think that the people we swore to serve would put us through so much.

"I'm not supposed to say anything," Theo quietly told me.

"Please, Theo," I begged. "I need to know something."

He sighed. "You'll be told eventually, but don't tell anyone else who comes in here from your year. She got thirty-nine lashes to her back. I am impressed that she woke up at all. She's been lying there for a day, and if you think she looks bad now, you should have seen her when she first arrived. And I know what you're thinking. You are the second one out. The rest are still being tested." He finished what he was doing to my ear and took his tray away, leaving me alone with Caleb, who was examining my leg closely.

The door banged open, making me jump and instantly sending a burning sensation through my body. Instead of a wheelchair, a stretcher was brought through the doors, accompanied by two agents and the Chief.

Caleb left me and hurried to the stretcher, yelling at the Chief— something most people didn't do. "If my future surgeon doesn't have his steady hands at the end of this, I'm going to stick you in an ice tank and see how *you* recover."

The Chief did nothing but laugh, probably because Caleb and Benjamin were from the same year and had a lot of history together. That was also probably the only reason Caleb dared to talk to the Chief in that manner. It was weird to think of the Chief having close friends.

Then what Caleb had said hit me. The person on the stretcher was Chuck!

I watched as they lifted him into a bed opposite mine and Elizabeth's. Doctors swarmed around him. No one was watching me. This was my only chance to see my best friend.

I sat up. My head spun, but I didn't let it get the best of me. I swung my legs over the side of the bed and closed my mouth as tight as I could, so no whimper would escape. I ripped the needle out of my arm and headed toward Chuck, dragging my bad leg and hopping on my good one. My chest started to throb, and I wondered if something was wrong with my rib cage. It hurt bad, but seeing Chuck was more important than my pain.

I hobbled over to his bed, and barely able to focus, peered around the swarm of doctors wrapping him in blankets.

"Get him in the tank and watch his heart rate," Doctor Caleb ordered someone. "See if you can get some nutrients into him."

No one had noticed me yet, and some of the doctors had moved away from Chuck's bed, probably preparing whatever the tank was.

"Chuck," I barely whispered from the end of his bed. His lips were completely blue, and his dark skin had gone pale. He looked unnatural, almost like he was dead. It scared me. He was someone who helped everyone and never asked for help in return. I prayed that he had passed the assignment. My guess was that he did.

Chuck always kept me up to date on what was happening in the hospital. The breakthroughs these doctors had made over the past decade were remarkable. They were still working on being able to fix bones in an instant, but they were getting close. Elizabeth and I would probably have completely new skin by the end of the week. I was easy to fix. I worried Chuck wasn't.

Caleb was still yelling behind me. I couldn't tear my attention away from Chuck for fear someone would pull me back to bed. He wasn't even shivering, which I knew was a bad sign.

The main doors banged open again. "Get back into bed, you idiot!" Darcy shouted, giving away my position. She was currently sitting in a wheelchair, being wheeled by an agent in through the hospital's double doors.

I turned away from Chuck and looked at Darcy, then saw Theo coming after me. "We'll have to strap you down if you're going to wander. There's too much going on for us to have to wonder where you are," Theo politely told me, seemingly sorry he had to take me away from Chuck.

Another doctor came over, and the two of them took my arms and helped me back to bed, my body aching the whole way. They lay me back down. I knew they were right, and I should probably stay put. At least I wasn't unconscious like Chuck or Elizabeth, who had finally stopped screaming. Doctors were busy poking and pulling the skin away from her back.

I looked away from Elizabeth and watched Darcy as she was rolled to a bed. She didn't fight. She didn't complain about being in a wheelchair, or that they didn't let her get herself into bed. She had her normal hard exterior.

Then I noticed her bare legs and arms.

She was wearing a black tank top and shorts, which were incredibly dirty. There were shiny gray things all over her body. I wondered what they were.

"Theo!" Caleb yelled. "Get Training Agent Bennet into X-ray and get going on that leg of his! I want that boy back on his feet!"

Theo and the other doctor who was still with me started to roll my bed out of the room and down the hallway toward the X-ray room. I had no idea what sort of healing journey lay ahead of me.

As we turned the corner, the door banged open one more time, and I heard Caleb yelling in outrage, "How many drugs did you stick in this poor girl?"

CHAPTER 25

My feet dangled off the edge of the bed. I reached up to catch the ball. "Here comes another," I told the others I was playing catch with.

The doors of the hospital swung open to reveal Oliver being rolled in, completely passed out. He didn't look too bad. We all watched him being pushed to a bed and lifted up on it. Doctor Caleb and another doctor came to examine his bare feet, and I realized most of his toenails had been torn out. I wondered what else had happened to him. Asleep, he looked sort of peaceful and less like the kid I hated. I thought about throwing the ball at him to wake him up.

"What do you think happened to him?" Lucas asked, catching the ball I threw to him instead.

All of us from our year—minus Oliver, who'd just arrived, and Austen, who we were still waiting for—were dangling our feet over the edges of our beds, playing catch around the doctors moving around the room. We'd been told we had to stay in our beds until the test was over. Something about how this was a super-secret test, and it needed to stay that way, so future years didn't know it was coming.

We were all wrapped up in different ways from our various injuries. Darcy was covered in tiny stitches where they had hammered nails into her skin. Lucas had had his mouth sewn shut and now had

171

red marks all around it. The doctors should have kept his mouth sewn shut, because he hadn't shut up since they removed the stitches. He had been in his test for six days. He'd just gotten back today and was dehydrated and starving. Thankfully, while he had been eating his soup, he hadn't been able to say much. Now that he had joined the game, his motormouth had been working overtime.

Mary had endured a very strange torture technique that her skin would take a while to recover from, although the doctors said she would be back to normal once they were done with her. Her torturer had carved pictures into her skin and then injected her with all kinds of hallucinogens. She was still not her normal self, and we didn't pass her the ball because her brain was working two seconds slow and the ball would have just hit her in the face. We'd learned that after throwing it to her twice.

Charlotte had undergone electroshock therapy. She looked rough and a little twitchy. Jane was probably the scariest, because they shaved her signature feature. Her long, beautiful hair was gone, leaving her completely bald. They'd also applied a red-hot iron to different parts of her body. I was curious if she was going to wear a wig once we left here, or if she was going to come up with some story to explain why her hair was gone.

Since Austen was still out there, I wondered if his test was going to be the hardest. After all, his future here was a lot bigger than all of ours combined.

"Ouch," Lucas said after he finished reading the clipboard that Caleb had left hanging at the end of Oliver's bed. Lucas was in a bed next to Oliver's but still had to ungracefully stretch to reach the notes. "It says that he hasn't slept in six days, and they used Chinese water torture on him. He got no food or water, and all of his toenails and fingernails were ripped off. Well," he finished, putting the clipboard back. "He'll be asleep for a while. Darcy, catch."

Lucas threw the ball a little too high, and Darcy had to stretch to reach it. She caught it like I knew she would, and we all saw one of her stitches on her left arm break, and then a little bit of blood started to run out. I thought about looking away, but I couldn't help but watch as the blood trickled down her arm. She wasn't even fazed. She reached for the needle and thread on her nightstand.

Before starting to fix her own stitches, she threw the ball at Elizabeth, whose whole top half was wrapped in bandages. Darcy didn't show any signs of irritation while she worked the needle and thread, nor did she alert the doctors. None of us bothered the doctors with stuff like that.

Chuck lifted his feet out of the water they were soaking in, and making the floor all wet, slowly walked over to Darcy. Carefully kneeling down beside her, he grabbed the needle and thread and finished the job while the rest of us continued the game without them.

The ball that we'd found was our only form of entertainment here. It was actually a stress ball that Charlotte had found in a drawer next to her bed.

"Thanks, Chuck," I heard Darcy whisper as Chuck grabbed a pair of scissors and finished up.

Chuck only smiled and headed back to his bed, catching the ball as it was thrown to him.

Darcy looked down at her new stitches and rubbed her arm. Then she walked over to my bed, a slight limp to her left leg. She sat down next to me, making herself comfortable by grabbing my blanket and wrapping it around her. I looked around, worried that a doctor might tell her off, and she would have to go back to her bed.

I didn't know when our friendship had moved so far forward. I was actually comfortable having Darcy sit next to me. A month ago, I would have been on high alert and ready to get torn apart. Two months ago, we weren't even talking. I liked being able to call her a friend and mean it. In fact, if I had to label it, I'd say she was becoming my second-best friend. Chuck used to be my second-best friend before Collin left me. Chuck moved up after the incident, so the second-best friend position had become available. I never would have guessed that the spot would be filled by Darcy.

"How's your leg?" she asked, giving it a little nudge.

"Better every day. I was a little worried when they started using a spray can on it, but it turns out you can regrow skin in a can. At least it's doing better than Elizabeth's back or Jane's feet." I looked over to Jane's bare feet dangling from her bed. She tossed the nail polish she'd gotten a doctor to smuggle in over to Mary who fumbled the bottle before it fell on her bed. Jane's feet were a nauseating purple color and were shriveled up from being burned.

"I would ask how you're healing, but if you keep tearing your stitches, we're never going to get out of here." I nudged her back. The doctors didn't want any of us leaving until we were all healed up, to help keep this test a secret. The only person that they couldn't completely fix was Jane, whose hair would take forever to get that long again.

Darcy fell back onto my bed, resting her hands on her stomach. I didn't know how many nails had been driven into her stomach, and I didn't want to know. With all of us wearing matching gray hospital gowns, I could only see her arms and legs, which looked like she had a terrible case of chickenpox because of the dried blood around some of her stitches that she had fixed without the doctors noticing. When Caleb finally came around to look us over, he'd probably give her a long speech about the importance of giving your body the time it needed to recover, just like he had yesterday after Darcy had torn open ten of her little stitches.

We watched Jane hurl the ball at Lucas's face. He tried to catch it and missed, sending everyone into roaring laughter when it hit him right in the nose.

I stopped laughing abruptly and sighed. "I'm falling behind on my training being in here," I told Darcy.

Darcy sat up and replied, "You know training isn't just punching people in the face, Bennet. It's an art to master—the art of going unseen but seeing everything. Take right now. Look at everything going on around you and take notes. That doctor by the sink, what color is his shirt? Who comes in and out of every door? What are the agents talking about in that corner?"

I tried to stealthily look around without moving my head. While playing catch, I tried to notice everything going on around me. "As an earpiece, I could just snap a picture and study it, but as a field, I have to memorize everything," I noted.

"Bennet," Darcy breathed, "you were a fantastic earpiece. Why are you giving that up?"

"Why do you keep asking me that?" I didn't make eye contact with her. I stared at Chuck, watching him laugh along with the rest of our friends.

"Because I don't like your answer. We have tons of people who know how to use a gun out there in the field, but not many people who know how to hack into the president's computer and are willing to leave the safety of the Orphanage."

I didn't know what to say to her. I had made up my mind.

"Do you know why I agreed to train you after your stunt with the knife?" she continued.

I shook my head, smiling at the memory of bending the rules.

"It's because you thought outside the box like a field should. Why can't you think outside of the box even more and combine two jobs into one? We have fields that specialize as dancers, accountants, government workers, and even cooks. Why can't we have a field agent who specializes as an earpiece? Imagine a former earpiece working out in the field." Getting up, she headed back to her bed because the last wheelchair was finally coming through the double doors of the hospital.

We all turned to look toward Austen rolling in. He looked awful, but not physically. He stared down at the floor like whoever had interrogated him had broken his spirit. Maybe they had loaded him up with a bunch of drugs, just like they had done to Mary.

"Alright, '01s!" Chief Benjamin called for our attention, entering the room behind Austen. River followed him with her typical armload of papers.

Doctors swarmed Austen and wheeled him over to the empty bed, lifting him onto it as they had done to us. He lay still, staring at the ceiling, making no sound. The doctors left his side as quickly as they had gone to it. They didn't attach him to any drips or give him any water. He didn't get any treatment at all, and Caleb passed by him without a glance. Nor did he take any notes on a clipboard about his condition. It all worried me.

Had Austen failed his test?

We all sat at attention, ready to hear whatever it was the Chief was going to say. I wanted him to say we were getting out today, because there was a rumor that the cafeteria was serving chicken burgers and fries, and I didn't want to miss the Coke they brought in special for that meal.

Chief Benjamin took the clipboard that River handed him, and she took a step back, giving the Chief center stage.

"I am pleased to inform you that you all passed the test. Never before had your loyalty to the Orphanage been tested like this, and I want to congratulate you on your impressive performances."

So, Austen did pass. That was a relief.

Benjamin continued, "This has been a tradition since the Orphanage opened the school here in America and will continue to be a tradition. Now, your loyalty will continue to be tested by your keeping this a secret. No one must know about what you went through except the doctors and the agents who were involved. You may talk about it among yourselves while you recover, but once you leave these walls, the past few days never happened. If asked where you were, simply say you were taken on a trip to Alaska for training. This has been the lie for the past thirty years and will be believable to those younger than you. If you even hint at these events, you will be taken back down to the basement and put through the test again, mostly as a punishment rather than a test. Do I make myself clear?"

"Yes, Chief," we all shouted in unison from our beds.

"Good." He handed his clipboard back to River. They both turned toward the doors.

"Chief?" Lucas asked, unable to keep his mouth shut.

"Yes, Training Agent Lucas?" the Chief responded, glancing back.

"What happened with Austen?"

We all leaned forward to hear the answer, curious to know the truth.

"Well," the Chief said, giving River a nod to tell her to get going and he'd catch up, "since he is the future head of the Orphanage here, we decided we needed to put him through something a little different. Instead of testing his body or mind, we tested his heart."

I looked over at Darcy, worried. She seemed perfectly unaffected by what the Chief was saying, almost like someone was telling her what the weather was going to be tomorrow. I noticed a couple of other faces. Chuck looked confused, and Mary looked nervous. You could have cut the tension in the room with a knife if any of us had been carrying one.

The Chief went on. "We sat him in front of some screens, and he got to watch all of you being tortured. Every hour someone would go into his room and ask for information on the Orphanage, promising that we would stop torturing you if he gave in. He watched all nine of you go through all of your testing, believing that one by one, we had killed you."

My heart ached for Austen. Mary's bed was beside Austen's, and she sat down next to him, brushing his black hair out of his eyes. Still, Darcy seemed unaffected. She just sat on her bed looking at the Chief with no pity for Austen. Her assassin side was showing, and I didn't like it.

Done talking, the Chief made his way toward the door. He hesitated with his hand on the door, then turned back to tell us, "Go easy on him. It wasn't easy for him to watch the people he cared about being tortured while he thought he could be the one to stop it all. He did his job, and you did yours. You should all be very proud. This is what you have been raised to do." He pushed through the doors and left.

"How can you look so heartless?" I murmured to Darcy.

She grabbed the pillow from her bed and chucked it at me, clearly mad at my comment. I hadn't been thinking; it had just slipped out. I should have been silent like everyone else with pity for Austen.

"You idiot—" Darcy started before Jane cut her off.

"If you want to be a field, you'll learn to keep your emotions to yourself!" Jane shouted at me. "You need to show the world that you have it all together. That could have helped you a lot the day Collin let the school explode!"

No one moved. Everyone was shocked at how brutal Jane had been. Most people had declared me too delicate to touch, let alone yell at.

I looked at Jane with my mouth hanging open and my heart beating wildly. Acting out of anger, something Darcy had told me not to do, I reached for the pillow Darcy had thrown at me and walked over to Jane's bed, fuming. Before I had the chance to throw the pillow at her, Darcy grabbed it from me, walked to Jane, and gracefully threw herself on top of her, smothering her face with the pillow and cutting off her airflow.

That's the story of how the doctors and agents had to break up a fight between Darcy and a bald Jane.

We finally got out of the hospital on Friday and rejoined everyone in time for the weekend. Anyone who hadn't fully healed had to wear long sleeves and pants to cover their injuries. Elizabeth had to make sure she didn't wear anything that showed her back, and I couldn't wear shorts because my new skin hadn't faded to match the rest of my skin tone. It sucked having to wear pants in the training room, but Darcy saw this as a good opportunity to practice fighting in a tuxedo. The tuxedos the Orphanage had created were wonderful and stretched to ensure a full range of motion, so it wasn't the end of the world.

Jane decided to go forth with her baldness and wear it proudly, claiming that she was bored with her hair and wanted a fresh start. She got a couple of snickers from some '03s, but those were quickly shut down when she filled their shampoo bottles with hair remover, and all the '03 girls got to walk around sporting the same look as Jane. She had to clean all the bathrooms in the dorm rooms as punishment.

We resumed classes, and Agent Asher let me join in combat training with the other fields in our year. I got teamed up with Austen, and that was when I really noticed the toll the test had taken on him.

We were practicing on the mats, and Austen was a million miles away. He took a swing at me, and I easily ducked. On my way back up, I swung my leg, making contact with Austen's side, sending him to the ground. He briefly touched the mat before rolling to get back up. At this moment, I was quicker. I threw a punch and hit his left cheek, making his whole body turn and giving me the chance to get behind him and get him in a chokehold.

I wasn't aware of what I was doing, or more importantly, whom I was doing it to. After my adrenaline wore off and I looked down and saw Austen's face, I quickly released in a panic and backed away. With him gasping for breath, we both stared at each other.

Agent Asher started clapping and told me that, even though Austen had gone easy on me, he'd noticed I was improving. If I kept going the way I was, I would make a decent field.

The encouragement would have felt a lot better if I hadn't noticed Austen's eyes. They were lost, searching, and in pain. During our fight, he'd seemed scared, not for himself but for me. I was worried that him having watched the rest of us get tortured would take longer to recover from than all of our physical injuries combined.

I made sure to sit next to him at lunch that day. Everyone at the table told and retold the story of our fight for those who weren't at our training session. They all congratulated me, and Jane even gave me a smile and a nod.

After lunch was over, Austen and I took all of our lunch dishes over to the dirty-dish area.

"Austen?" I said. "Have you gone to talk to Agent Stephen since . . . everything? He helped me a bit when everything went down with Collin."

Austen muttered, "I haven't been to see him since our testing. Chief Benjamin wants me to go. I'm worried what will happen if I do."

"What are you worried will happen?"

"That the truth will come out," he confessed. "I don't know if I can be the Chief. It's a job filled with pain, but you're not allowed to act like you're in pain. I've signed up for a life of reading everyone's final statements and sending people on assignments I know they may not return from. I will be the one agreeing to torture training agents to test their loyalty. It's a lot, and I don't have a choice in any of this."

"I'm sorry," was all I could say.

He never mentioned it to me again, though I saw him sneak down to Agent Stephen's office that evening. Austen's future was already set for him, just like all of ours were. He would need all the help he could get.

Other than Austen, everything was back to normal. Darcy and I were training again, and let me tell you, riding a motorcycle through the forest while trying to shoot targets was harder than it sounded, and it already sounded hard.

"And that is how Agent Haddy saved the Orphanage from a serious security breach. That ties in with your next assignment." Agent Asher was leaning against the whiteboard at the front of the classroom, half talking to us and half marking our latest assignments, which he held in his hands. "I want you to come up with a way to take down the Orphanage. Include blueprints and outlines of everything that you would use. Attached should be an essay detailing every step. I want lots of thought going into this assignment, because while this is to get you to think about how to break into somewhere with over-the-top security, this is also for us to look into whether or not your ideas are possible and to fill any holes in our own security system. Dismissed."

I tried not to groan out loud while we gathered our books. A class that was only two hours long had felt like it had taken all day.

Since Darcy and I were the last to leave the room, we walked back to the dorms together to drop off our books before heading for dinner. Tonight was grilled cheese and tomato soup, with way too many vegetables for my liking. I choked them down anyway.

Darcy and I took the least amount of time in our rooms putting our books away and were the first to claim a table for our year. We sat quietly, exhausted from the day, trying to regain our strength before training that night. I was scooping soup into my mouth like a famished dog when I saw Oliver walk into the room, talking with Austen, who was starting to look like his old self.

Motioning toward the two of them, I asked Darcy, "What do you think of Oliver?"

I had been meaning to talk to her about Oliver for a while. Every time we were alone, I forgot, and when we were with the others, I was afraid she wouldn't tell me the truth. Or that she'd punch me in the arm for being rude.

Without missing a beat or looking up from her soup, she murmured, "Like a punch in the gut every time I see him."

I snorted, and a little soup came out of my nose, making Darcy laugh hysterically. I reached for a napkin and laughed at myself.

"What did we miss?" Oliver asked as I put more soup into my mouth.

That made me start laughing again, causing me to snort more soup through my nose and starting another round of laughter. This time the others all joined in.

"Come on, you idiot," Darcy said, chuckling, "finish your soup, and let's get some extra training in."

In unison, we lifted our trays and discarded them, thanked the cooks, and headed toward the training room.

"Pick up the axes," she told me, picking up two of her own.

We stood on the mats and danced around each other, almost like we had practiced a routine. I was pleased with how graceful I was becoming. I still had a ways to go to be as graceful as Darcy—especially considering I'd spilled tea all over my favorite sweater that morning just walking down the hall.

"You're not balanced with your axes," she told me, reading my mind.

Her ponytail swished around, and in response to her comment, I made a lunge for it, trying to cut the end of it off with my sharpened ax. She sidestepped me and slapped me on the back with the flat of her ax. Laughing, she twisted both of her axes in her hands and pointed one at me, daring me to try again. I closed my eyes and took a deep breath, trying to remember all I had learned from anybody who had ever trained me, before running at her. Keeping one ax in front of me and one ax behind, ready to swing, I reached her, and we were at it again.

"Strong like Collin," I grunted, kicking my leg up and hitting Darcy in the gut.

She staggered back and regained her balance.

"Swift like Jane," I said, rolling on the floor and standing up on the other side of her.

"Calculating like Austen." I took the flat side of my ax and whacked her on the back, just as she had done to me.

She used the momentum from the hit and spun on me, kicking me in the chest, causing me to land on my back. Then she was on top of me, with one of her axes at my throat.

"Graceful like Darcy," I finished, flinging my legs up and wrapping them around her neck. Twisting around on the ground, I ended up on top of her, with both axes to her throat for the first time ever. I smiled in triumph.

"Good job, Bennet," she hissed. "You did everything everyone else would do. But what would you do?"

"Huh?" I asked before a sharp pain hit my side.

Flinging me off, she rolled on top of me to prove to me—and the rest of the room—that no one could get the better of her. Getting off of me, she picked up both of her axes and twisted them in her hands again.

I stood up and looked down at my shirt. A tiny bit of blood had soaked through. "You actually hit me," I said, shocked.

"Calm down. It's not deep. I've done worse to you. You can't fight like everyone else," she yelled at me. "You need to fight like Bennet, like the kid who charged the target with the knife and outsmarted me into training you. Where is that kid when we fight?"

"That kid was an earpiece! That kid hid behind a desk!" I yelled back, throwing my ax at her in anger.

She sidestepped it with rage in her eyes. She threw her ax at my head, and I had to dive out of the way.

"Go clean the weapons room," she ordered me, clearly wanting me out of her sight.

"Why does this always end up with us yelling at each other?" I yelled back at her.

"Why do you want this?" she demanded, still holding one of her axes threateningly. "Why do you want to be a field? Why do you want to be anyone but yourself? I don't care what you say. It's your answer, not mine. I just want to know."

How long could I keep the answer to myself?

I sat down on the floor and chucked my ax to the side. Looking down at the tiny stain of blood on my shirt, Darcy joined me on the mat. She lay down with her arms and legs spread out like a star. We were both emotionally exhausted with each other.

I knew it was now or never. I let out a sigh and told Darcy the truth.

"Because when I first lost Collin, I could still remember him," I said quietly. "I could remember his laugh when I did something stupid, his grin when I got excited about a new comic book. I remembered his daily routine, and how we could look at each other and just *know* what the other was thinking. I could remember thinking I should call him, and then he wouldn't pick up, because at that exact same moment, he was trying to call me. I could remember it all. But then," I lay down next to Darcy, "I started to forget what his soft snoring sounded like and the snarky remarks he would say at the lunch table. I started forgetting what his laugh sounded like and where the moles were on his face. I forgot whether his hair was long or short. I was forgetting everything. And then I realized, if I tried to become him, I wouldn't need to worry about forgetting him because I would *be* him.

I decided that the best way to hold on to him was to become a field agent, because Collin didn't even know how to take apart a computer, much less hack into a security system. I had to lose me to find him. Does that answer finally please you?"

She chuckled—a response I wasn't expecting. "That's dumb!"

"I thought you said it was my answer, and you didn't care."

"I don't care what your answer is, but I can still have an opinion. You'll never truly be with people unless you are yourself. Stop trying to be like me, stop trying to be like Austen or Jane, and most definitely stop trying to be like Collin. Collin is dead, okay? We need to move on. Now, I have no problem training you, but I am training *you*, a computer genius. So, start acting like one. Start acting like *you*."

I sat up, angry. Everywhere I turned, Collin was being taken away, whether it was Jane yelling at me or Oliver taking over our room. The last person I expected this from was Darcy. I thought she, of all people, would understand.

Standing up, I left behind my ax and cut our training session short, unable to look Darcy in the eye. I could sense that, behind me, she hadn't moved and wasn't about to call after me to tell me to stay. Letting my anger carry me, I marched back to my room, knocking shoulders with Toby on my way out of the training room.

When I stormed into my dorm room, I didn't notice anyone else there. I walked straight to the sink, turned on the tap, and splashed water on my face to calm myself down, not knowing if my emotions were going to win, causing me to cry.

Staring at my dripping face in the mirror, I leaned my hands against the sink, ignoring the pain in my side from where Darcy had struck me with her ax. My face didn't remind me of myself but of my brother. There was a rage in my eyes that reminded me of Collin when he got frustrated during training. A battle took place inside me as part of me tried to hold on to Collin, and another part missed who I used to be. I didn't know who I was anymore, and it was killing me. I reached up and slammed my fist into the mirror, wishing for nothing more than for this reflection to go away.

The glass shattered into a million pieces, falling into the sink and onto the floor. For three seconds, it was nice to not look into a mirror and see a reflection I had once shared with my brother. Then came pride. I, Bennet, was capable of breaking a mirror with my fist. The next thing I noticed was my aching hand. I lifted it up to see pieces of broken mirror stuck in my bleeding knuckles. I started to pick them out and throw them across the room as a new rage filled me, a rage to prove Darcy wrong, to prove I could be myself.

"I never liked that mirror anyways," said a voice with an annoying English accent.

I sighed and looked up, wondering how God could possibly punish me more. I turned around and faced Oliver, who was sitting on his bed, holding a package. I ignored the elephant in the room and asked, "What's in the package?"

Oliver pulled out a picture of a duck. "I told my sister about how the rooms have absolutely no character, and she sent me this horrid picture. I think I will hang it above my bed," he said, holding the picture above his bed to see how it would look.

In all my years living there, we had never decorated our room. I didn't know if we weren't allowed, or if we really didn't care. The Orphanage supplied us with everything we needed, and decorations weren't on that list. I guess regular boys decorated their rooms with posters of soccer players or bands they liked.

Oliver asked, "Does it ever bother you?"

I looked at him, wondering what he meant. "What?"

"Not owning anything? It seems kind of sad not having anything. I mean, people come into your room once a week and wash your clothes and replace your sheets, but nothing here is truly yours."

This was our first true conversation since he'd arrived, but this, coming on top of what Darcy had said, was too much to deal with. Unable to answer him, I sat down on the edge of my bed facing his.

Silence hung between us. I sat there, sort of numb and unsure of what to do next. I had nothing I really wanted to say to him, and I had originally come back here hoping I could have some peace and quiet. My guess was that he knew I wasn't a big fan of his. I was just glad he wasn't forcing a conversation about my brother.

I picked at my bruised and bloody knuckles while Oliver continued to stare at his picture from his sister. Packages weren't a normal thing around here. None of us had family to get packages from. Would Oliver send a package back to her? What could he even send to her? He could always take a picture of a lighthouse from one of the hallways. It's not like any of us would miss it. There would be another one in a different hallway to replace it.

A pang of jealously hit me, and I tried to ignore it. Oliver owned things. It was obvious which bed was his the moment you walked into our room. It was sprinkled with trinkets that gave you a glimpse into his life. A family picture was on his dresser along with letters from his mother that he got weekly. He had a picture of one set of grandparents behind his bed, and now he also had the picture of a duck. I knew then that my life would have looked completely different if I had been born and raised into the British Agency.

The rest of the beds in the room were practically identical. Little things gave it away to whom they belonged to. A medical book was hidden under Chuck's bed, and I had a recycling can beside my bed for Coke cans when I was lucky enough to get my hands on any of that glorious, refreshing nectar. We were taught at a young age how to make our beds, and every morning that is how we made them. When Lucas had something on his mind, he usually left his bed a little more unkempt than the rest of ours, but he still tried in his own way. Austen's was always perfect no matter what was going on. Every shirt in his dresser was perfectly folded, and all his socks were correctly matched and in the correct drawer. But none of us really had things that we called our own.

"What do you even like?" Oliver asked, breaking the silence and actually sounding curious.

I couldn't answer, because at this moment, I didn't know who I was apart from my brother. Then it was like Oliver had hit the nail on the head. Everything came rushing in, and I knew exactly what I had to do.

"I've got to go," I told him.

Excited, I headed for the door. As I reached for the knob, I glanced back at Oliver, then at the broken mirror, and asked, "Could you clean that up for me?" Then I popped out the door, but before I closed it behind me, I stuck my head back in and said, "Oh, and I like superheroes and computers."

I raced down the hallway and climbed the stairs two at a time, unable to wait patiently for the elevator. People watched me sprint past them, and I practically knocked over Maria and Mason, who had found an inconvenient corner to make out in. Rounding the corner to the training room, I quietly sprinted up to Darcy, who was standing in front of a punching bag, grabbed her, spun her around, and punched her square in the face with all the force I could gather.

Why *couldn't* I be both an earpiece and a field? Darcy was right.

I'd realized, with Oliver's help, that Bennet was someone who was constantly changing his mind. Bennet was someone who loved superheroes and doing the right thing to help others. Bennet was someone who cared deeply about his friends and who didn't always know the answer but could always figure out how to find it. Bennet was someone who was willing to change so that he could always better himself. But most importantly—as I'd found out the day I had decided to ask Darcy to train me—Bennet was someone who didn't play by the rules, and that was exactly what I was doing here.

I thought way back to when I was throwing knives at a target to get Darcy to agree to train me, and how I'd thought I was acting like Collin. Collin would have hit the target right in the middle. As an earpiece, on the other hand, I always found my way around the obstacle I had to face, and that was exactly what I had done that day. I'd figured out that the best way to beat Darcy was to fight her when she didn't even know we were fighting.

Pulling my fist back from her face, I swung my leg around and kicked her right in the gut. She bent forward, and I had a perfect shot to kick with my other leg at the back of her legs behind her knees, sending her flying to the floor, where I climbed on top of her back and pulled her arms behind her.

A hush went over the room. Darcy, surprised, was unable to get out of the trap she was in. Out of nowhere, I heard a slow clap start to form. Looking up, I saw the whole room break into applause as people who had watched me trying for two months to take Darcy down finally got to see me win.

I released Darcy. She turned over and said, "I knew you would come to your senses."

CHAPTER
27

After smearing strawberry jam on my sourdough toast, I took a giant bite. It wasn't often that we got to leave the Orphanage for something as mundane as going out for breakfast. Darcy had managed to swing it with one of our teachers and had brought some cash she had left over from a previous assignment.

As I was taking a big gulp of orange juice, my second batch of eggs and shredded hash browns came out of the kitchen. The food was so good that I couldn't help but overeat. Darcy, on the other hand, was content with one helping and a black coffee. She did order a donut to start with, so I felt like maybe that was her moment of indulgence.

"I'd put some ice on that," I told Darcy, pleased that it was finally me telling her to take care of a black eye.

Picking up one of the sugar packets on the table, she chucked it at my head and grinned. We were happy at that moment, like two kids who were actually kids, enjoying breakfast before the day started. She sat across from me, sipping her coffee, letting her smile fade into her cup. The black eye and swollen nose were unusual features on her face. Her ponytail was a bit of a mess too—something else I was not used to.

We'd stayed up all night going over techniques for surprising your target. We'd talked about what it would look like to combine being an earpiece and a field agent. We'd laughed and goofed off until we'd completely lost track of time. When we'd noticed that my stomach was growling, we'd decided that we needed a break. Hence us taking a car and grabbing breakfast.

I speared the last sausage on Darcy's plate with my fork, dipped it into her ketchup, and took a bite.

"Use a knife, you animal!" She grabbed my fork and stuck the rest of the sausage into her mouth.

Returning to my plate, I cleaned up the rest of my food. Then I noticed that some of the truckers seated at the tables were giving us sideways glances. We were teenagers eating at a diner in the middle of nowhere, one of us with a very noticeable black eye. If only they knew that, only a few weeks earlier, Darcy was sporting nails all over her body, and I had a beautiful skinned leg, then they'd *really* be staring. They had no idea we lived at a secret facility that trained agents. Why would they? I mean, "secret" was our goal.

"Can I get you anything else?" the waitress asked, standing at the end of our booth.

"Ah, n-no thanks," I stammered at her.

She had to be in her early twenties. The messy bun on top of her head gave her a relaxed, approachable look. Her apron hugged her, showing off her figure. I could tell by the bags under her eyes that she had been working all night. She was a different kind of beautiful—the kind that, if you looked at her quickly, you wouldn't notice, but the longer you looked, the prettier she got. I'd had plenty of time to stare at her while we were eating breakfast. I hoped I wasn't too obvious.

"Actually, if I could get one more refill, that would be awesome," Darcy said with a smile.

"Sure thing," the waitress said, heading behind the counter to grab the pot of coffee and coming back to fill Darcy's mug.

"We're going to be late," I told Darcy after the waitress left.

Darcy took a big sip of coffee. "I have a training idea for you."

I picked up a packet of sugar and played with it. "Right here, right now?"

"You're going to flirt with the waitress."

I dropped the sugar packet and stared at Darcy, baffled. "You have got to be kidding me."

"This will be great for you. Someone you don't know and will never see again. She's perfect for you to practice on."

"I can't flirt," I told Darcy. There was no way I was going to do this.

She put down her cup and said, "Oh, come on. You flirt with Mary all the time."

I looked back at the sugar packet. Mary was cute, but I didn't think I had been flirting with her all this time. Had I?

"I'm not going to do it," I told Darcy. The poor waitress deserved better than having some weird sixteen-year-old practice flirting with her.

"You have two options," Darcy said. "You either flirt with her or kill her."

I chuckled. "I'm not going to kill her."

"Those are your options. You'd better choose quickly."

Was she serious? I couldn't tell if she was joking anymore. Was she just trying to bait me into flirting with the waitress? This was really taking the fun out of our breakfast.

"Don't sit there and judge me, Bennet. You were a witness to many murders on a computer screen back when you were a simple earpiece. Now you are on the other side of the screen. You should know this by now, Bennet. The Orphanage doesn't believe in justice. It believes in tying up loose ends."

She had to be joking. The waitress wasn't a loose end. She had been nothing but nice to us since the moment we'd walked in.

"Why do you do it?" I asked, tossing my sugar packet aside.

"Why do I do what?" Darcy asked.

"Why do you kill people?" I whispered, scared to raise my voice.

Darcy sighed and leaned back in her chair. She looked out the window of the diner and said, "Because I'm an assassin, Bennet. My job is to kill."

She stopped talking as if that was a perfectly reasonable answer. But I needed more.

Seeing me look at her with hurt in my eyes, she went on. "Fine. You want to know the truth? The Orphanage made me this at a very young age. If I lived out in the real world, who knows? I might have ended up insane or a serial killer. I've come to terms with what I am. Thankfully, I have another option. I can use the madness that lives in my head for good, kind of like all those superheroes you read about. I can kill bad people. I like what I do, Bennet, and I'm not sorry about it. The Orphanage is well aware of what I am. If you ever get the privilege of viewing my file, they've labeled me 'unstable.'"

"I'm sorry, Darcy. I didn't know." I wanted to reach out and grab her hand to comfort her.

"Well, now you do."

"But I don't know if I can just kill someone," I said.

I watched her weigh what she was going to say next, clearly calculating what I needed to hear against what she wanted to say. Gathering her thoughts, she asked, "Do you ever expect to succeed at the Orphanage?"

I thought about her question. Did she think the only way to victory was through killing?

"Yes," I told her. "But I want to help people, not tear them apart without a second chance."

"Ah," Darcy said. "But we can only give people so many second chances. Now go flirt with her."

I banged my head on the table. Having come full circle, I was still going to have to flirt with the waitress.

"Forget about what I just said. I was only joking," Darcy told me, though whether that was true or whether she regretted letting me see the monsters inside her head, I didn't know. "I'll make it easy. You can use paying as your excuse to flirt. It will be good for you to talk to a girl." She put two twenties on the table and waited for me to go.

I steadied myself, allowing Darcy to sweep our conversation under the rug. It might be gone, but it wouldn't be forgotten. It must have been hard for Darcy to grow up feeling like that.

Grabbing the two twenties, I asked, "How do I look?"

Darcy smirked, shook her head, and said, "Like you've stayed up all night."

I pursed my lips together and clicked my tongue. "I guess that's as good as it's going to get."

Leaving the booth, I gathered my courage and walked up to the counter, where the waitress was drying cups. There were only a few truckers scattered around the diner. I prayed they weren't paying any attention.

"Can I help you with something?" the waitress asked.

I quickly glanced at her name tag, cursing myself that I hadn't noticed it before. "Um, yes, Stephanie. Um, I would like to pay the bill if that would be okay." This was not going well.

She smiled politely and said, "Of course. Come this way to the register."

I followed her to the end of the counter. She punched buttons on the register, and our total came to thirty-two dollars and eighty-five cents. I handed her the forty dollars I had, and our hands brushed when she reached for it. I snatched my hand back. My cheeks became very warm. "Keep the change," I told her, racking my brain for something else to say.

"Thanks. Did you enjoy your breakfast?" she asked. Her smile was stunning.

I gulped and rubbed my sweaty palms on my workout shorts. "The eggs were great. Do...do you cook them?" What a dumb thing to ask.

"No." She smiled, clearly cluing into what I was failing at doing. "We have a cook in the kitchen. I just serve everything to the customers."

I looked back at Darcy for support. She was trying her best to hide a smile. I was going to kill her later for this. This was worse than any training session she'd ever put me through.

I turned back around and said the first thing that popped in my head. "So, breakfast. That's pretty great. Right?"

Stephanie picked a rag up from behind the counter and started wiping things down. She was trying her best not to laugh; I could tell. "Yeah, it is pretty great."

"You'll have to excuse my brother." Darcy popped up behind me, grabbing me by the shoulders. "He's had a long night."

"I think he's cute," Stephanie said, smirking at me.

That was a tiny victory, at least.

"Thanks for everything," Darcy said to the waitress, steering me out of the diner.

Opening the door and entering the crisp morning air, I was finally able to breathe again. We walked toward the car, stuffed from breakfast. I was worried that I might throw it up after talking to the waitress, but now, out in the fresh air, I started to feel better. My cheeks weren't so warm, and my palms not so sweaty.

"So, that could use more practice," Darcy said, trying to hold in her laughter.

I sarcastically said, "Thanks."

We hopped into the blue sports car Darcy had picked out of the Orphanage's garage. She teased me the whole way home, and I rolled my eyes at every comment she made. I told her next time I would need her to teach me by example, and she said, "Not in your wildest dreams." For a terrible training session, it was sure funny.

The car ride home was short and sweet. Something that should have taken an hour was only twenty-five minutes with Darcy's heavy foot. Every Orphanage vehicle came equipped with a device that scanned for police cars to alert us when we needed to slow down and blend in. We came across none on our way home. The back roads were almost always clear since no one came out this way except to head to the Orphanage. It was a peaceful drive through a forested area. The main thing we had to worry about was deer walking across the road.

Back at the Orphanage, we ditched the car in the garage and slumped back to the dorm rooms, completely exhausted. People were wandering around, heading to breakfast or working on assignments. My feet ached, and my eyes were ready to close permanently. I cursed myself for staying up all night. It would be a challenge not to fall asleep in class that day. But even if staying up all night had been a huge mistake, I was glad that it had brought Darcy and me even closer.

I gently opened the door, not wanting to disturb anyone in the room who might still be sleeping, then flopped down on my bed. I closed my eyes and breathed into my pillow before rolling over and facing the ceiling.

Chuck was still in bed, and Lucas was in the shower. I decided I could get in a quick nap before getting ready for class. I opened my eyes for a brief moment when I heard a crash from the bathroom. Lucas must have knocked the shampoo bottles off the ledge.

Before closing my eyes and returning to my nap, something grabbed my attention. I drew myself up and leaned on my arm, twisting my body to look above my headboard. There, hanging in a black picture frame, was a small photo of Spider-Man.

I laid back down, thanking the person who believed that we needed to decorate our room to make it our own. Maybe Oliver wasn't so bad after all. Only time would tell.

CHAPTER 28

Time passed in a blink of an eye as we prepared for the end of the school year. Teachers loaded us up with homework and extra training, leaving almost no time to do other things like organizing another match of "cops and robbers" or laser tag. My dresser had more books in it than clothes.

Chuck was spending most of his time in the hospital, and Lucas was in the workshop, leaving Austen, Oliver, and me to study in our room. Austen was back to his usual self, minus random moments when he would look at me like he wondered if I had told anyone about him being scared to become the future Chief. I wouldn't dream about telling anyone about that, because even though we were all trained in keeping countries' secrets, gossip at the Orphanage spread like wildfire. I hoped he knew that he could always talk to me if he needed to.

It was funny, because on the one hand, we were all open books, with files about everything that had ever happened to us. The Orphanage had every minor detail about us recorded. They knew our strengths and weaknesses, our bad habits and our good ones. On the other hand, we were still people, and we all had things we loved and things we feared, whether or not the Orphanage knew about them.

My routine with Darcy was still going strong. I was surprised one day when I looked in the mirror and actually noticed some abs trying to form. I was rather proud of them and showed them to Chuck right away, who thought it would be a good idea to punch them. I toppled over, surprised and clutching my stomach. Chuck was incredibly sorry and couldn't stop apologizing—in between laughing. Once I caught my breath, I laughed along with him, thinking how comical it was that, after all this time, Chuck could still take me down. It taught me an important lesson: I should always be prepared for anything.

I had spent the early morning in the lounge, working on the assignment Agent Asher had given us to come up with a plan to destroy the Orphanage. I had spent the past month trying to write a kill formula to crash the network the Orphanage used and was failing miserably. I'd spent a week trying to come up with a method a field would use, but Darcy was right. I needed to be a field while still being me, and what I would normally do is attack the best way I knew how: by hacking.

I threw the laptop I was working on onto my bed and grabbed a muffin and tea from the cafeteria before heading to class. I was going to be late because I had gotten carried away in the lounge. Agent Asher was going to announce something today, so everyone from our year was supposed to be there.

Shoving the last bit of muffin into my mouth before Agent Asher could yell at me for bringing crumbs into his classroom, I entered the room and took my seat next to Chuck, who was resting his head on the desk beside me. He hadn't come to bed the night before, and when I'd woken up, he still wasn't there. I wondered if he had stayed up all night in the hospital working on his year-end project for Doctor Caleb.

"Sit down and shut up," Agent Asher demanded, hobbling through the open door with great purpose.

Mary and Lucas, who were arguing in the back of the room, walked to their seats, and then everyone was silent, waiting for what our teacher was going to announce.

Agent Asher stood at attention, which was strange, because when he taught, he either paced around the room and threw things at people or sat behind his desk with a coffee cup filled with something that probably wasn't coffee. He was incredibly brilliant but unpredictable, which made him a scary but wonderful teacher.

In walked Chief Benjamin, with River following him, her hands full of case files. The class quickly clued into what was going on. This was our year-end assignment from the Orphanage.

Our assignment would take place outside of the Orphanage, and we would not get help from anybody except others in our year. Every year looked different. In our first year of training, when we were five, all we'd had to do was gather information about a stranger the Orphanage thought was taking children from playgrounds. We were basically victims—guinea pigs—but we had the training to keep ourselves safe until actual agents moved in.

As we moved up, our assignments got more interesting. Last year, for our year-end assignment, Darcy, Chuck, Collin, and I got grouped together. Darcy and Collin had to break into a hospital and steal a patient, and then Chuck had to perform open-heart surgery on him, because he'd just had a heart attack: the reason why he was in the hospital in the first place. What the hospital didn't know was that he was an organizer of human trafficking. We had to get him safely back to the Orphanage, where actual agents would deal with him. I, of course, was the earpiece and dealt with all the technical stuff.

"I suspect you all know what this is about," the Chief began, "so let's get to it. River, the files, please."

Everyone knew that River was the one who put together the year-end assignments, and the Chief just looked them over and okayed them. River stepped forward and gave him half of the files before stepping back to her regular place as his shadow. She shoved her free hand into the giant pocket of her sweater, resting the remaining files on her hip.

Benjamin looked strange carrying the stack of files; he often carried one file around the Orphanage but never a stack of them. That was what River was for. He looked down at them. "Oliver," he called out and plopped a file on Oliver's desk.

We all looked at Oliver and wondered what was in the file.

"Elizabeth," the Chief continued, placing the next file on her desk. "Jane, Lucas, and Charlotte," he finished, putting files in front of them all.

That was half of our year gone, meaning maybe that they were all on one team, and those remaining were on another.

Chief Benjamin addressed the class, answering my thoughts. "You five are Team Orchid. Inside your files, you have your instructions in detail. You have one week to prepare. Next Monday morning, you will leave and will be expected back by Friday at 0900 with your proof of completion. Your assignment, in brief, is to break into the president of Germany's private estate in Rothenberg. We have discovered that, during World War Two, a Nazi stole pieces of art and hid them behind the art in that house. To avoid any embarrassment of the German president, we will quietly retrieve them and return them to their proper owners. You have trained hard, and I have faith that you will complete this assignment without anyone being alerted to your presence in Germany.

"Oliver, you are the team leader. Jane and Elizabeth, we have invitations for you to attend a party at the residence on Wednesday night. Lucas, you are on surveillance, and Charlotte," the Chief turned to look at her, "uh, have fun."

Charlotte smiled and turned to Oliver. Lifting up a piece of paper, she rather obnoxiously pointed to it. Agent Asher, Chief Benjamin, and River chose to ignore her. It was a rather colorful picture of a bomb. She probably had some crazy idea of a distraction for their assignment. From what I knew of Oliver, he probably wanted to go in stealthily. He'd have his hands full with Charlotte.

Turning to River, the Chief motioned for the rest of the files. She stepped forward to hand them to him, then stepped back to listen to what he had to say.

"Now," Benjamin boomed in the voice he used when he was making announcements in the giant auditorium, "Darcy, Chuck, Mary, Austen, and Bennet." He handed out the remaining folders with our names on them, giving me mine last.

I stared down at my folder, knowing that this was my first assignment as a field. I was both excited and nervous. My leg bounced underneath the table from it all. I couldn't believe I was finally getting my chance to use everything I had been learning.

"You five are Team Eleven and will be heading to Canada to take care of a little oil problem. You have a picture of a woman in your folders: Jessica Chadwick of Chadwick Family Oil Company. She inherited the company after her father died in a tragic accident two years ago. Oil companies have mysteriously been going out of business, and Chadwick has been collecting a few too many of them. Your assignment is to shut down her main operations center in Alberta, and if need be, to take care of her. She has no other family to pass the business on to."

Sitting behind a desk, this sounded simple enough. Knowing I had to jump into a snowsuit and venture into the depths of Canada was a little too real. I prayed no one noticed my hesitation. I couldn't drag my team back. Thankfully, Darcy was with me, and I could count on her to kick my butt all the way to Canada.

"Austen," Benjamin said, "you will be acting Chief for this assignment. Chuck, you're medical support. Mary, you're transportation. Darcy and Bennet, you need to get into the base of operations and shut it down, taking care of Jessica if she needs to be taken down."

This wasn't an assignment for a training agent. We had talked about warring oil companies a month ago. This was a big deal. News stations had been talking about this and feared what this would mean for gas prices and countries' relationships. I didn't know if it was a good thing that the Chief thought that I was up for the challenge or a terrible, terrible mistake.

"Are you serious?" Darcy shouted at the Chief.

Her voice echoed off the walls and filled the silence. Everyone leaned forward, suddenly tense at the sound of someone as young as Darcy yelling at the Chief.

She continued like this was a normal thing to do. "He's barely trained!" She pointed at me in case anyone was confused about who she was talking about. "Start him on something small but not this! This is suicide!"

The Chief stood a little taller: an intimidation technique, although he was probably also annoyed by being yelled at by a training agent. "If he dies, it's because he's an idiot."

That stung, and I was curious if he knew that was something only Darcy called me. Him being the Chief and knowing absolutely everything that went on here, he probably did know that and had used it to make his point.

"What if I die?" she asked, still not backing down. "I'm your best training assassin. You can't afford to lose me."

"If you die," the Chief said, "it's because you were foolish enough to try and save him. Now, he either goes back to being an earpiece and working behind a desk, or he takes the assignment and passes this year of school."

I couldn't go back to sitting behind a desk. I knew it was going to be hard, but Darcy was going to be there to call me an idiot and help me through it. This was the best time to see what I was made of. If I died, I got to join Collin, and if I lived, I could finally prove myself to the Orphanage.

"Chief," I said, standing up, "I can do this. I can shut it down. Thank you for giving me this opportunity."

Chief Benjamin nodded. "Good luck, Training Agent Bennet." He turned and walked out of the classroom with River following.

This was our moment to prove ourselves before our final year of school. I couldn't let it be my fault that my group didn't pass. We would have to put everything we'd learned to good use. It was my job in this mission to shut down the company and ensure that Darcy didn't need to kill our target.

I looked around at my teammates, and they all looked back at me, worried. We five would be alone this time, with zero help from the Orphanage for our most intense assignment yet.

Hopefully, this one wouldn't end with a bang.

CHAPTER 29

Aiming the piece of popcorn, I tossed it toward my target. Everyone in the room was sitting still in anticipation. Cheers erupted when the popcorn landed perfectly. Celebrating, we stood up, and high fives were passed around.

"You have been trying to get a piece of popcorn in Austen's mouth for fifteen minutes, wasting half the bowl, and all we have planned is that we are going to take a plane to Canada. Bravo guys, bravo," Darcy sarcastically congratulated us, bringing us all back to reality.

The five of us were hanging out in the lounge, trying to finish our plan—and by "finish," I really mean "start." Between finishing projects for different classes and studying for exams, we'd had little time this week to figure out a plan for our final assignment. Austen had told us to finish whatever classwork we had during the week so that the weekend could be dedicated to preparing for what next week would throw at us.

Austen and I had spent the past little while goofing off with our group's snack while Mary and Chuck cheered along. Darcy had stepped out of the room to grab coffee for everyone, and I could tell by the disappointed look on her face that she felt like she needed to be our babysitter.

She placed the cups on top of our files and paperwork, clearly not worried about getting them wet. "I expected more from our future Chief," she said, letting the comment hit Austen hard.

I watched his face as he tried to keep his reaction inside. He stood up, grabbed his coffee, and turned to look at the painting of a lighthouse on the wall. I knew how deeply Darcy's comment must have cut him.

"Today's practically over," Austen told us, still looking at the lighthouse painting. "We need a plan, and we need one now. Oliver was already bragging last night that their team has finalized their plan and are gathering supplies."

I was sitting on a couch with Mary. She sat cross-legged, knitting something purple. Chuck was sitting in a rocking chair, and Darcy was standing, holding her cup of coffee, almost as if she was ready to pounce on something.

I opened up my file and reached for the photo of Jessica Chadwick. Her picture was plain. She wore a blazer and a necklace with a ruby in it. She was nothing special, but the power she held was very special. Through the file, we'd learned that she owned, whether through the company she'd inherited from her father or from other companies that she owned secretly, seventy-five percent of the world's oil. It turned out her dad had been moving in and slowly collecting and blackmailing other companies when he passed away, and his daughter had stepped right into his shoes and continued. Digging deeper, we found that she owned companies that owned companies that owned other companies like weapon manufactories, as well as water rights in many locations and several prisons around the world.

Darcy was very much on board with just putting a bullet in her head, and Austen was leaning that way, too. They thought that no one should hold that much power. I argued for just bringing her back to the Orphanage and letting her sit in the basement. Chuck and I both thought that we should focus on the problem of shutting down her base.

Our team was torn, and Mary seemed to have zero opinion except what type of plane we should take to Canada and what snowmobile we should use. She was a little upset when she learned we weren't going far enough north to need snow gear and that Canada actually got hot in the summer.

"We can't just kill her," Chuck begged.

"Then what do you suggest we do, Doctor Chuck?" Darcy mocked. In my opinion, she needed a nap.

Chuck ignored her, and rocking in his chair, continued, "We could always drug her up. I've got plenty of stuff you can use. Engineering just shoved some poison darts in a ring. That could be fun."

"Ahh," I moaned, and everyone turned to look at me.

"Would you like to say something, Bennet?" Darcy said, her tone still mocking.

I picked up my coffee cup and took a sip. It was too hot, and it burned my tongue. I needed as much caffeine as possible to help me get all my work done before Monday. "We can't just do the assignment halfway and leave it for someone else to clean up," I told the group. "Our assignment is to stop whatever it is Jessica Chadwick and her company is trying to accomplish by having a monopoly on the world's oil. We have to shut down her base of operations."

They all looked at me and then at each other, having a conversation with just their eyes. They were all in on some sort of secret.

Finally, Mary spoke up, putting her knitting down. "That sounds great, Bennet, but we have no one to do the complicated stuff like manipulating security cameras or hacking into their fire alarms. If a door is locked, we are going to have to blow it up or spend time picking it, instead of you opening it with the click of a button. Austen can do the basics as an earpiece, but there is no way he can do what you're capable of. Our best bet is to get rid of Chadwick and maybe blow up the facility."

Chuck chimed in, joking, "Or we can buy up the rest of the oil companies and never sell them to Chadwick."

Austen choked on his coffee and glared at Chuck, who wasn't helping the situation at all. I ignored what he'd said and let what Mary had said sink in.

It was true. Our team wouldn't succeed if no one could hack into their computer systems. We had devices that could shut down security cameras, but it was easier to steal their feed and plot the safest route.

Darcy looked at me and smiled. My guess was that she wanted to give me the honors of telling everyone what I had planned for my future.

I looked at Mary and answered her concern. "I'll be doing all of the earpiece stuff."

"So, you'll stay on the plane with Mary, Chuck, and me while Darcy breaks into the building?" Austen asked, hopeful.

"No," I replied. "I'll be doing all I can on-site next to Darcy. Why can't I do both?"

No one answered my rhetorical question. Mary and Chuck just turned to look at Austen, as though they were asking him if it were allowed. I looked at Austen too, and waited for his response.

"Alright, hotshot," Austen said. "What do you propose?"

I smiled and moved from my spot next to Mary to the coffee table with all our blueprints and information. Picking through the papers, I found the map of the premises and flattened it out for everyone to see.

The building was huge, with only two stories, plus a basement. It was the headquarters for Chadwick, but when I pictured companies like this, I pictured a floor in a downtown skyscraper, not a military fortress in the middle of nowhere.

The fortress was surrounded by trees for miles, and the forest was also well-equipped with security cameras, and guards, and whatever else her money could buy. We would have to look into seeing if there were any guard dogs, because I would not be okay with that.

Overall, the place looked like a mini version of the Orphanage, meaning that it should be impossible to get into. But there was one hole, one opportunity to get in, and one opportunity to get out. We had a small window, and if we screwed up, we would be trapped.

I found the spot on the blueprints that had sparked my interest and pointed at it. "This is our best bet."

Four sets of confused eyes looked up at me like I was crazy.

"This better be good, you idiot," Darcy muttered, pacing slowly back and forth, looking at the blueprints.

"You want us to… what? Bomb the mainframe room? Parachute onto the roof?" Austen asked, leaning his elbows on his knees and resting his head on his fist.

I looked up at him. "You think my plan is to bomb the building or parachute onto the roof? Now who's the idiot?"

Chuck, Mary, and Darcy chuckled before Austen cut them off with a look that could cut glass; I'm guessing he'd learned that from all his years working with the Chief.

"Does anyone remember that project Agent Asher gave us?" I asked. Then I smiled. "Oh, and we're going to need a flock of Canada geese."

My stuff, along with the rest of the team's equipment, was loaded on the plane of Mary's choosing. Both teams stood in line at attention, waiting for the Chief to send us off. Agent Asher and the rest of our teachers were standing off to the side, waiting for our final assignment to begin so they could celebrate a week off. They'd had to deal with this all morning, sending all the agents, from ages five to eighteen, off on their assignments to determine whether or not they would move on to the next year. Training agents mostly came back successful. Sometimes people needed intensive hospital care, but they still came back and were one step closer to graduation and becoming an agent.

I was itching to get on the plane. We had a two-hour flight, and I planned on using those two hours with Chuck to plan our summer reading list. When I say "summer reading list," what I really mean is comic books. We had recently gotten into *The Fantastic Four*. I would be spending most of my time training and studying this summer, minus the camping trip my year had planned.

Standing at the end of my group beside Darcy, I looked over at the other group. They all looked like themselves. Charlotte was sporting a concert T-shirt from a band she'd probably never even heard of, Jane was wearing a blazer, Elizabeth had her hair in a bun, Lucas was losing concentration, wrapped up with some unknown idea in his head, and Oliver looked stone-cold and ready to go. I guessed that their team would beat us back to the Orphanage. They had gotten lucky with their assignment, and our whole team wished we could have had something as simple as retrieving hidden paintings.

A sneeze came from behind us, and none of us dared turn around to see who it was. River and the Chief made their way to us. Agent Hannah, with a duffle bag in hand and a look that clearly said she wished she could be on any other assignment than being the pilot for training agents, was also following a step behind. She sauntered up to the plane the other team had decided to take, climbing up the stairs and disappearing.

"Alright, '01s," the Chief's voice echoed throughout the hangar, "Your final assignment of the school year will indicate whether or not you will pass on to the next year, your final year of training."

We continued to stand at attention, waiting for him to finish and send us on our way. The teachers moved forward to stand behind the Chief and Agent River.

"I wish you luck on your assignments. Get the job done. I don't want to have to come along and clean up your mess. The only thing we will clean up is dead bodies—hopefully not yours." He looked at me when he said that, reminding me that the last time I was on an assignment away from the Orphanage was when my brother died.

He continued, "Be back here by Friday at 0900, or else you will have failed. Do not show up late. You may not contact the Orphanage at any time during your assignment unless a team member dies.

"Team Orchid, Agent Hannah will be taking you to Germany, but you may not use her for anything else. Everything else is fair game. Good luck to you all." He motioned for us to enter our aircraft. Then, just like that, the Chief and River turned and headed to the next year to wish them luck.

Our two teams looked at each other and gave one nod for goodbye and good luck.

My team didn't look back as Austen led the way to our plane. I brought up the rear as we all walked up the stairs and entered what would be considered our base for the week. Mary headed straight to the front of the plane to get ready for takeoff, and the rest of us headed to the main room to strap in.

The plane had two decks, with the top deck holding the bedrooms and the main room, with a conference table, workstations, and a kitchen. At the front of the main room, close to the cockpit, were a few comfy chairs, where we strapped ourselves in. The lower deck held the vehicles, equipment, and weapons, as well as our Canada geese. Chuck had suggested knocking the birds out until we needed them, so we didn't have to hear them squawk the whole trip.

"Systems are online and ready to go," Mary said into her headset to the agents working in the tower who would open the ceiling for us to fly out. "Copy that. We will wait till AA9402 has taken off before we go."

I was leaning forward against my seat belt, trying to get a better view of Mary and everything she was doing. Darcy, sitting in the chair next to mine, was already getting herself ready for a nap with a neck pillow and blanket.

Austen was grinning away, excited to be leaving the Orphanage. He rarely got sent on assignments and instead was stuck in the office, overseeing earpieces and helping organize countless agents. The whole Orphanage would be watching to see how he would do on this assignment and what it would mean for his future as Chief.

A loud rumble came from above us. I knew it was the ceiling opening up to let us fly out. I looked out the window and saw the other team's plane pull forward. The plane didn't need to gain any speed since it was designed to take off straight up. It rose up and away from the Orphanage, leaving us behind.

It was our turn next.

"AA9402 has taken off and left the airspace. AA8671 is starting its ascent," Mary spoke into her headset.

The chair I sat on started to vibrate, and the engines grew louder and louder, working hard to lift us off the ground. Mary tilted the plane up, making us all lean back in our chairs. We took off, slowly gaining speed. Out the window, I watched the open garage dwindle, the people inside it becoming too tiny to spot.

"Wake me when we get there," Darcy told us, rolling over and facing away from me.

I worried about the person who would have to wake up sleeping Darcy. Maybe Austen could do it. It would be good training for him.

"AA8671 has successfully taken off, and we will be signing off until our return flight," Mary said. She clicked away at switches before removing her headset and climbing out of her seat to join us. Grabbing her knitting from a bag next to her chair, she told the team, "Coordinates for our destination have been plugged in, and the autopilot is on. The plane will alert us when we are thirty minutes out and will hover one hundred kilometers outside of our target zone with camouflage mode on."

I loved hearing Mary talk in technical terms while she knitted. She looked like a badass granny with her knitting needles flying away.

"Well," Austen said, "we've got two hours to kill."

Chuck smiled at me and unbuckled his seatbelt. I unbuckled too and followed him to the conference table. Before sitting down at the table, Chuck reached above one of the computers on the far wall and opened a cupboard. He pulled out a stack of comic books and plopped them down on the table.

"Do you want to start or should I?" he asked me.

Typically, when we started a new series, one of us would read one book ahead and then pass it to the next when he'd finished.

"Go ahead and start," I offered. "I'll grab some snacks."

Austen's head jerked up when he heard me mention snacks. "Grab some cookies for me, please."

"There better be cookies left for the flight home," Darcy mumbled. "That food might have to last a bit longer if something goes wrong with our plan."

Ignoring Darcy, I wandered to the kitchen. We mostly had pre-packaged food like astronauts would use, plus a few treats like pop in the fridge and chips and cookies in the cupboards. Grabbing the Oreos, a bag of salt 'n' vinegar chips, and two cans of Coke, I headed back to the group and handed Austen the cookies.

Chuck was already well into the first comic. I opened the chips and my pop and waited for him to finish, scarfing down some chips and chugging half my pop while I sat there. I reflected on the fact that I hadn't even noticed that, over the past couple of weeks, things like eating and sleeping had slowly become easier and normal again. Things I'd almost had to force myself to do, I was slowly enjoying again, and I smiled at my progress. Collin would be proud to see how far I had come.

As soon as Chuck finished, I picked up the comic and started reading. Throughout all these years of us sharing comic books, we had gotten a good rhythm going. As soon as he finished his next one, I had finished my first. We spent the whole two hours doing this while Darcy slept, Mary knitted and occasionally checked the controls, and Austen read over files for the assignment. Austen needed a hobby that had nothing to do with agent work because all he seemed to do was agent stuff, like work out or train or read old assignment files. Maybe Oliver had a hobby that Austen would have liked, but the only thing I could picture Oliver doing was something super British and boring like cricket or polo.

While we were all deep in our activities, Mary's alarm went off, making her jump a little. She got up and headed over to the controls and sat down in her captain's chair. Flipping a couple of switches and moving things that I didn't understand, she focused on the screen that popped up on the window in front of her, displaying a map of where we were.

"Bennet," Austen called to me, looking ahead at Mary, "see if you can get into a satellite that has eyes down here. Mary, make us invisible and hover the plane. Chuck, please wake up Darcy."

Chuck and I put down our comic books, and he looked at me with fear in his eyes.

"Good luck," I told him, getting up and patting him gently on his shoulder.

Heading back to my position as an earpiece, I pulled a chair out in front of a decent-looking computer and went to work, scanning for a satellite that could give us eyes on the ground. The earpiece stuff kicked back in quickly, and I felt right at home.

"Are you kidding me?" I heard Chuck yell. Darcy quickly blurted out an apology.

A few seconds later, Chuck was sitting at the workstation next to me with an ice pack on his nose. "Who knew the first bit of first aid I would have to perform would be on myself?"

I smiled and went on typing away. Bringing up the video feed, I sent it to the screen on the conference table where Darcy, still wrapped in a blanket, Mary, and Austen were already sitting.

Chuck followed me and sat as far away from Darcy as possible. Darcy's ponytail was messy and falling down. She was too sleepy to care. She had her feet up on the table and was leaning back dangerously far in her chair.

The hologram screen in the center of the table could be seen wherever you sat. It showed a forest covered in trees and a winding river that led to a waterfall. Just off to the side was a gray building. Movement was noticeable, but I would have to try to zoom in to get a better view.

"Good job, Bennet," Austen spoke. "Can you record this for the next twenty-four hours? Darcy and I will study the footage while you, Chuck, and Mary check on the geese downstairs. We will sleep in shifts. Darcy and Bennet will have the last shift before they prepare to enter the field. For the next hour, we will finalize points in the plan. Are we clear?"

"Crystal," Darcy smiled, tightening her messy ponytail before leaning forward to grab the leftover bag of chips.

CHAPTER 31

We stood in silence around the Canada geese. No one dared speak for fear they would be forced to do the horrible task ahead of us.

The geese had no idea what was coming. They were awake and squawking away inside their cage, probably annoyed that they were trapped, though soon enough, all but one would be free to fly away. Well, they would all fly away, but one would be very dead as it did so.

"So, we thought of drugs to knock them out during the flight, but nothing to let one of them slip away nicely. We are truly geniuses," Darcy said.

I spoke next, a little worried that they would make me do what I was about to ask. "Should we just wring its neck? Is that the best way to do it? We could use a knife, but we need it in one piece."

Again, no one spoke. We all just continued to stare at the geese in the hope that one would spontaneously die of old age.

We only had so much time before Darcy and I would be jumping out of the plane, and we needed to fit whichever goose we picked with its flight suit. We didn't have time to stand around sentimentally worrying about a goose. But it was hard.

"Darcy, you do it." Austen tried to sound commanding. "You're an assassin, after all."

"I kill people, not geese," she protested. "I vote the future doctor does it."

We all turned to look at Chuck, seeming to agree that it should be him. I felt bad that I'd turned on my best friend but not bad enough to change my mind.

Chuck looked at us and let out a big breath before asking, "Do we have any marshmallows?"

Everyone looked baffled at the change of topic, but I smiled knowingly and raced toward the kitchen. Kind of conveniently, we did have marshmallows, because as the one in charge of bringing snacks, I'd piled the cupboards full of junk food. I had made sure to get everyone's favorites. There was Coke for me and Oreos for Austen. Chuck had discovered Pop Tarts last summer when we went camping. Mary loved Nutella, and she usually had a jar of it hidden under her bed, and Darcy, conveniently, loved s'mores.

I reached the kitchen, flung open the top cupboard, and grabbed the extra-large marshmallows. Racing back to the group with the bag in hand, I tossed them at Chuck.

"Alright, doc, what's the plan?" Darcy asked skeptically.

Chuck, looking slightly ashamed, answered as he opened the bag and pulled out a giant marshmallow the size of his palm. "One time—I don't know if we were eight—but when we went camping one summer, Bennet and I decided to go feed the ducks, and… well, all we had were marshmallows."

Mary, Austen, and Darcy waited for him to keep going with his story. The geese were still squawking away, and I felt a little sorry that one wouldn't be squawking soon. As someone who wanted to be a field, I really needed to control my emotions if a dead goose was already making me nervous.

"Well, umm," Chuck said, "we fed the ducks marshmallows, and that's when we discovered that, well…"

"Well, what?" Darcy snapped.

"Their throats weren't big enough. They choked on the

marshmallow and died."

The three of them looked at Chuck and me in shock for keeping this secret for all these years. Even Collin never knew, because we had been so scared at the time of having accidentally killed a couple of ducks. We had panicked then, but now we laughed about it. Finally sharing the story was weird since it was something that we'd thought we would keep till our graves.

Austen was the first to start laughing. Darcy joined in, and Mary managed a couple of chuckles. I joined in as well, but Chuck just stared at the marshmallow in his hand. As the four of us laughed at our embarrassing childhood mistake, Chuck decided to take matters into his own hands, and looking at the geese, without any warning, tossed a giant marshmallow to one of the birds.

We immediately stopped laughing and watched the closest goose, who had successfully taken the marshmallow in its mouth and swallowed. Right on cue, it started choking. We could see the lump of the giant marshmallow in its long neck as the goose freaked out in the cage. Outside of the cage, we were also freaking out.

"Oh my gosh!" Mary screamed.

"What the heck!" Austen exclaimed.

"Should I try to take it out?" Chuck responded.

"It has to die!" I yelled over Mary's constant screaming, and the geese squawked louder, watching their friend slowly die in front of them.

"It worked," Darcy whispered, interrupting our screams.

We stopped and looked at each other and then at the goose that was now lying quite dead inside the cage. Its foot twitched slightly, and its eyes were still open.

"Does anyone want a marshmallow?" Chuck quietly asked.

Austen grabbed the bag and stood in front of the cage facing us, serious again. "Mary and Chuck, I'll help you get the goose ready for takeoff. Darcy and Bennet, you've got one hour before your jump. Go get ready."

Leaving behind what had just happened, we all turned and went back to work. A layer of seriousness came back down on us now that the problem of the dead goose had been dealt with. The real assignment of breaking into the building below and getting out alive was our next step.

I followed Darcy back to the main floor. She grabbed our packs and tossed one to me. I stuffed some food packages into it. I also grabbed a Coke out of the fridge and started to drink it, just in case it was my last. Heading to my bunk, I opened the drawer underneath my bed, packed my extra set of clothes, and grabbed my gear to change into.

Darcy came out of the bathroom when she was finished changing. We both wore black pants, combat boots, a black toque, and black gloves—and that was just the beginning of everything we had to put on. Thank goodness it wasn't winter, or else we would have had to add ten extra pounds of clothing just to keep warm.

Darcy chucked me a bunch of leather straps, and I started the five-minute job of putting on all my extra pockets to hold my knives, guns, tech gear, and whatever else I needed. Darcy was also working away, but she was much quicker than me.

We didn't need tons of stuff, mostly tech and weapons. We had no intention of camping overnight outside in the woods, so we didn't need to bring a tent or sleeping bags. We had coin-sized GPS units attached to our pants with carabiners, and we had our headsets to keep us in touch with Austen, Chuck, and Mary aboard the plane. I opened my mouth and stuck my mic into my back molar, where it fit perfectly.

Heading back to the lower level, I rounded the corner and grabbed the final thing we needed: our jumpsuits. I picked up two and tossed one to Darcy, who was already standing in front of a wall that was covered in weapons, picking out the ones she wanted to take. I hoped Mary and Chuck were making progress with the goose. Chuck would be dissecting the goose, and Mary would install the flight suit, leaving Austen to supervise.

"Take these two," Darcy told me, putting two guns in my side holsters, invading my personal space.

I noticed Darcy already had five different guns in various places, and those were just the ones I could see. She put another one in one of her boots. In the other boot, she placed a knife. Joining in, I put my Coke down, grabbed two knives, and placed them in sheaths on my back.

Last but not least, we slid two grenades each into our belts. We were locked and loaded and almost ready to go.

I gulped and took a deep breath. I didn't exactly want to jump out of a plane, but it was the next step in the plan. Plus, people jumped out of planes every day with gear that was way less safe and advanced than what the Orphanage had. I would be fine. I would probably just need a little push.

Darcy finished zipping up her jumpsuit. "Nervous?"

I didn't know how to answer that. Should I lie and try to come off cool? Collin would have been fine. I wished that I could have been doing this with him, just as the Orphanage had always wanted. It would have been fun to storm the castle with my brother by my side. The truth would have to do, because although I had started becoming a field agent to stay close to Collin, I knew now that I would have to be me, or else I would never succeed.

"Yes," I quietly replied, not wanting anyone else to hear. "Do you think I can do this?"

"You'd better, because I am not dying for you."

I tried to smile at her attempt at what I hoped was a joke. I needed to tell her something, and now was the only time before we jumped out of a plane and risked our lives. "Darcy, just so you know, I'll always be your family."

She looked up from adjusting one of her knives in her boot. "Thanks, Bennet."

I sat on the end of the bench, and Darcy took up the rest of it by lying down. We took some of our last moments to relax.

"Meet Maliki," Chuck said, walking up to us with the dead goose in his gloved hands.

"That's disgusting," Darcy muttered, sitting back up on the bench and turning to face Chuck and the others.

Austen was pulling the cage with the rest of the geese, and Mary was holding the remote that would control the goose in Chuck's hand. I looked at the poor geese still squawking at nothing in particular. Soon they would be free, and the dead goose would be helping us get past the many layers of security that waited for Darcy and me.

"This is it," Austen said. "As much as I want to stay down here, I'd better get up to the conference room and start setting everything up. Good luck."

I could sense a bit of worry in his voice that I definitely didn't need to hear before I jumped out of an airplane toward maybe the worst idea I had ever had.

Austen let go of the cage, walked to the stairs, and headed up. Mary pressed a button on the wall. The floor lowered. We were hovering over our target, so there was no wind, but the roar of the plane's engines holding us in place was suddenly deafening.

Darcy and I walked over to put on our parachutes. I put mine on over top of my backpack. It was a little uncomfortable, but it would only be for a little bit. We'd ditch the parachutes once we were on the ground. I double-checked the straps to make sure they were extra tight.

Our last pieces of equipment, our air tanks, were already attached to our parachutes. Jumping from so high up, we needed air tanks, otherwise we would pass out after thirty seconds of falling. The tanks were pretty small since we only needed air for about five minutes. There was a small section of my jumpsuit to zip the hose into so it wouldn't flap in the wind. I worked the hose under my arm and up to my chest. With it securely in place, I put the facemask on, letting it dangle from my neck since I didn't need it just yet.

The hovering plane's engines were so loud with the floor open that we had to yell to communicate with each other. Chuck put the dead goose on the floor, then positioned the cage of geese right on the edge of the lowered ramp. Mary flipped on the remote, and the dead goose came to life. Amazingly, the thing actually made a convincing bird.

Our plan was that this flock of geese, led by their deceased friend, would fly over our target. The dead bird would drop out of formation and land on the building below. Since it was a bird and not a drone, we hoped the security team wouldn't be too desperate to get rid of it. What the security team wouldn't know was that the special tech we'd grabbed from the Orphanage to put in the dead goose would temporarily freeze their system, giving us a twenty-minute window to get inside the building.

"Everything's ready up here," Austen told Darcy and me through our headsets.

I looked at Chuck and gave a nod. Chuck picked up the flapping dead goose and threw it out of the plane, and we watched it fall straight down. Mary engaged the motors in the goose's flight suit before it fell too far. Its wings started flapping, and just like that, it looked like any other goose. She flew it around and back to just below the open floor of the plane.

"Well, it works," Chuck announced. "Time to release the flock."

Darcy and I moved to the cage, positioning ourselves at the back, away from the opening. Together, we reached forward and opened the cage door. The geese, realizing what we were doing, started to go insane. As we slid the door open, they flooded out, heading into the open air. Mary flew the dead bird away from the opening, and as we'd predicted, the other geese formed a V shape, with our dead decoy goose in the lead.

Mary had the coordinates that would take the flock right over Jessica Chadwick's headquarters. On the screen of the remote, she could see through a tiny camera everything the lead goose was seeing—or would have been seeing if it weren't dead.

While keeping an eye on the remote, Mary pushed the button

to close the opening in the floor. She'd programmed the autopilot to start gaining altitude as soon as she did this, and the roar of the engines, momentarily lessened by the closing ramp, suddenly grew louder again.

It would take us a few minutes to climb to the much higher altitude we'd be jumping from so we wouldn't be detected from down below. Mary and Chuck left us, moving up to the second deck. There was an airtight hatch between this deck and that one. As soon as they were out of the way and the hatch had been sealed, Darcy and I put on our oxygen masks. Darcy pushed the button that started lowering the air pressure in the compartment to match the outside.

I knew that, in just a few minutes, I would have to jump out of the plane. I had jumped out of a plane in training, and I didn't enjoy it. I would much rather have stayed in the thing that was keeping me safe.

Austen spoke up. "Everything looks good. Mary, keep me posted if anything changes on the geese. Darcy and Bennet, you're up."

Darcy chucked a pair of goggles at me. She was already wearing hers. The goggles were more than just to protect our eyes from the rushing wind as we fell; they would also digitally show us our proper jump course and notify us when the goose had successfully completed its assignment. The right lenses were telescopic, so we'd be able to zoom in on things happening beneath us. The people below had no idea we were coming. We wanted to keep it that way.

I pulled on my goggles and the display lit up, showing me how many feet it was to the ground and when was the last safe moment to pull my chute. It would be making calculations all the way down. It was both a comfort and a gentle reminder of how close I could be to my death.

The air pressure equalized with the outside. The roar of the engines lessened. We were at our jump altitude. Darcy pushed the button to open the ramp again, and she and I walked partway down it. We stood there and looked out at the setting summer sun.

"Wait," I told Darcy. "I have to pee." I was trying to buy time.

"Hold it," she told me seriously.

I leaned a tiny bit forward to get a good look at the drop. We were so high up the Earth below looked like it wasn't even real.

"Darcy," I said, loud enough for only her to hear—and Austen unfortunately, as he could hear everything through the headsets.

"What?" There was not a hint of worry in her voice.

"I can't do this." Panic set in. "What was I thinking? I'm an earpiece, not a field agent. I'm not Collin. Oh, man, I need Collin." I could feel my breathing getting shallow. My mind closed in around me, and nothing made sense except that I needed Collin.

"Bennet!" Darcy shouted, grabbing me by the shoulders.

I caught my breath to listen to her. She had concern written on her face instead of the anger I feared would be there for my cowardice.

"Do you trust me?" she gently asked.

I didn't even have to think about the answer. "No."

She smiled. The gentle concern that was there a moment before was gone. Now she looked like the Darcy I was used to, the one who would kick my butt. "Smart man."

Still holding me by the shoulder, she twisted her arms toward the opening of the plane. I lost my balance, fell, and rolled out into nothing.

CHAPTER 32

The thin air rushed past me as I fell headfirst, faster and faster. Chadwick's company base was a horrible place to try to land on. If I missed, there were no open fields to land in, only trees to crash into and most likely break something.

"On your left," Darcy laughed in my ear, zooming past me and then spreading her body out to slow herself down and allow me to catch up.

I was both grateful she had pushed me out of the plane and rather annoyed. Part of me wanted to see if I could actually jump, but another part of me knew that it would have taken up too much of our time, and our window to land on the roof would have gotten smaller.

I looked down. Zooming in with the telescopic right lens of my goggles, I could see the geese flying over the building. The timer in my headset activated, notifying me of the drop. I watched the lead bird descend toward the building's roof. I prayed there was enough padding around the device inside the goose that it wouldn't go splat when it hit. Mary did enough prep that she should have thought of everything.

The other birds kept going, a new bird taking the lead. It seemed that no one below cared that a bird was falling to its death in their airspace. The building below was quiet and still. Security would be roaming the halls, and the daily workers would already be heading to their housing. Through our research, we'd learned that the few people who worked here were flown in for weeks at a time and stayed in cabins a short distance away. The only ones working besides security would be janitors and perhaps chefs, cleaning up after dinner.

I watched the goose hit the building.

A deafening buzzing started in our ears.

"What is that?" Darcy yelled.

Austen spoke up. "Problem with the device. The computers are telling me that it is offline, and we can't activate it. If you keep falling, their radar will pick you up."

"How much time do we have?" I asked Austen, trying to remain calm.

We heard some clicking in the headset, and I wondered what Austen could be doing. "Three minutes to get it back online."

"Can Mary fix it?" Darcy chimed in.

I thought about it. Though Mary was incredibly smart, I doubted she knew how to access the device in the bird. She knew how to work the remote and press the button at the right time to shut down the security system in the building below, but if the remote was not getting a signal from the bird, we were done for.

"Well, Bennet," Chuck began. He must have been sitting with Austen, watching everything from the conference table. "You said you could be both a field agent and an earpiece. I guess you need to prove it to us a little sooner than you thought."

I took a steadying breath and slowed everything down in my head. "I got this, but I can't focus on my landing target and get the bird reconnected."

"Umm, Darcy?" Austen said.

"I got this," she told us, echoing what I'd said.

While falling through the sky, I had to fish my tablet out of my backpack and reconnect the bird. There was still a chance it wouldn't work. If that was the case, when we landed on the roof of Chadwick's company, security would be alerted, and we would have to run like hell through our assignment. Things were not going well.

Darcy and I made eye contact and nodded once, acknowledging that what we were about to do was insane, but it had to be done. Darcy spread out her body to slow down, then steered herself above me. Once positioned, she brought her arms and legs in and headed toward me.

"Brace yourself," she told me, then slammed into my body and grabbed on.

This whole situation was more than uncomfortable. My brother's old girlfriend was clinging to my back. It was probably the closest I had ever been to a girl without fighting one.

"I need you to grab my tablet out of my backpack, and please don't take my chute off," I told Darcy, kicking myself that my backpack was buried.

She got to work, sliding her hand between my chute and down my jumpsuit toward my backpack. Despite the cool air around me, sweat formed on my brow. Darcy dug around, and I felt things moving on my back. What scared me the most was the loosening of my parachute pack, making everything on my back—my sweater, my jumpsuit, and my backpack—shift.

"What are you doing?" I yelled at her.

"Calm down, okay? I'll tighten it once I put your tablet back. Besides, I've got you." Her saying that did not make me want to calm down. I didn't have any other choice, though. I wasn't about to wrestle her off of my back while hurtling toward the earth.

"Here," she told me, pulling herself closer and handing me my tablet.

I put my hand out for her to put the tablet in. Holding on to it for dear life, I turned the device on and gave a little thanks that the Orphanage tests all our equipment at different temperatures to ensure they'll work; otherwise, it would have been way too cold for the poor thing.

Getting to work, I started to track the bird. The signal was easy to find, but it kept cutting in and out. I couldn't keep it long enough to fix it. I punched away at my tablet, working very hard to dance around the network in the building below. According to our research, if they identified an unwanted user, they would reboot everything and go into lockdown. I fleetingly wondered if they were hiding something more down there than just their desire to control the world's oil.

"It's connected," Austen shouted in excitement. "Oh wait, it's gone again."

The buzzing in my ears cut in and out, along with the connection.

A warning light flashed in my goggles. Our air tanks were empty, and we were low enough that we didn't need them anymore. I pulled off my mask. "Darcy," I said, "I need you to reach into my backpack's side pocket for a USB drive. The green one, not the pink one."

She let go of my body and grabbed onto my chute. Again, I could feel her hand shuffling around in my backpack, and soon a zipper was being moved. As she stuck her hand in and started to dig around, a horrible, slow sensation set in: the straps of my parachute were lengthening.

Then the slow sensation gave way to a sudden jolt as the straps snapped full-length, sending Darcy away from me and my tablet slipping from my hands.

"No!" I shouted, desperately reaching out into thin air.

I slowed my fall like Darcy had, taking her by surprise and crashing into her. She instantly understood that I was trying to get my tablet back, though she had a bit of a different idea. She moved her feet onto my back until she was crouching on top of me. Then, kicking out, she used me to propel herself toward my tablet.

"Got it!" she said. "Brace yourself."

She said that, but she didn't give me time to do it. Again, she crashed into me, slamming my loose parachute into my back as well. She handed me my tablet, and I held onto it even tighter this time while she held tightly to me.

Darcy handed me the green USB drive, and I quickly plugged it in and got to work.

"Austen, check again," I told him.

"It's connected," he acknowledged. "The device will be activated in five, four, three, two, one."

I handed Darcy my tablet to put away, and the terrible buzzing finally stopped. Our glasses showed that we were a little off course and Darcy, still holding on to me, moved through the sky to correct our position. I looked straight down at our target: the dead bird on the roof.

Darcy, not seeming to want to keep me posted on her moves, let go of me and opened her parachute. The ground below was clear and easy to see. My glasses alerted me that I had five seconds to open my chute. I reached back to pull the ripcord and remembered that my parachute was no longer tight against my back.

"Pull your chute, Bennet!" Austen cried.

Finally reaching the string, I pulled. The only problem was, as my chute emerged into the airstream, my arms started to slip out of the straps. The only thing that felt secure was the belt fastening it around my waist. Nothing about this felt good. I looked up at my parachute. It snapped fully open, whipping me forward, pulling my arms out of the straps and leaving me dangling only by my waist. I was trying my best to adapt to my new circumstances rather than complain about them, but this really sucked.

Everything that could go wrong had. I prayed this would be our last hiccup, but even as I thought it, I knew it wouldn't be. Now I just needed to focus on landing on the roof.

"Just double-checking on the bird," I gasped, not wanting to lose my concentration.

"The bird is on, and the timer is going," Austen informed us. "You have eighteen minutes to get inside the building before the motion sensors and security cameras come back on."

I was ahead of Darcy at this point, and my glasses were flashing red. I knew deep down I would not make the roof, no matter how much I kicked through the air. At this point, I needed to focus on not getting stuck in some trees. I cursed my poorly constructed parachute straps. I was going to report this to whoever was in charge of checking equipment at the Orphanage. This was ridiculous.

I looked down and braced myself for landing. One foot hit the ground, and I thanked the Lord that I'd made it safely, but as I reached with my other foot, a gust of wind gently lifted my parachute back up and sent me tumbling along the ground. Like the idiot I was, I held on to my parachute, hoping it would stop, instead of unclicking the belt buckle. It did not stop, and I continued to get dragged. Luckily, it pulled me closer to the building. Unluckily, I smacked right into the wall before I finally clued in to unbuckle myself.

I came to a stop close to the building. Since no alarms were blaring, I assumed that my bird device had worked and the guards inside were still unaware of us.

Standing up, I looked at the roof and watched Darcy. She vanished from my sight as she landed on the roof, but a moment later, she was looking down at me over the edge. "You idiot. You missed the roof! How could you miss the roof? It's huge!" she yelled at me, not making the situation any better.

I tried to tell her off. "Is this really the best time to argue about it?"

Plan A was completely off course, and just then, to add to our mess, the goose exploded behind Darcy, sending bits of feathers and metal in all directions and alerting everyone in the building of an intruder.

CHAPTER 33

I watched in horror as a feather floated above Darcy's head. For a couple of agents out in the field, we were honestly off to a terrible start. The easiest of our eleven plans was to go through the roof. Now we just had to compromise. We'd made several backup plans, mostly in case I screwed up.

"I thought you said we had eighteen minutes," I complained.

"Was that the goose?" Austen asked nervously.

"Yep," Darcy calmly responded, walking to the middle of the roof and out of my sight, apparently moving to plan B.

I started to move back so I could see her. Before I'd taken two steps, her black shape appeared at the edge of the roof. She leaped off and plunged two stories to the ground—or almost to the ground: her parachute, which she must have quickly anchored to something on the roof, snapped her back just before she hit, leaving her dangling. She undid the straps and landed gently. Now when the security team came to the roof to check out the ruckus, not only would they find goose feathers, but they'd also discover a parachute. I had to give it to Darcy—she was great at adapting to her circumstances.

Darcy came to stand next to me, and we watched lights start to flick on in the building. Confusion and chaos must have erupted in there. They'd seen nothing on their computers, but now an explosion was indicating something was seriously wrong. The goose had been a great decoy to allow us to make our way into the place.

"Well," Darcy said, "since everyone is heading up to the roof, let's go through the front door."

We each took a big, calming breath before we dashed toward the building.

Pulling my backpack around to my stomach, I unzipped one of the pockets and reached inside for two badges. I tossed one to Darcy while we ran and clipped the other one onto my jumpsuit. We both ripped off our toques and gloves, and I stuffed them into my backpack. Then I grabbed a baseball cap and jammed it on my head before stuffing my backpack into my jumpsuit. Darcy handed me her backpack, and I awkwardly shoved hers into my jumpsuit as well. The two backpacks stuffed inside my clothes made me look kind of pudgy, but that was part of the disguise.

We matched our pace as Darcy clipped her badge to her jumpsuit, tightened her ponytail, and put on a hat that matched mine. She also managed to apply a terrible shade of lip-gloss but forced me to stop running while she applied a coat of mascara.

Walking again, we rounded the corner to the main entrance. Two armed guards stood in front of the doors. They both had the same buzz cut. My guess was that they were ex-military.

They saw us walking their way and pointed their guns at us. Immediately we stopped, trying to look terrified, and put our hands up, showing that they were completely empty.

One of them came closer, and in a booming voice, asked, "Who are you?"

My voice shaking, I grabbed my badge and pointed at it. "We're . . . we're part of the janitorial staff!"

Darcy followed suit, and hand slightly shaking, pointed at her badge as well—not that they could make out the pictures on them as far away as we stood. The guards had no reason to question us based on our appearance. Our badges said that we were janitors, and since we'd done our research, our jumpsuits looked exactly like the ones the janitorial staff here wore.

"What are you two doing outside at this time of the evening?" the closer one asked.

I looked at Darcy as if I needed encouragement. "We needed some, um, privacy," I stammered, hoping they'd read between the lines. By their slightly impressed expressions, I figured they got it. "We were walking around when we heard this loud bang. I think it came from the roof. Anyways, we tried to get back inside the way we came, but the door was locked, and our key cards wouldn't work. We figured the front door was the best place to try."

"Please let us in," Darcy pleaded in a high-pitched voice that didn't belong to her. "We still have a bit more work to finish up."

"Sorry about the door, sweetheart," the man said, speaking directly to Darcy. "We went on partial lockdown, so your key card won't work until we reboot the system. Here, let me help you back in."

With his gun in his hand, he led the way, and the other man opened the door for us. As far as they knew, we were just silly newbies who didn't have a clue about the regular routines and procedures of the facility. Luckily enough, a flight had brought in some new workers that morning. The main thing that would have given us away was our key cards, if they had looked closely. I had spent the day before snooping through social media until I found a photo of someone who worked here. It showed a man and a couple of his work buddies playing a card game during a break, and they were all wearing their badges. It took some simple copying and pasting to make our own. Ours didn't work on any of the doors in the building, but in a lockdown like the one we'd triggered with the goose, no key card belonging to janitorial staff would open an outside door.

Darcy smiled at them as we walked through the doors, and I gave one nod to say, "Thank you." We walked down the hallway and heard the door shut behind us. The building was quiet, but we knew somewhere inside there was a security team frantically trying to reboot the system. With our knowledge of this place, I figured we should be able to avoid them for a while. I had faith that my skills were superior to theirs.

"Austen," I whispered, "we're in."

We turned a corner and were out of view from the main doors. Getting to our next destination wasn't going to be a problem after all the studying of the building's floorplans we had done. I looked up and down the hallway to make sure no one was coming, and Darcy casually leaned against the wall. A downside to such a high-security building was that the security team always wanted to know who was opening every single door—even the door to a janitor's closet.

Unzipping my jumpsuit so that I could reach into my backpack, I grabbed my tablet and something that resembled a credit card attached to a cord. I plugged the cord into my tablet and stuck the card into the card reader on the door. A red light flashed. I worked quickly to trick the door into opening. A moment later, the door beeped, and the little light turned green.

While I was putting my stuff back into my backpack, Darcy opened up the closet door and walked in. She was barely in there for five seconds before emerging with the final piece of our disguise: the yellow cart the building's janitors typically pushed everywhere they went. I pulled the backpacks out of my jumpsuit and shoved them into the garbage can on the cart.

A janitor was a common disguise for an agent because no one bothers to look at janitors. People are too busy to notice anyone they consider insignificant.

The downside to the bird exploding earlier than it was supposed to was that the security cameras would be back up and running soon. If they had face recognition software, they would spot us quickly. We kept our heads down to avoid eye contact with any of the cameras.

We moved off without a word, me pushing the cart and Darcy leading the way. We were walking at a normal pace down a long hallway, when up ahead, three people turned the corner and started walking toward us. My muscles tensed as we walked closer and closer to the group. They were talking among themselves, too quietly for me to hear what they were saying. They looked bored, and I couldn't figure out what that meant.

The space between us shrank. There were two ladies in their late twenties and a man who seemed older. They wore the same kind of white clothes the cooks wore back at the Orphanage. They looked worn out, and one of the women had brown stuff splattered all over her. From that, I assumed they were coming from the kitchen.

"I don't remember us getting new janitors. Did someone quit?" the woman in the middle asked.

"Maybe," the other woman said, stifling a yawn. "Kitchen staff and janitorial staff hardly mix."

Darcy smiled at them and answered their question. "We just started working here today. So far, it's pretty easy, but it's going to be a bit of an adjustment living where we work."

The woman in the middle responded, "Well, welcome to the middle of nowhere."

They walked away, clearly just getting off their shift and tired from being on their feet most of the day.

Darcy smirked at me and quietly whispered, "Idiots."

I couldn't help but smile to hear her call someone an idiot other than me.

CHAPTER 34

INSIDE CHADWICK'S HEADQUARTERS
JUNE 12
9:28 P.M.

We had barely left the group of cooks behind when Darcy pointed at our next door. This was my time to shine. I reached into the garbage can and pulled out my backpack to once again take out my magical door opener. Darcy casually leaned against the wall, keeping watch. The security cameras were moments from coming back online, and we wanted to look like regular janitors.

I had the door open in seconds, and we both entered, bringing the janitor cart with us and shutting the door.

"Austen?" Darcy whispered. "We're on to phase two."

No sound came through our headset. I realized we hadn't heard from Austen since we'd entered the building.

Darcy tried again. "Come in, Austen. Austen, do you copy? We are on to phase two."

There was still no response from Austen or anyone else on the plane. I looked at Darcy questioningly, trying to figure out the problem in my head. It dawned on me, and the horror of our new situation set in.

"Darcy," I said to get her attention. She was still trying to reach Austen.

Her look said she knew I was about to give her bad news.

I did. "We're locked in."

Her brow tightened. "What do you mean?"

"I mean, there was one thing I didn't account for when making this plan. I thought their system was similar to the Orphanage's security system. At the end of the day, ours is better, but—"

"But what, Bennet?" Darcy demanded.

I bit my lip, trying to decide how to explain what was happening. "You know when parents accidentally lock their keys in their car with their baby still inside? Well, we're the baby, and the parent purposely locked us in the car. Oh, and the parent is also in the car."

I felt like she was about to call me an idiot. To avoid that, I changed my tactic. "The system knew something was wrong when we blocked it. The backup system kicked in and is now blocking anything that doesn't belong."

"That makes no sense," Darcy told me.

After a quiet, breathy scream of frustration, I told her, "We can't communicate with our team, and our team can't communicate with us. We're on our own."

"Okay." Darcy tried to stay rational while I was on the verge of freaking out. "Let's finish our assignment and worry about communication later. There's always another plan."

I nodded. We didn't have many options here except to move forward.

I tossed Darcy the key card, and she caught it and put it in my backpack. Then she pulled out something the size of a pen. Taking it from her, I used my hand to measure five feet from the left corner. I held the tip of the pen against the wall, and with a small hiss, it began to cut through the drywall.

I cut out a rectangle and gently removed it from the wall to reveal a large pipe. Putting the pen against the pipe, I cut out a rectangle, big enough to stick my hand in. I put the piece of pipe on the floor next to the piece of the wall. Inside the pipe were a bunch of different-colored wires, which I knew had all sorts of purposes.

I handed the pen back to Darcy, and she handed me a tiny box the size of an old-fashioned flip phone, which had a thin cable with crab claws on one end. I put the tiny box in the pipe and squished it between some of the wires to keep it there. I then took the cable attached to the box and moved it strategically toward one of the yellow wires. When I clipped the claw onto the yellow wire, it cut through the insulation and wrapped around the wire inside.

"Your tablet says it's connected," Darcy informed me.

I took the tablet from Darcy. The yellow wire connected to the building's security cameras. Their displays popped up on my screen. I started making each camera show a ten-second loop. I had to ensure that each camera had nobody on it: security might get suspicious if a person kept walking up the same hallway over and over.

Darcy waited for me to finish, occasionally fidgeting with the stuff on the cart and rolling it back and forth in the small space.

"Done," I told her. I grabbed a roll of tape from the cart and taped my tablet to the handles so that I could push the cart and watch the live feed at the same time.

"Is the hallway clear?" she asked with her hand on the door handle, ready to go.

"The coast is clear," I confirmed. She opened the door, and I pushed the cart out of the closet.

We had two places to go: the mainframe room and Chadwick's office. We quickly made our way to the elevator that would take us to the basement. After we were done down there, we would have to make our way to the second story to Chadwick's office.

Darcy hit the elevator button, and the doors slid open. She entered first, and I followed, still pushing the cart. Darcy pushed the button for the basement, the doors closed, and the elevator started to descend. If anyone joined us, we'd previously agreed to strike up a conversation about pizza places in New York City.

The elevator let us out, and we casually made our way to the mainframe room. A sign on the door read, "Do Not Enter: Authorized

Personnel Only." We started the process of opening it. If we failed and were caught, I hoped the security team would get better locks for their doors. I was having way too easy of a time breaking in.

Once the door was unlocked, Darcy barged into the room, leaving me to pack up my stuff. I pushed the cart into the room and shut the door behind us.

Joy filled me as I ditched the cart by the door and walked down the many aisles of mainframes. They were giant and beautiful and everything I wanted in life. I wanted to take them all apart, look at all the wires and circuits, and put them back together. The beautiful little lights that glowed from the machines reminded me of Christmas, and I felt like a kid in a candy shop, wanting to touch everything.

"Focus, Bennet," Darcy said through the whirling and buzzing of the machines.

I snapped out of my trance. While I searched for what I needed, Darcy browsed up and down the aisles. She didn't care to watch what I was doing. She just wanted to move on to the next part of the assignment.

I found exactly what I was looking for after a bit of wandering. Bending down in front of the machine, I grabbed my backpack and pulled out my USB drives. I had packed two pink drives and one green one. The green one was meant for my tablet, and the two pink ones were meant for here and Chadwick's computer.

Reaching for a couple of wires, I worked on switching around what I needed to. I hesitated for a second and was about to call out for Darcy to grab me something from the cart when she appeared at my side with exactly what I needed. She handed me my tablet and a cord, and I took it from her and got to work plugging it into the mainframe. After attaching it, I opened up my kill program and plugged my USB drive into an empty slot on the machine. The two devices connected, and I hit ENTER. Once my beautiful code was scrolling across my screen, I hit CONNECT, and the code got to work, busily working its way into the system of Chadwick Family Oil Company.

I looked up. "All done," I told Darcy.

I handed her my things. This time she took control of the cart. We headed out of the mainframe room, making our way to our next location: Jessica Chadwick's office.

Flipping through security cameras, I made sure that our path to her office was clear. If I had to make changes to our route to avoid people, I quietly let Darcy know, and she followed me without question.

The building we walked through was rather beautiful. There were paintings on the walls and the occasional flower bouquet on a desk. The building had a feminine touch to it—in fact, it was almost homey. It was a lot cozier than the Orphanage, and I was slightly jealous of the people who lived and worked there.

"Last room on the right," I reminded Darcy.

Doing our same routine as the last three doors, Darcy tossed me the key card. I fumbled it a little before I attached it to my tablet and knelt down in front of the door. It took a little longer for my system to figure out the code to open this door, but it got there after a minute or so. During that time, we nervously stood there in the open. Even though we knew no one was coming, it was uncomfortable to be so exposed.

The little light on the door finally turned green, and Darcy opened it. We put everything back into the cart and rolled it into the room. Darcy got to work snooping through Jessica's things.

Right away, I noticed that her office was even nicer than the rest of the building. She must have hired one expensive interior decorator. That or she had a very good eye for this kind of stuff, but I felt like she had more important things to worry about than picking out flower vases and desk trinkets. Taking over every single oil company probably took up a lot of her time.

I ditched the janitor's cart and walked over to her desk. Sitting down in her chair, I cracked my knuckles, then got to work hacking her password. Her computer desktop was big and beautiful, and I debated for a second shoving the whole machine into the garbage can and taking it back to the Orphanage to set it up in my dorm room for computer games.

Once I'd figured out Chadwick's password, I stood up and got Darcy's attention. "Pass me the pink USB drive."

She moved away from the bookshelf and walked to my backpack. She found the pink thumb drive and tossed it to me, and I caught it without fumbling it. Sliding my fingers along the side of the computer, I found the port and quickly slid the drive in.

I was still waiting for it to open when Darcy slammed a book down on the desk. Looking up at her and then down at the book, I tried to figure out why she was showing it to me. The open pages had a bunch of letters and numbers on a chart, and some of them seemed familiar, but I couldn't quite place them.

"What is this?" I asked her, still looking at the book. I turned the page, and the numbers and letters kept going.

"They're the same codes that the Orphanage uses to log weapons," Darcy informed me. "Can you find anything about this on her computer?"

I minimized my program and started to search through Jessica's files, looking for anything on weapons. "Her company has produced enough to arm multiple countries," I said. "But it doesn't show that she has sold them to anyone. So, what is she saving them for? Or who is she giving them to?"

"What do you get when you add a ton of weapons to control over the world's oil?" Darcy asked.

"Chadwick could start and control a war," I said, horrified.

"Correct."

I looked back at the computer and then back at the book. I smiled in spite of the situation, finding it ironic that one of the most peaceful countries was housing the potential for World War Three.

My program jumped around on the screen, alerting me that it was ready. My class project for how I would destroy the Orphanage was perfect for destroying Jessica's company digitally. All their mainframes would be completely wiped, and any information on them would be lost.

Darcy grabbed the book and threw it into the garbage can, wanting to take it back to the Orphanage for evidence and information. I got back to work uploading my program. I hoped it would also take care of the program preventing us from communicating with the rest of the team, and we would be able to easily get out of this place and get picked up.

"Give me my tablet," I commanded.

Darcy went over to the cart, but as she started to unstrap the tablet from the handle, she paused.

"What's wrong?" I asked.

"We've got company coming."

"How many?"

"Ten guards," she told me, handing me the tablet. "They know we're here."

I had to work fast to get everything set up. If this was happening, I needed the program to start.

"Strip off the jumpsuit," Darcy commanded. "This is going to end in a fight, and we might as well have easy access to our weapons."

I did as Darcy instructed me, tossing my jumpsuit to her. She threw mine and hers in the garbage can. Then she took a gun in each hand and pointed them at the door. I ran behind the computer and hid there to keep working.

A picture of a skull and crossbones came up on my screen, letting me know that my program was ready to start killing any information on their system.

The door burst open. "Freeze," I could hear one of the men shout.

But Darcy didn't freeze. I heard a gunshot. I looked at the security footage on my screen and saw Darcy was doing pretty well.

I entered a few more codes into Chadwick's system and started my program. A time bar came up, letting me know how long it would take. My heart sank when I saw it said it would be done Friday evening, which was long after we needed to be back at the Orphanage.

Sliding one of the drawers open, I hid my tablet under some papers, hoping it would be safe for the time being. I also moved a vase on Jessica's desk in front of the pink USB drive. Praying it would kick in and work faster, I grabbed one of my guns out of its holster and prepped myself to enter the fight.

Jumping up, I turned to face Darcy and the seven men who were still standing. I pointed my gun at one who was getting close to Darcy, and my whole body shook at the idea of actually shooting a person, something I'd never done. I had shot a gun lots of times, especially over the past few months, but never at a real live person.

"You're holding a loaded gun, you idiot!" Darcy shouted at me, and all the men turned in my direction. "Act like it!"

With that horrible encouragement, I aimed and shot the guy closest to Darcy in the shoulder. Moving on, I shot another guy in the leg. I couldn't bring myself to kill them, but I figured hurting them wasn't that bad.

Realizing I was a threat and not just a skinny nobody, two of the guards came at me. One of them jumped at me, making me drop my gun. I struggled under his weight as he punched me in my delicate nose. As he punched me in the face a second time, I reached for my utility belt, grabbed my favorite thing, a taser, and stabbed him in the side.

Shaking, he fell onto the floor beside me, but now the other one was closing. Shifting the taser to my left hand, I reached for my other gun with my right—and mistakenly pulled out one of my knives. Holding it, I gave the second man a worried smile as he skidded to a halt in front of me.

The smile he returned was a lot less worried than mine as he pointed his gun, not at my chest, but at my leg. My body acted before my brain could and threw the knife. It hit him in the chest. A month before, Darcy had spent two days training me to actually hit a target throwing knives. Turned out, all the practice paid off.

Fighting the urge to vomit at what I'd just done, I faced the next guy who was charging toward me. Clearly, these men were under orders to keep us alive. None of them were shooting to kill. Instead, they seemed to hope we'd surrender. Whoever had sent them probably wanted to question us. We had to make sure that didn't happen.

Darcy was holding her ground. The two guys I had shot were up and attacking, not letting bullet wounds to a shoulder or leg stop them. Darcy grabbed a giant book and a statue of a rearing horse from the bookshelf and used them to whack the first guy I had shot in the shoulder, sending him flying into the wall. He slid to the floor and didn't move. The next guy dove and knocked her down. Lying on her back with the man on top of her, she jabbed the statue into his eye. Blood poured out, and he cried out in pain, but not for long because Darcy then slammed the statue into the side of his head, knocking him out.

I had taken care of two, and Darcy had taken care of five, which left three for us to deal with.

Two of them teamed up against Darcy while the other came after me. I tried to do what Darcy did and find something to use to knock him out, but I had a hard time deciding what to grab. There was so much nice stuff in this room, and I didn't want to wreck any of it. In the end, I grabbed the only thing I could think of: the computer. I prayed the USB drive had sent everything it needed to my tablet.

Screaming like a madman, I threw the computer with all of my strength. It hit my attacker in the head, and he fell on top of Chadwick's desk. I grabbed a picture frame holding a photo of her dad and smashed it onto the man's already-bleeding head. He rolled off the desk and joined the other bodies piling up on the floor.

I laughed in relief, right up until a foot kicked me, driving me back onto the desk. My attacker leaped at me, ready to punch. I rolled, and his fist slammed into the desk. I leaped up and did Darcy proud, holding my ground against this skilled man as we fought around the room.

After a couple of minutes, I shouted, "Stop!"

Completely taken by surprise, the man stopped, staring at me with his fist in the air, ready to strike.

"Thank you," I said, trying to catch my breath. "I need a little break."

I leaned against the wall with one hand. A bang echoed through the room, making me jump, and my attacker collapsed, revealing Darcy standing behind him, holding a gun that was now pointed at me. Breathing heavily, she snapped, "No breaks in life-or-death situations."

I didn't allow myself to think about the ten men lying either dead or unconscious on the floor. I raced over to the broken computer, removed the pink USB drive, and prayed everything had gone through. As I headed over to check on the tablet, the lights in the room and hallway suddenly turned off, leaving us in total darkness.

"Did you turn off the lights?" Darcy whispered.

"No," I whispered back, trying to see her in the dark.

"Then we have a problem," she said, and an instant later, the lights came back on to reveal the hallway full of men with guns aimed at us.

We had no choice but to surrender. Darcy stuck her arms in the air, and I did the same. Two men came forward, holstering their guns, while others in the hallway kept theirs pointed at us. They handcuffed our wrists behind our backs. They searched us, removed all of our weapons from their various locations, and threw them across the room. They pulled a comb out of Darcy's boot and held it up, giving her a questioning look.

Darcy shrugged. "It's just in case I needed it."

Knowing better than to trust a sixteen-year-old girl who had broken into their highly secured facility, the man pulled the comb off the handle, revealing a sharp knife.

"Like I said," Darcy said with a smile. "Just in case."

The man didn't like Darcy's sass. He slapped her across the face with the back of his hand. That wiped away her smile, and she glared at the man with hatred. I didn't like to think about what she would have done to him if she hadn't been handcuffed.

The men in the hallway parted, making a pathway for someone. They still had their guns aimed at us, so I didn't dare move. The two men who had handcuffed us now moved behind us, drew their guns, and pointed them at our heads.

An elegantly dressed woman appeared in the hallway. Her whole look screamed that she meant business. I recognized her right away as Jessica Chadwick, the mastermind and the reason we were here. Her hair was elegantly arranged on top of her head, and her high heels clicked with every step. She walked right up to us and looked us over from top to bottom. She glanced around at the bodies on the floor and the destruction of her well-decorated office before turning to look at us again.

She half-smiled. "Let me guess," she said, and there was something that could only be described as joy in her eyes. "The Orphanage sent you?"

"How do you know about the Orphanage?" I blurted out, earning me a kick from Darcy.

"Because," she said, "two years ago... they killed my father."

CHAPTER 35

"I have to pee!" I shouted at the top of my lungs.

We had been locked away for more than twenty-four hours, no one had come to interrogate us yet, and I desperately needed to pee. Drinking a Coke before leaving on the assignment had probably been a bad idea.

"I'm going to get a bladder infection!" I yelled.

"Shut up, Bennet," Darcy moaned, leaning her head against the wall we were handcuffed to.

We were sitting on the floor of what I could only assume was what they used for a prison here. I was curious how often this cell was used. My wrists were killing me, and sitting here for so long with my hands above my head had made them fall asleep. I couldn't feel my fingers.

We had spent too long in here. Maybe they were busy figuring out what I had done to their system. I'd be surprised if they found anything. My program was made to hide behind a firewall, making it impossible to find. They would never be able to stop it. What I had created was unique, and I reveled in its beauty.

The events in Chadwick's office had haunted us a little. We didn't know what to make of an outsider knowing about the Orphanage. Who else knew about it? About all our secrets? We had to warn the

Orphanage about Chadwick. If she was on the verge of starting World War Three, she needed to be stopped.

There was also the matter of her father. In our heads, Darcy and I had gone through as many past assignments as we knew about to see if it was something that the Orphanage had done. It wasn't in the file we had received for our assignment.

Too much information was coming out of this assignment, and I felt way off course. Were we supposed to just kill Chadwick and get out of here? If so, we could have simply sent Darcy to do that, and we'd already been back at the Orphanage drinking hot chocolate and enjoying our warm beds instead of a prison floor. Again, I was jealous of the other team and their simple assignment. All they had to do was get some paintings, not get caught, and bring them back to the Orphanage. Our assignment had had so many uncertain factors and twists and turns that I wondered if either the Orphanage didn't have the whole picture or if they wanted to give their future Chief a challenge. Austen was probably going insane back on the plane, not knowing what was going on.

When the guards had searched us in Chadwick's office, they had taken our equipment from the janitor's cart, including the book we had stolen. We had nothing left except the clothes we wore. The only thing they'd missed were the tiny pieces of metal in our ears and teeth that connected us to the plane. Too bad they weren't working.

"I thought they would come faster than this," I hissed at her. "I mean, for goodness sake, I have to pee."

Darcy rolled her eyes and looked at the door. We'd taken turns sleeping. While awake, Darcy had spent most of her time staring at the door right in front of us, several yards away.

The room, thankfully, was well lit. It sucked for sleeping, but it was nice when we were awake. The walls were a bright white and the floor tiled in light gray. Obviously, the decorator of the rest of the building hadn't been allowed to get their hands on this room.

As well as desperately having to use the bathroom, I was also starting to get incredibly thirsty and hungry. I couldn't wait to get back to the plane to Mary, Austen, and Chuck and eat whatever cookies Austen hadn't eaten—after I went to the bathroom, of course.

"Do you think Austen is planning anything to get us out? How could he possibly know what has happened?" I asked. All I could think about was my full bladder and my hopes of getting some relief soon.

"No," Darcy responded coldly.

I turned my head and looked at her. "What do you mean, 'no'?"

She let out a huge breath and refused to meet my eyes. "I mean that Austen and I agreed that, if we didn't get out by Thursday evening, he had to make sure Chadwick was in the building and then release the bomb we got Charlotte to make for us. That way, at least he, Chuck, and Mary will complete the assignment and move on."

"So that's what you meant when you said, 'There's always another plan.'"

She nodded.

"But we wouldn't move on," I pointed out. "We would be dead."

Darcy looked at me with pity in her eyes. "Isn't that what we both want?"

I turned away from her, unwilling to let her see the pain written on my face. How could she sentence me to death like that? If Austen called the Orphanage, they could get us out. We would fail, and for Austen—the future Chief—that would look really bad, but at least we would be alive.

But what Darcy said made sense. Chuck and Mary would probably put up a fight, which was probably why Darcy and Austen had kept this information between the two of them. Now I had to ask the important question: Was I ready to die?

If you had asked me back in January, I would have handcuffed myself to this wall. Now I wasn't so sure. My heart still occasionally ached for Collin but not like it had when everything was still raw. I had worked too hard to get where I was to give up. If I were trapped with Collin instead of Darcy, he would never give up, especially on me. If Collin knew I was trapped here with his girlfriend, and we were about to die, he would want me to do anything I could to get her out, even though most people would assume it would be Darcy getting me out. I couldn't give up on Darcy, and I couldn't roll over and let Chadwick get away.

"It isn't what Collin would want," I murmured. Turning my head to look at Darcy, I told her, "It's time for us to get out of here. I'm tired of playing the damsel in distress."

Darcy smiled. "Good. Come on, you earpiece field agent. Get us out of here."

I looked around the room again, as though for the first time. This time I didn't look around as someone who desperately needed to pee but rather as someone who needed to get his friend out alive. The camera up in the corner was trained on us. That was when my horrible and slightly embarrassing idea came to me. I prayed it would work.

"Darcy," I said with a sigh, "look away."

She did the opposite of what I'd asked and instead looked straight at me.

"I'm going to pee," I told her.

"And what the heck is that going to solve?" she objected.

"Well," I began, "hopefully these security guards won't want a video of me shimmying my pants off and peeing all over their clean floor."

Darcy had an argument ready right away. "You have been yelling at them forever, and they haven't cared that you have to pee. And frankly," she lowered her voice, "I also have to use the bathroom, but you don't see me yelling at the camera to let me out."

"Exactly. All talk and no action," I said.

We could sit here and argue all day, accomplishing nothing, or I could get us out of here and finish our assignment. If we happened to find a bathroom along the way, that would also be nice.

"Well, it's your choice to look or turn away," I told her. Looking directly at the camera, I shouted, "I guess I'll just have to go here!"

Praying that my hunch about these people preferring not to clean up a mess was correct, I started to weirdly rub my pants against the wall, trying to slide them off.

"You are disgusting," Darcy moaned, turning away, not wanting to look at the horrifying scene.

My pants started to shimmy down my hips, revealing my underwear. The wall was not as cold as I thought it would be against my skin. I worried that no one would come and get me, and I would just end up peeing all over the floor. At least the pressure would be gone.

"Please stop," Darcy begged.

"I'm almost there," I informed her, even though I wasn't even close.

She continued to shout at me, randomly calling me an idiot, as I wriggled against the wall and floor to show whatever security guard was watching that I was serious. I mean, if they wanted us dead, they probably would have killed us already instead of locking us up. They were waiting for something, and I was just moving that along.

The door burst open just as I felt my butt cheeks make contact with the floor. In walked the same man who had let us in the front door. The door shut behind him, and I knew by the classic-looking hotel card slot that, in order to get in and out of this room, you needed a key card.

"Please do not use the floor as your personal bathroom," the guard demanded. "I'll take you to the bathroom, but any funny business, and I'll come back and shoot the blonde." He took his gun out of the holster and pointed it at Darcy to drive the point home.

I nodded my head, agreeing to his terms. He walked over to me and took out his keys. When he opened my handcuffs, I let my arms drop right down, feeling the blood rushing back into them. I moved my tingling fingers around.

The guard reached down and grabbed me by the shoulder, lifting me to my shaky feet. With one hand, I pulled up my pants. Darcy watched as the guard dragged me to the door, his gun pointed at me. My arms were free, and I would have to make my move sometime on the way back from the bathroom. I would have to get the key to Darcy's locks and his badge for the door. Cameras would pick me up, so I would have to move quickly. This was our chance to escape.

We were at the door, and the guard was taking his key card off of his shirt when Darcy, in a sweet and innocent voice, spoke up. "My nose is really itchy, and clearly I can't reach it. Would you mind?"

The guard looked at her skeptically but clearly decided that, since she was small and chained to a wall, nothing bad could happen.

It's dangerous to underestimate kids.

The guard shoved me down onto the floor. "If you move, I'll shoot her," he said.

I nodded, scared to say anything that would set him off.

He walked toward Darcy with his gun aimed at her. I kept as still as possible considering my full bladder. There was no fear in Darcy's eyes as this muscular man stood towering over her. I watched him bend over, and with his free hand, scratch her nose. That was when Darcy ruined my plan of dealing with him after I used the bathroom.

My mouth fell open as Darcy lifted her legs, wrapped them around his neck, and twisted them behind his head to lock them in place. Darcy was still cuffed to the wall, and the man used that to his advantage, leaning back and pulling Darcy with him. He started gasping for air, and the back of his neck began to turn purple. Darcy, stretched out in the air with her wrists bent in her handcuffs and her legs wrapped around the guard, was quite the sight to see. She let out a couple of grunts, either in pain or just to try and catch her breath. The man, remembering he had a gun, started to lift it.

My body suddenly decided to start working. Charging forward, I took the guard by surprise by tackling him from behind. He crashed down to his knees. I reached for the gun but was too late. He fired twice, both shots hitting the wall right beside Darcy.

Annoyance passed across her face. She jerked her whole body to the side. A slight noise came from the man, and his lifeless body hit the floor with a thump, his head twisted at an odd angle. I backed away from him, trying not to pee my pants. Darcy had snapped his neck.

I looked away from the body on the floor and up at Darcy, who had an expression on her face that said, "Hurry up!"

I bolted forward and took the keys from the dead guard's belt, knowing we were on camera and more guards were probably on their way. My hands shook as I sorted through the keys to find the one he had used on me. Once I found it, I shoved it into Darcy's lock and opened her handcuffs, releasing her from the wall.

"Thanks," she said, rubbing her sore wrists and shaking her hands out, encouraging blood to flow.

"I was going to take him out in the hallway," I informed her. "And I have to pee, so that takes priority. Let's go." I grabbed the guy's key card and raced the few steps to the door.

I had never felt such relief as the feeling of no longer having to pee. I waited outside the bathroom we'd found after a few minutes of running through the halls and getting as far away from the prison as possible, traveling up from the basement to the top floor. I held the gun that we'd taken from the dead guard and had it ready in case someone came down the hallway. Darcy was using the bathroom now, and I was waiting for her to finish up so we could somehow make it back to Chadwick's office and get my tablet. If it was still there.

An alarm had been ringing since we'd left the cell, yet security guards were nowhere to be seen. I wondered why we hadn't been caught yet, especially with our little pee break.

Pacing back and forth, I debated the best course of action. Even if we did complete my plan, we still had everything else to worry about: Chadwick mass-producing weapons to start World War Three, the Orphanage killing her father, and her desire for revenge was just a short list of our problems. We also had to worry about how Jessica knew about the Orphanage and whether or not she had told anyone else. This was an organization that had stayed a secret since 1826, and now, all of a sudden, an outsider knew about us.

While I was pacing back and forth, a hand reached out from

behind me and dragged me into the bathroom. I almost dropped the gun but then swung around with it, ready to fire.

"Seriously, Bennet," Darcy complained, snatching the gun from my hand. "Who else would be dragging you into the bathroom you are supposed to be guarding?"

"What are we doing in here?" I asked, ignoring her comment. "Chadwick's office is that way." I pointed out the bathroom door.

Darcy climbed on top of the sink counter, reached up with the gun, and poked open the grate covering a vent. I gave a little half-smile at our new route to Chadwick's office.

I hopped up on the counter with Darcy, and she cupped her hands to give me a foothold. I put my foot in her hands, and she used her strength to lift me up. Gripping the edge of the vent, I pulled myself up. Once in, I had to carefully turn around in the tiny space to help Darcy up. I held out my hands. She grabbed them, and I pulled as she kicked off the counter.

Once we were both in the vent, she said, "This way," and crawled off. I followed, the alarm still ringing in the background.

My pants were getting dustier with every move I took. I looked up to see if Darcy was also covered in dust, and the only thing I saw was her butt right in my face as she stopped dead in her tracks. I crashed into her. "Why did we stop?" I asked, rubbing my nose.

She was looking down through a slotted grate. The light coming through it painted stripes on her face. She started moving again, and I shuffled along after her, pausing briefly to see what she'd been looking at. I had to squint a little because it was so bright down below, but once I did, I could easily make out rows and rows of guns of all different shapes and sizes. Off to the right, I spotted a couple of rocket launchers and some missiles.

How could such a sweet-looking person cause so much destruction? I liked the old movies where it was the hideous and strange people—the people who clearly looked like villains—who were the bad guys. When villains came in all shapes and sizes, it made things trickier to decipher.

At first, I'd prayed that Austen would ignore Darcy and not leave us here, but now I kind of wanted him to blow this place up if we couldn't get out. If they blew it up, at least everything they stored here would be gone. The only problem would be everything they might have stored in another location. Who knew how many warehouses full of weapons Jessica had? We needed to get our hands on that book of hers.

My knees were sore from all the crawling. This building was huge. I wanted to complain about how uncomfortable and warm I was, but I couldn't complain to Darcy. If I did, she probably would spend all summer training me to crawl through the vents at the Orphanage. And those had lasers in them.

Reaching our destination, Darcy awkwardly turned around to face me, with the grate between us. We both looked down and saw Chadwick's office below. We slid our fingers into the hinged grate and lifted it up. It opened toward Darcy, and she had to back up to quietly put it down on the metal.

Darcy dropped into the room, and I followed. As I made my way to the desk, Darcy stood by the door, gun ready. As I scrabbled through the drawer I'd hidden my tablet in, my heart dropped. It wasn't there. The room had been cleaned and put back together. There was even a new desktop computer.

I stood there, unable to think of what to do next. Unless we came up with an idea, we would just have to wait until midnight for Austen to blow the place up. It would make a huge mess, but at least Chadwick would be dealt with, and the secret of the Orphanage's existence would hopefully die with her.

I let out a sigh at the idea of being with my brother again. I missed him so much at that moment. He would have known what to do. I closed my eyes and tried to picture him. It was easier to picture traits than what he looked like. It seemed like forever since I'd seen him, and I didn't even keep a picture of him by my bed. Maybe if I made it out of this, I could ask Oliver for a picture frame and fill it with a photo of Collin.

Things are really bad if I'm thinking of turning to Oliver for help, I realized.

"Hurry up so we can get back into the vents," Darcy whispered from her position by the door. "Maybe we can find a way out through them."

"Seriously? You returned to the scene of the crime? How stupid could you be?"

Darcy and I both froze at the sound of Jessica's voice. Darcy didn't turn and shoot as I would have expected. Instead, we both slowly turned our heads and watched Jessica Chadwick casually emerge from a secret alcove behind her bookcase.

CHAPTER 37

CHADWICK'S OFFICE
JUNE 14
5:22 P.M.

Jessica stood in front of us, the secret door behind her displaying a bed and bathroom. She seemed totally unfazed by us breaking into her office. Had she been expecting us?

Darcy raised her gun. Chadwick didn't flinch as Darcy pulled the trigger and the bullet buried itself in the books beside her head. I jumped, a piece of me buried from last December wanting to run away from the loud noise.

Chadwick stood her ground, staring Darcy down. It was weird, like she was completely in control of the situation even though we were the ones with the gun.

After the bang, we all stood still, waiting for someone to make the next move. Darcy kept her gun aimed at Chadwick's head, and Chadwick stood as though this was perfectly normal, a smirk on her face and her hip cocked to one side.

The tension rose until Jessica finally said, "If you're going to shoot me, just shoot. It doesn't look good, standing there like an idiot."

Darcy's face tightened, and I knew it was game over for Jessica Chadwick.

"No!" I shouted and charged Darcy before she could shoot.

We landed in a tangle. I grabbed the gun from her, and rolling around on the floor, used every ounce of training she had bestowed on me to ensure she wouldn't kill Chadwick. We needed her alive. There was too much we didn't know, and if we brought her back to the Orphanage, we could interrogate her.

I put Darcy in a chokehold. I could feel the anger coursing through her. Chadwick just stood and watched us patiently as we wrestled for possession of the only weapon we had.

Having gained complete control of the gun, I stood up and pointed it at Darcy, who lay on the floor, looking up at me with disgust and hatred. Her ponytail was completely ruined, and I was sure I didn't look any better. We both wanted the same outcome—to shut down Chadwick's operation—but Darcy wanted to do it by killing her, and I wanted to do it by destroying all her hard work.

"We... we are not going to kill her," I panted, trying to regain my composure. "We need to take her back to the Orphanage."

"The Orphanage doesn't care," Darcy spat. "The Orphanage doesn't believe in justice. It believes in tying up loose ends. And once you get that through your thick skull, you will have a much easier time doing your job. Shoot her so we can clean up this mess."

I looked over at Chadwick with my gun still trained on Darcy. I had no clue what her deal was. She hadn't moved during our whole fight. She seemed to think she was in control of this whole situation.

Turning back to Darcy, I debated what my next move would be. I couldn't shoot her, but I couldn't let her have the gun. For her whole life she had been trained to aim and shoot, and that was exactly what she wanted to do now. I couldn't blame her for that. I just wanted to take a different path, and I wished she would let me.

I thought back to Collin and what he would do. I thought about him bravely getting everyone out of the school while he stayed to save it. I thought about how he didn't even have to think twice about it. He had put everyone else before himself.

Unfortunately, I also thought about the pain and the hole he had left behind. Though he had put everyone else before himself, to me, he had seemed incredibly selfish, because he had left me here alone. No matter how hard I tried, no matter what I did, whether I became a field agent or left to join Google, I would still miss him. Right here, right now, how could I honor him properly? How could I be selfless like him?

"Darcy," I said, looking down at her with pain in my eyes, "the Orphanage can deal with me when we get back if they don't like the call I made. They can put me behind a desk and make me an earpiece, but I can't let you kill her."

I knew Darcy could take the gun away from me if she really wanted to. It would come down to whether or not Darcy would let me win.

I waited to hear her response.

Darcy lifted her head and reached up to redo her ponytail. "Fine. We'll do it your way."

I reached down with my free hand to help her up, and she took it. Pulling her to her feet, I smiled at her.

"This is nice and all, but I think it's time I take over," Chadwick said.

I looked over. Chadwick had a gun in her hand. I spun toward her with my own weapon, but I was too late.

She fired.

I screamed in pain and dropped the gun as the bullet slammed into my right shoulder, spinning me around. My shoulder bloomed red. Blood oozed between my fingers as I clapped my left hand to the wound. I had never been shot before, and I had already decided that I never wanted to be shot again. This sucked.

Darcy made a move toward the gun, and Jessica calmly spoke up, taking a delicate step forward in her high heels. "If you reach for that gun, I will pull the trigger, and the next bullet will go through this young man's heart."

Darcy stood straight, reassuring me that she wasn't going to put my life in jeopardy. Our purpose in life was to die for the Orphanage, and Darcy could have chosen that moment for me to fulfill that purpose. Thankfully, I was still breathing. I was in pain, but I was still breathing. Chuck would now have another task on this assignment besides dissecting a goose.

"Please, have a seat," Chadwick told us, motioning with the gun toward two chairs in front of her desk. "It's a good thing you took the vent to get here. Every entrance and exit is sealed with a metal door. Not even I can get out. We are stuck here until a friend of mine comes by."

We slowly moved to the chairs, and I carefully sank down in mine, still using my left hand to apply pressure to my bullet wound. Jessica gracefully moved around her desk to sit in her big office chair, keeping her gun trained on me the whole time. I did not care to be the victim in this situation. It was annoying how she already had our roles figured out. Just once, I would love it if someone thought that I was the tough guy, and Darcy was the assistant in our relationship.

"How on earth did you break into my facilities undetected?" she asked.

"Acted like we were part of the janitorial staff," Darcy replied. "At a place like this, you always have big tough security guys who think they are too good to learn about people they consider lower than them. It would help if your security team studied up on everyone who works here." Darcy sounded snide. "Even the new people."

Jessica nodded as though what Darcy had said was the most important thing she'd heard all day. We sat awkwardly while she typed one-handed on her new computer, keeping the gun trained on me the whole time.

She finished typing. "Any questions?" she asked.

"Umm, I have one," I said. "Why did you leave us so long in the cell without questioning us?"

"I was curious to see what you would do. There was nothing on TV, and you guys have created some *much*-needed entertainment around here. That, and you are going to be a present for a friend of mine who should be arriving any minute."

"Are you going to call security?" Darcy asked. She sat with her hands on the chair's armrests, ready to push herself out of the chair and attack at a moment's notice.

Chadwick tilted her head to the side and kept a beautiful smile on her face, outlined in red lipstick. "Would you call for security, or would you deal with the problem yourself?"

Darcy didn't answer, but she looked slightly impressed.

"That's what I thought. Strong people don't need other people to clean up their messes. They do it themselves."

"What happened to your dad?" I asked, trying to distract her and get information at the same time.

"You killed him," she informed me. "The Orphanage is a ruthless task force that destroys everything in its path. Just look at her." She motioned toward Darcy with her gun. "She was going to kill me just because they probably told you to take me out. But do either of you really know anything about me?"

"I know enough," Darcy said coldly.

"Well, did you know this?" Chadwick snapped. "My dad was a man of business, and just because his dreams were too big, the Orphanage decided to kill him."

"So, what's your role in all of this?" I asked. The amount of blood coming out of my shoulder was beginning to worry me a bit.

"I am the one who took my father's dream and made it bigger!" Chadwick shouted. "I saw two sides to the story and played both of them. I will be both the supplier of oil and of weapons when the day comes. And when countless people are thrown into prison, I will be there to use them to build my empire!"

Darcy shook her head. "You can't be in this alone."

Chadwick got up from her desk and backed up to the bookshelf. Keeping the gun on me, she reached behind her, and at random, grabbed books and tossed them on the desk. I looked at the titles. They were all history books. Chadwick came back to the desk, holding one final book that she tossed onto Darcy's lap. "Do you think your organization acts alone?" she taunted. "No. You have people all over the world who are in on your little secret and have been throughout your history. You take street rats, orphans, and babies who deserve to die off in a corner where no one will miss them and train them to become killers, to act without thinking, to follow orders. Don't look at me with your nose up in the air when you are just as guilty of destroying the world as I am. I just want to come out on top when the world is destroyed. Lots of us do."

"You keep talking, telling us your plan, which isn't helping your case. Why?" Darcy demanded.

Chadwick answered her question with another question. She looked directly at me and asked, "Have you ever considered that you may be on the wrong side? You could do great things if you weren't being held back."

I looked at her like she was crazy. I could never betray the Orphanage. I had proved my loyalty to them, and I would prove it again. This was my life, and I hadn't left it even after Collin died. I wasn't on the wrong side.

"Like this," Chadwick said, opening a drawer with her free hand and pulling out my pink USB drive. She held it up. "This is incredible. Imagine what you could do if you were given free rein."

"I am free," I said.

"You created something that could send the world into a frenzy. You could shut down anything you wanted. Do you realize how much power you have? How much you could control with just a laptop and your mind? Or should I say, tablet?" She reached back into her desk and pulled out my tablet.

I could see on the screen that my program was still working itself into her system. Soon, all of her work would be lost.

"This is very interesting. I would really like this to be destroyed, but my computer techs couldn't crack it. So, what do you say?" Chadwick said. "I know some people who would love to have you join them. Of course, you would be more independent than you are at your precious Orphanage. You could have the world at your fingertips. And the best thing is, if the Orphanage ever came after you," she tossed the pink USB drive into my lap, "you would know how to deal with it."

She made some good points, but I could never leave Darcy. I stared at Chadwick, and feeling like I was speaking blasphemy by saying the name to an outsider, told her, "The Orphanage would never hurt me because I am loyal to them. The Orphanage tries its best to do what's right, to help save innocent people from the things that hide around every corner. And you are one of those things. I can't join you, because that would mean leaving my family to join a villain, and I don't know if you've ever seen any superhero movie, but it never turns out well for the villain. Why don't you quietly come with us? Hopefully, the Orphanage will be gentle with you."

"If your organization sees me as a bad guy, then that is what I am going to be to you." Calmly, she fired again. This time the bullet skinned the top of my right shoulder. I screamed.

At the moment Chadwick was distracted by her own gunfire, Darcy leaped out of her chair and over the desk. In her three-inch heels, Chadwick tottered back against the bookshelf, where Darcy easily overpowered her and took her gun. Out of pure hatred and revenge, Darcy started to punch Jessica in the face over and over again.

I scrambled to find the other gun in the room. Picking it up, I ran around the desk to where Darcy was beating up Chadwick and pointed it at Darcy. "Darcy, stop!" I shouted. "My opinion on all of this hasn't changed! We need to bring her in!"

Darcy pulled back, rage in her eyes at the fact I was aiming a gun at her after she had just tackled my shooter. More blood poured from my right shoulder. This whole thing needed to be over soon before I passed out.

With Darcy moving away from Chadwick and closer to me, I aimed the gun at Chadwick, who was slowly getting up. One eye was swollen shut, and blood poured from her nose.

"Darcy, give me your gun. Jessica, please take my seat," I politely said. "Darcy, you sit down, too."

Darcy tossed me her gun. As she and Chadwick moved to the chairs Darcy and I had been sitting in earlier, I sank down into the boss's chair, feeling quite powerful. The tables were turned, and I could get back to more important things. Chadwick and Darcy sat watching me work away on my tablet, completing the program and the original plan.

"What are you doing?" Chadwick asked.

"Basically, I'm putting your entire system down the drain and turning the garbage disposal on."

"I can still call security."

"No, you can't," I told her. "The security cameras in here have been deactivated, and as I see from this memo… you weirdly sent everyone home for the rest of the week—except for the guard you had watching us in the cell—because of this friend you are expecting." I turned my tablet around, showing her private emails.

"Who's coming for dinner?" Darcy asked her. "Must be someone pretty important and private if you want no one to know they're here."

Chadwick sat still and didn't say a word.

"You let us rot for twenty-four hours chained to a wall," I said, thinking out loud. "Maybe we should let you do the same. After all, we are the only ones here until your surprise guest shows up. You can keep the dead security guard in there company." I put down my tablet and picked up the two guns, pointing them at her.

Jessica looked straight at me with such malice that I feared for my life for a moment, even though I was the one with the guns. But she didn't go for me. She reached down, ripped off one high-heel shoe, and jabbed it into Darcy's left shoulder. Then she flung herself at Darcy, sending both of them crashing to the floor.

And I, being new to these situations, just sat there like an idiot with two guns in my hands. I dropped one and leaped to my feet holding the other.

Jessica was on top of Darcy, choking her. Darcy looked over her shoulder, her bulging eyes pleading for me to do something.

My hands shook. Everything came back to this, killing Chadwick, no matter how hard I tried to avoid it. Life just wasn't fair. If it was, Collin would be here instead of me.

I couldn't lose Darcy too. Aiming the gun at Chadwick's back, I closed my eyes and pulled the trigger.

Chadwick's body collapsed on top of Darcy. Her blood ran onto the floor and Darcy. I came around the desk, pushed Chadwick's body to the side, and helped Darcy up.

Darcy was unfazed by the dead body on the floor and the fact that she was covered in blood. She got to work doing her second-favorite thing after shooting people: snooping. She picked through the books Jessica had thrown on the table and grabbed the USB drive from where it had fallen and stuck it in her pocket. Then she headed over to the bookshelf and started sorting through the books to see if there was anything important. Grabbing the book with the charts in it, she skimmed through it and smiled. "Of course, she would clean up her whole office and put everything back in its proper place. So predictable!"

My hands shook. I dropped the gun. I didn't know if I was dizzy from the blood loss or because I had just killed someone. Jessica's lifeless body was lying right in front of me, and I was the one who had put it there. Would someone miss her the way that I missed Collin? "We need to get out of here," I told Darcy faintly.

"She said all the exits are sealed," Darcy replied. "What are our options?"

We each grabbed a gun. Darcy had the book, and I had my tablet. We stood there, trying to figure out how to escape.

CHAPTER 38

Darcy started for the office door.

"Wait," I exclaimed, holding my good arm with my gun in it out to stop her. "No one is here," I reminded her. "This is our chance."

She frowned. "Chance to what? We completed our assignment."

She couldn't see the big picture, only the fact that her target had been taken care of. All I could think about was when she had told me not to complain about circumstances but rather to adapt to them. Our target had changed, whether the Orphanage had told us so or not. We couldn't just leave the weapons stored here for someone else to take.

"Darcy," I pleaded, hoping she would see things through my eyes. "Adapt."

"I can't," she cried.

It was my turn to shake my head. "You can't what, Darcy? You can't walk away from someone without killing them? You can't do more than what you were asked? You can't let yourself feel for those you kill, or for their families who have lost someone dear to them? Stop being an assassin for one second and be Darcy! Someone with her own opinions and choices to make! Someone who thinks that, in five years' time, she could be somewhere totally different! Don't let everyone make your decisions for you!"

"I can't lose you like I lost Collin!" she shouted, backing away from me. "This *is* me adapting to my circumstances rather than complaining about them. I am not complaining about losing Collin, but I am going to make sure as hell that I don't lose you too, because you are my family, and I know how important family is to you. So, please," she begged, "let's get back to the rest of our family!"

I understood the pain she felt, because I didn't know what I would do if I lost her, but how could we walk away from this knowing everything we'd left behind? Someone important to Chadwick was on their way right now. My guess was that this person was in on the whole World War Three power plan. It would be awesome if all of this— Chadwick's headquarters with the guns and weapons and whatever other mysteries she had stored here—were gone before they got here.

"That's it!" I exclaimed.

Her eyes widened in surprise. "You agree with me? We're leaving?"

"Charlotte's bomb!" I said. "We can use the bomb to get rid of the place, like you and Austen planned."

"Sure. We just have one problem. We're locked in here, and your program is busy shutting everything down, including the security measures to reopen the doors. We're stuck."

I looked down at my tablet, alerting me that, in thirty seconds, all of Chadwick's work would be gone from the mainframe. We'd done what the Chief told us to do, and now we were going to die if we couldn't find a way out.

And then it hit me.

If Chadwick had kept my tablet and USB drive, then maybe she had kept some of our other items. I put my gun into my waistband and jogged over to her secret room behind her desk and looked around.

The place was tidy, with a made bed, pillows properly fluffed, and a rack of clothes organized by color on one wall, and a leather sofa with a liquor cart beside it along another, facing a massive TV. It seemed like a nice place to relax while working overtime. It really paid to be the boss.

Nothing would be in the bathroom I figured, but the dresser drawers next to the rack could be a place to start. I ran over there first, Darcy on my heels and wondering what I was doing. I tossed my tablet on top of the dresser. Throwing open the top drawer all I found was jewelry delicately laid out. I moved on to the next drawer and found towels and extra bedding. So far this was useless, but Darcy got the idea and joined in tearing the place apart. She ran to the bed and looked for anything that could be hidden underneath

Making it to the bottom drawer of the dresser, I flung it open and found what I had hoped for. I knew I had recognized the gun Chadwick first pulled on us. It was one that I had tucked into my holster before her security team took it away. If she had kept one of my guns, perhaps she had also kept the grenades that Darcy and I had brought along.

Riffling through our weapons, I found a cloth bag. Pulling it out of the drawer, I undid the bow and pulled it open to reveal our new exit strategy.

"Hey, Darcy," I called to her. "Feel like blowing open a hole in Chadwick's office?"

Getting up off the floor from looking under the bed, she walked over to me and looked in the bag I was holding. "That's one way to leave."

Reaching into the bag, we each pulled out a grenade and went ahead with the only idea we had.

"Wait," I said, feeling panicked, remembering that Chadwick's body was still in the other room.

Easily annoyed, Darcy tilted her head back and grumbled, "What now?"

"I don't know about you, but I would rather not throw a grenade into a room with a dead body in it. Don't really feel like walking through the mess after it goes off," I informed her.

"Agreed."

Placing the grenades we were holding on the bed, we quickly walked back into the main office and over to Chadwick's lifeless body. Standing at her feet, I tried not to cringe while I reached down to pick up her legs. Darcy had grabbed both of her arms and we lifted together and easily carried her to her secret room. The carpet where she had once been lying was stained dark red. I did my best to avoid stepping in it, but the trail of blood that we created from carrying her was a little harder to avoid. I created a couple of footprints on our way back. Her open eyes, staring at me and stirring up guilt deep within me, was the worst part of it all.

Leaving her on the farthest side of the secret room, we hurried, and each grabbed a grenade from the bed. It seemed heavier in my hand than usual. I looked at Darcy for reassurance, and she nodded once before we went to find the safest place to throw them from.

We stood against the wall right beside the secret door, both with a grenade in hand ready to pull the pin. Taking a deep breath, we nodded, pulled the pin, and threw them at the farthest wall in Chadwick's office. Quickly covering my ears and closing my eyes, the grenades went off, causing unknown damage to the office.

Opening my eyes, I looked at Darcy, hoping our plan had worked. I walked over to the dresser to grab my tablet before joining Darcy to walk out and look at our new opening. The office was a disaster. Books had flown off the shelves and the curtains that had once covered the windows were shredded and smoldering. Debris left the carpet a mess, and random office supplies were scattered throughout.

We walked right up to the opening and leaned down to see the two-story drop.

"Really?" Darcy said. "There is no way you can jump out of a second-story window with bullet holes in your shoulder."

I looked at her. "Sure, I can."

"Fine. Then you go first." She motioned for me to go ahead.

Not knowing if I could actually make the jump, I grabbed the book out of Darcy's hands and tossed it out, hoping Darcy would go after it.

"You have got to be kidding me," she complained. She made a move to grab my tablet in retaliation.

"Woah, woah, woah," I said, holding it above my head. "Do you know how much information this has on it? You can't just chuck it out a window."

As I held it over my head, it started beeping. I looked at the screen and saw that all I had to do was press ENTER, and everything would be complete. It was a waste of time, considering we would be blowing the place up, but a piece of me wanted to wipe the Chadwick Company from history.

I looked over at the history books now scattered around the room and smiled at the idea of Chadwick's hopes of making history being completely destroyed by two sixteen-year-olds. With a grin in Darcy's direction, I hit ENTER, completing my program.

My moment of triumph was short-lived. The sound of a helicopter came through the homemade window. Chadwick's friend was close, and we didn't want to stick around to see if her friend brought other friends—the kind with guns. They wouldn't be too happy that we'd killed Chadwick.

Darcy looked out the hole in the wall, down at the book I'd thrown, and glared at me for having thrown our most important piece of evidence out the window. "Now what, genius?"

I sighed and walked back into Chadwick's secret room to grab the bedding from the dresser. Tossing some sheets at Darcy, we worked at tying the ends of them together. Making our rope as long as we could, I anchored it to a pipe that stuck out from the exposed wall, hoping that it could hold our weight. Darcy proceeded to throw the other end of the rope out the window.

"Time to go," she said, pushing me toward the opening.

I took a deep breath, shoved my tablet into the waistband of my pants beside my gun, and grabbed hold of the bedding. Dangling my feet out the window, I started using my feet to push myself out to help me walk down the wall.

The helicopter noise was getting louder, notifying us to hurry up. Moving fast, Darcy came after me, and we worked our way down the two-story building toward the green grass below.

My feet hit the ground and I backed off, giving Darcy room to climb down. She let go of the rope and dropped down when there was only a few more feet for her to go. She bent down and picked up the book, and we took off running toward the cover of the forest.

"That was the most unattractive exit I have ever made," Darcy told me.

I laughed at her. "At least we are alive," I responded.

Static started to howl in our ears as we got farther and farther from Chadwick's. Darcy started to call desperately for Austen to come in. Nothing came back but more static. Our trackers were in our backpacks, which the guards had taken, so I was still trying to figure out how to send Austen, Chuck and Mary our location if we managed to get ahold of them.

The occasional branch whacked me across the face as we sprinted through the forest, trying to get as far away from the building as possible. Darcy was still calling for Austen or Chuck or Mary. Having to make the trek back on foot was looking like a possibility. I wondered if we would be allowed to pass even if we were a few days late.

"Darcy, finally," Mary's voice came in. "Austen, it's Darcy."

"Is Bennet with her?" I heard Austen ask. Their voices came in very crackly, but at least we could hear them, and they could hear us.

"I'm here," I told Austen. "We need you to blow the place up. Use Charlotte's bomb."

"You have a bomb?" Mary said, shocked.

I had forgotten that this was a plan Austen and Darcy had made, leaving the rest of us in the dark.

Austen ignored her. "Are you still in the building?"

Darcy let me do all the talking. I was glad she approved of my plan. Hopefully, the Orphanage would side with me when we got back and filed all our paperwork. With World War Three on the horizon, I thought they would approve.

"We are out, and Chadwick is taken care of," I informed our future Chief. "Blow the building."

Austen calmly held his ground. "I need more information,"

"Austen," Darcy snapped, "we don't have time for this. Blow up the damn building, and we will fill you in later!"

"Fine." Austen tried to keep his cool. He hated being told what to do, especially by Darcy. I didn't blame him at all, considering he was supposed to be in charge of her and not the other way around. "Mary, set a course. Our target is the center of the headquarters. The bomb is already loaded."

"Great," Darcy said. "Now, pick us up at the lake south of Chadwick's operation."

"The lake?" both Austen and I asked.

"Don't hesitate," Darcy said to me and raced off through the woods. I chased after her.

She ran faster than me with the book still in her hand. Ahead lay a clearing of some sort. She leaped into the air as she reached it—and dropped out of sight.

I didn't let my brain think about it. I copied Darcy's action and leaped, clutching my tablet for dear life as the ground below me disappeared.

I looked down to see what I was falling toward and held my breath at the last second. As my feet hit the water, I heard an explosion from up above. I plunged deep into the lake and had to remember to swim up to the surface.

"I lived through that, right?" I asked, spitting water. I lifted my tablet out of the lake. It had completely died. I shoved it in the back of my pants beside the gun that was still there.

Darcy had surfaced long before me and was laughing—genuinely laughing—at me. In spite of myself, I joined in. We must have looked silly, both of us treading water, Darcy trying to hold the book above her head to keep it from getting wetter than it already was and laughing for no other reason than the fact that we were alive and together.

Off in the not-too-far distance, smoke was rising, and we heard the loud noises of a building collapsing. It looked like some of the trees had caught fire, but as long as everything Chadwick had built was gone, it was totally worth it. I wondered briefly if the guest Chadwick had been expecting had been caught by the explosion. We would have to check with Austen about that later.

"You all right down there?" Austen asked, hearing us laughing away.

Both of us looked up and saw our plane hovering above our heads. The ramp opened, and Austen descended on a cable to pull us out of the water.

"Hey, Chuck," I called into my headset. "You there?"

"I'm here, buddy," Chuck called back, excited.

"If you could have some needle and thread and a whole lot of painkillers ready for when we get up there, that would be awesome."

Darcy continued to laugh and smile, and I had never before been so happy while in that much pain. Her smile was contagious, and as Austen joined us in the water, he also started to laugh, probably because of how ridiculous we looked.

"Let's head home," I told my family.

CHAPTER 39

"Seriously? These are the paintings you were sent to retrieve?" Austen asked.

"Unfortunately, yes," Oliver said with a sigh.

Our whole year sat in a classroom staring at the paintings the other team had recovered. They were absolutely disgusting. I couldn't imagine the disappointment they must have felt when they got a good look at them. We'd all assumed they would be some lost and forgotten pieces by Monet or Van Gogh, but these were something else. They were five paintings by Edvard Munch's favorite niece, who had apparently been a big fan of dogs dressed up in people's clothing.

The dogs were either terrifying or looked incredibly disproportionate. The paintings did not look like they were worth tons of money, but I guess the stuff made by people who are important to you is priceless. If I'd ever had a niece who painted me pictures like this, I would have stuck them on my fridge for a week and then tossed them as soon as she was gone.

"Everyone to your seats," Agent Asher boomed, hobbling into the classroom.

We all sat there waiting for him to give us our last class before we were dismissed for summer. Both our teams had made it back in time, and we were just waiting to hear any comments the Chief or any of our teachers might have about our reports, which we'd written the Friday we came back. We were also waiting for Agent Asher to give us back our papers about how we would break into the Orphanage. Since my idea had pretty much worked in real life, I had a feeling that I'd passed.

The group of us had spent the weekend watching movies and chilling in one of the lounges, enjoying any of the leftover junk food we hadn't eaten during our assignments. Since I had bought five whole cases of Coke, we had plenty to go around. It was a nice weekend, just the ten of us hanging out. I even enjoyed Oliver's company. I didn't want to be close friends or anything, but he seemed to fit into our little family well.

The weekend was perfect for recovering from the fun of being shot twice. Chuck had drugged Darcy and me as soon as we got on the plane and had done a good job on our stitches. We'd had to go to the hospital once we got back just to be checked over. Oliver was also in need of medical attention, because Charlotte's flamethrower had malfunctioned while it was in Oliver's backpack, giving him a terrible burn. We enjoyed a few hours of trying to entertain each other while the doctors rushed around, helping others coming in from their year-end assignments.

Without a word, Agent Asher started to walk by our desks, handing out our assignments as he went. I watched everyone pick up their papers and start to flip through to read the comments. Asher dropped my paper on my desk, and I quickly picked it up. I was pleased to see that he hadn't made any corrections to it. But then I flipped through the whole assignment and couldn't find any comments either, which worried me. What if he hadn't marked it because he thought it was bad? What if he was going to call me out in front of the whole class?

My worst fears came true when Agent Asher, now back at the front of the classroom and leaning against the whiteboard, said, "By now, you have heard of Bennet's plan during their year-end assignment. What some of you may not know is that the plan that his team executed was actually the one he designed for the assignment I just handed back.

"Now," he continued, starting to shuffle down the rows. "What did Training Agent Bennet do that made his project so different?"

The question hung in the air, and I looked around, hoping someone would answer. No one dared shuffle a paper for fear of being called on. I tried my best to think of the answer, but nothing came to me.

"Someone put their hand up before I call on someone at random," Asher said.

Jane stuck her hand high in the air. The rest of us just sat like we were trained to: looking straight ahead at the teacher.

"Jane?" Asher said, giving her permission to speak.

She lowered her hand to the desk, folded it over top of the other, and answered, "Because Bennet used his strengths to his advantage."

Agent Asher didn't look pleased with her answer. "Continue," he ordered.

"Though he is a training field now, he still knows everything about being an earpiece. If I wanted someone to hack into someone's computer, I would ask Bennet to do it. He was able to combine two things—his knowledge as an earpiece and a field—into his project." She looked rather confident with her answer, and I felt confident for her because that was exactly what I'd done. It was exactly what Darcy had encouraged me to do. There was no reason why I couldn't be an earpiece out in the field.

But it turned out that wasn't the answer that Agent Asher wanted. "Good try, Jane. How about Darcy? Someone closer to the situation."

Darcy looked at me like she was searching me for the answer. Agent Asher and the class waited for Darcy. I wanted to give her the answer, but I couldn't even figure it out for myself. It was just something I did, not something I'd planned.

"Because he multitasked," Darcy tried as an answer. "He

remembered his paper and thought he could use it in a real-life situation. The rest of us did the exact same project of breaking into the Orphanage, so why didn't *we* use it to break into our targets on our final assignment?"

Agent Asher smiled at Darcy and then looked at me. "Would you like to continue with the answer, Bennet?" he asked me.

I thought Darcy had answered the question, so I didn't know what he wanted me to say. I thought about what Darcy had said about applying my recent project to our assignment. I didn't know what Agent Asher wanted, but I knew I needed to say something. And that's when it hit me.

"There's no point learning new stuff if we don't apply it to our jobs. Everything we learn is for our future working here. If we can't apply what we create, like my paper, then why do you bother giving us these projects?" I looked up at Asher.

"Yes, Bennet, and thank you, Darcy and Jane, for helping him get there." He made his way back to the front of the classroom. "We spend years teaching you to be the best. We want you to think for yourself and build plans and goals for yourself. We can't spoon-feed you when you are out in the real world. Take the assignments we give you seriously. Use them in your jobs whenever you can. Because we don't just make up these projects for fun. We give them to you for you to use them."

We all let that sink in. We were heading into summer, and time would tell how much of this we would remember. We wouldn't be back in this classroom until September, and we would enjoy every second of our free time. I already knew Elizabeth planned on studying under another agent for a couple of weeks, Austen was working with the Chief, and Lucas and Mary planned to build a self-driving motorcycle. Summer was a time where we could work for fun.

"Now," Agent Asher continued, "as for your final assignments, we were all very impressed with your abilities to improvise. You all had great plans outlined, and both of your plans went horribly wrong, yet you still made it back. I look forward to what you will be capable of next school year. Thanks for an interesting year. I can say it was definitely one of a kind." He gave me a look. "Now, it's time to head off to the auditorium for the graduation ceremony." He headed out the door, assuming the rest of us would follow.

We all pushed back our chairs and then tucked them back in before following him out the door. There were other classes heading to the ceremony, making the hallway busy. We shuffled through as best we could, sticking together the whole time. Like most of the other years, we ignored the elevator and headed for the stairs, climbing the rest of the way.

On the main floor, we started bumping into agents who were heading to their seats as well. Any agents free and in the building were obligated to attend the graduation ceremony. It's short, sweet, and to the point, and kind of exciting to watch as friends move on up and are finally able to be called "agent" instead of "training agent." It's like they're finally getting rid of their training wheels. I couldn't wait for when it would be our turn.

"It's summer!" Lucas cried out, and our year and others joined in thunderous cheering, celebrating the beginning of something new.

"We leave next Monday for camping, so we need to plan a day to make a list of food we need to take and who's cooking when," Austen said. "I talked to River, and the Chief is going to let us go without any agents to supervise us this year—"

"Yeah, yeah," Lucas cut in, not really caring about the small details. "Where are we going this year? I was thinking Brazil or Costa Rica. Any other suggestions?"

Our year talked away about plans for camping and what fun things we wanted to do this summer while we walked to the auditorium. We got carried away with plans of taking a boat and finding a deserted island to camp on or maybe going up to the Arctic for something totally different.

"Happy birthday, Bennet," Darcy leaned forward and whispered in my ear for only me to hear.

No one else had acknowledged my birthday, because I'd asked them not to. I was officially older than Collin, and I always would be. We were forever apart in age.

Darcy wishing me this quiet "happy birthday" was something different. It was our private secret that we both hurt on this day when someone we both missed couldn't be here to celebrate. I knew the rest of our friends missed Collin, but their feelings couldn't compare to mine or Darcy's. Our shared love for my brother was something that connected us, and nothing could ever break that.

I took my seat in the auditorium with Darcy on one side and Chuck on the other. We sat where we had all those months ago when we'd gathered for Collin's final statement, but this time, we had a new member added to our family: Oliver. We sat quietly but excited, waiting for the graduation ceremony to begin and dreaming of our camping trip and our futures.

CHAPTER 40

THE ORPHANAGE
JUNE 22
6:44 P.M.

I had been called into Agent Stephen's office, and I had no idea why. I hadn't run out of the cafeteria crying. I hadn't destroyed any property or done anything out of character. I was truly fine. Even the new photo that Oliver had helped me get of Collin that was now in a picture frame above my bed hadn't made me cry yet.

I sat waiting for Agent Stephen to arrive. We hadn't talked since the last time I'd been there.

"Well, Bennet," Agent Stephen said, opening the door and closing it behind him. "You have made quite the commotion here at the Orphanage. I wanted to personally congratulate you on everything you've done."

I didn't say anything while I watched him walk over to his chair. Nervous, I played with my right shoulder to see if I could still feel any pain from being shot twice. Nothing ached as I moved it back and forth. The shots wouldn't leave a scar. I loved having easy access to advanced medicine, though I didn't like the reason why I'd needed it.

Agent Stephen, seeing that I wasn't jumping into the conversation, kept talking. "I knew it would take some work, but when you were in my office forming your little idea, I had faith that you would surprise everyone," he told me, gesturing in my direction.

I was happy that Agent Stephen could see the progress I had made. "When I was sitting here back in March," I said, "did you know that I wanted to do the impossible and become a field?"

Agent Stephen leaned forward in his chair. "Who do you think told Chief Benjamin to let you switch career paths to get you to stop moping around?" he said. "Collin wouldn't have wanted that for you. He would be so happy to know that you run to the training room because you are excited to learn. If he could have seen you on your year-end assignment, he would have been so proud."

"But I asked the Chief," I said, still focused on the first thing Agent Stephen had said.

He chuckled and asked, "Do you really think the Orphanage would let you switch career paths? You would be surprised how much I get away with because I say it will help my patients' emotional well-being."

I looked at him in shock. He'd guessed what I was thinking that day. I supposed it was good that, as a therapist, he knew what his patients were thinking and could stay one step ahead of them. Agent Stephen was truly incredible. I owed him a lot for my new purpose in life, but I knew all he wanted for me was to go out and live.

"Now, I believe Miss Darcy is waiting in the training room. Have fun this summer with your training." He motioned toward the door, excusing me from our meeting.

I got up and smiled at the man who had changed my life for the better, then headed toward the door. Making my way through the hall, I kept smiling at how different my life was now. I could never go back, and right now, I didn't want to. Agent Stephen was right. Collin would have been proud of me.

I passed lots of agents bustling around and came across Chuck walking toward me. We had great plans that summer to read through so many comic books and try to get permission to go to Comic-Con in San Diego. We knew it was a long shot, but we thought we might as well ask.

"Hey, Chuck," I called, and we casually high-fived as we passed. Since he had what looked like a heart in a jar in one hand, my guess was he was heading to the hospital.

"How was therapy?" he asked, walking backward for a moment to stay with me.

"Better than I thought," I told him and broke into a jog to make it to the training room faster.

When I got there, I found Darcy standing in front of the targets, throwing knives. I didn't know if she was doing it as a joke or if it was just a coincidence that this day was kind of similar to that day so long ago.

Not wanting to get her attention just yet, I quietly sneaked around the room. There were other people working out and making plenty of noise. Some looked up from their workouts and training, wondering what I was doing.

I made it to the stand that housed some of the weapons, including a bow. I picked it out and took an arrow from the stack that, instead of a sharp point, had a tiny tennis ball on the end. Taking aim, I released and watched it fly, getting the satisfaction of seeing it hit Darcy right in the back. She flinched ever so slightly, her stance for throwing knives helping her keep her balance.

She turned around and spotted me right away, and without missing a beat, hurled the knife she had in her right hand at me. I decided to hold my ground and not show any fear. My hypothesis was correct: The knife landed right between my feet. I looked down at it, smiling, then glanced up at Darcy. She walked toward me with her classic blonde ponytail swishing through the air.

I picked up the knife and twirled it in my hand. It had left a nice little hole in the floor that, hopefully, no one would ask about. This room had plenty of bumps and bruises, so one more really didn't matter. I gave Darcy back her knife, and then we stood facing each other in silence. Clearly, we needed to train, but there were things I needed to say first.

"Why did you hold back when you fought Chadwick?" I asked. "You had plenty of chances to take her out, but you always hesitated."

She shrugged. "I did it for you."

"For me?"

We stood practically toe to toe. After all these months of getting closer and having her legs wrapped around my neck while training, personal space was no longer a thing between us.

Darcy continued, "You look at me and see something better. Someone who isn't just a killer. I was hoping you were right. But in the end, we did kill her."

It made me feel a little bit better that Darcy took some of the responsibility for killing Chadwick. It was hard knowing that I had my first kill behind me. How many more would I have to do before my career was over?

"Collin tried to get me to do better, but at the end of the day, when he looked at me, he saw an assassin. I loved him, and he loved me, but when I look at you, I see family. It's a weird feeling to not want to disappoint your family," Darcy confided. She was a beautiful person with many layers; they just took time to peel off.

"Family" was a word I usually just threw around in my head. It was nice to hear it out loud from someone else. Darcy truly was my family. Collin hadn't left me all alone, and though he'd wanted me to leave this place after his death, I think in some way, he knew that I would be taken care of.

Darcy stepped back and said, "Catch," then tossed me something.

I managed to snatch the tiny object from the air. It was my pink USB thumb drive that Darcy had taken from Chadwick's office before we left.

I frowned. "You told the Orphanage this was destroyed. The Orphanage told me never to make a new copy and to abandon this idea, because anything powerful enough to destroy the Orphanage shouldn't be kept around."

"Relax, Bennet," Darcy said. "You made it. You deserve to decide if it should be destroyed or not. Think of it as collateral. Now you have something to threaten people with if anyone comes after you."

I chuckled at the idea of me needing to arm myself against personal enemies, considering the world didn't know that I existed. Jessica Chadwick had never learned our names, nor did she ever ask. All we were to her were kids sent by the Orphanage that had killed her father. She hadn't cared about us at all.

"Good plan, by the way," Darcy said, referring to our year-end assignment and completely changing the mood. She headed over to get rid of her knives, and I put away the bow I was still holding.

"Are you serious? It barely worked. My program took too long, and we ended up killing Chadwick and blowing the whole place up. If I weren't on the team, you guys would have blown up the building and killed Chadwick anyway. All of my contributions were pointless."

We headed over to the mats, and without Darcy even having to tell me what to do, we got ready to fight. I dodged or blocked every punch she threw at me.

"You're not pointless, Bennet," Darcy told me. "I need you. I would have shot Chadwick on sight. You held me back, and look at everything we found out. Now we have work to do this summer. I volunteered us to track down the locations of her other warehouses and get rid of them."

Darcy threw me down on the mat, and I landed right on my butt. I put my hands back so that I could lean on them and sit comfortably.

"The Chief let me have a look over that book we took from Chadwick's office," Darcy informed me. "The only other thing that's written in it, besides Chadwick's notes, is inside the back cover. It says, 'From the Shepherd.' Now we get to figure out what that means."

I looked up at her and smiled at her attempt at a pep talk. "Looks like it's going to be a thrilling summer."

I raised my arm. Darcy lifted me to my feet, and we got to work on our last summer of freedom.

ACKNOWLEDGEMENTS

I never knew what I wanted to do once I graduated high school. There were too many options, and they all had their pros and cons. I wandered around for a few years, lost and unsure. Once I was brave enough to sit down and put words on a page, I realized I could be anything I wanted to be as a storyteller. These words on these pages wouldn't be possible without so many people who probably aren't even aware of the affect they've had in my life.

Mom and Dad, thanks for giving me space and time to follow my dreams.

Luisa, thanks for being the first set of eyes to view this story.

Gavin, you had such a big part in me completing this. Thank you for cheering me on and for being there when I wrote the very last sentence. Your friendship will always hold a special place in my heart.

My best friend, Megan, who I first told the story to while we were shopping in Sephora when I was too embarrassed to tell the world my love for writing stories. Thank you for always listening to me.

Thank you, Emily, for volunteering Austin to proofread my work. Austin, you tore apart my work in the most delicate way possible.

Alexis and my dear sister Stephanie, thank you for being my Darcy.

Thank you, Carly and James, for encouraging me every step of the way. I couldn't have asked for a better team.

Alyssa, thank you for making a book cover of my dreams.

To quote Lizzie McGuire, "This is what dreams are made of."